PIRATE TARGET: EARTH!

No galactic traitor had ever escaped from the permafrost prison planet Gastonia. And nothing could threaten the coronation of Empress Stanley II—the most tightly secured event in the history of the Empire of Earth.

Or so it was commonly believed—until thousands of pirate warships exploded into Earth's orbit the day of the ceremony. Operation Annihilate could only be stopped by some fast blaster-work from SOTE's top weapons for counterintelligence and pirate-catching: the superagents of the *Family D'Alembert!*

NOVELS OF SCIENCE FICTION
by
E. E. "DOC" SMITH

•

The Lensman Series

TRIPLANETARY
FIRST LENSMAN
GALACTIC PATROL
GRAY LENSMAN
MASTERS OF THE VORTEX
SECOND STAGE LENSMAN
SPACEHOUNDS OF IPC
CHILDREN OF THE LENS

The Skylark Series

THE SKYLARK OF SPACE
SKYLARK THREE
SKYLARK OF VALERON
SKYLARK DUQUESNE

The Family D'Alembert Series
(with Stephen Goldin)

IMPERIAL STARS
STRANGLERS' MOON
THE CLOCKWORK TRAITOR
GETAWAY WORLD
APPOINTMENT AT BLOODSTAR
THE PURITY PLOT
PLANET OF TREACHERY

#7

THE FAMILY D'ALEMBERT SERIES

E.E. "DOC" SMITH

WITH STEPHEN GOLDIN

PLANET OF TREACHERY

BERKLEY BOOKS, NEW YORK

PLANET OF TREACHERY

A Berkley Book / published by arrangement with
the author's estate.

PRINTING HISTORY
Berkley edition / May 1982

ISBN: 0-425-05301-6

A BERKLEY BOOK® TM 757,375
The name "BERKLEY" and the stylized "B" with design are
trademarks belonging to Berkley Publishing Corporation
PRINTED IN THE UNITED STATES OF AMERICA

This one is for the Cohen family: Kal, Esther, Betsy, Jon and—by marriage—Joe.

—S. G.

1

—— *Encounters on a Pirate World* ——

As the man left the camouflaged doorway of the elevator tube from the pirate base and headed out into the jungle, he got the distinct impression he was being watched. The prickling of the small hairs on the back of his neck, the suspicious absence of movement, the too-quiet stillness all around him—all these were danger signals to his wary mind. He'd gone through too many perilous situations before, had put his life on the line too many times, to ignore his instinctive feeling that something was not quite as it should be.

He stood stock still for a moment in a seemingly casual pose—but his hand was no more than a few centimeters from the hilt of the stun-gun tucked into his belt. Turning his head slowly he surveyed the landscape before him, alert for a myriad of possible dangers.

The pirate base was organized along very utilitarian lines. All the important areas—headquarters and strategy, supply depots, communications, living quarters for the chief pirate officials—were buried below more than a hundred meters of solid rock, secure from all but the heaviest weapons the Empire could throw at them. Closer to the surface were the barracks for the "enlisted men," the pirate hordes, representing nearly a thousand worlds. At this base alone there were more than twenty-two thousand people, men and women—alumni from the toughest planetary and Imperial prisons, graduates all from the school of survival-at-any-cost. Ringing the base in a series of underground silos were the ships the pirates used for their expeditions—more than five hundred of various sizes, ranging from small, swift scouts to large cruisers brimming over with destructive capacity.

No expense had been spared to set up the base—and this was only one of several that this particular pirate knew about. He also knew that the business of looting spaceships was nowhere near lucrative enough to support an operation of this scope and magnitude. This all had to be a part of something bigger and more diabolical—but despite his best efforts he'd been unable so far to pierce that mystery.

As he stood now on the surface and looked around, there was little indication of human activity on this planet. The elevator tube from which he'd emerged was disguised to look like a wide tree set at the edge of a clearing. Around it were many other real trees—tall, with dark brown trunks and broad, serrated leaves of a strange color closer to blue than green. Strung through the tops of the trees were the red slithervines that all the pirates learned to avoid within a short while of coming to this world; the vines exuded a strong serum that could even soak through clothing, and left a person's skin red and burning for a week or better. Local birdlife was abundant, flying between the trees in their brilliant plumage and raising their voices in raucous cries. Insects and small animals added their own buzzes, clicks and whistles to the jungle cacophony, all contributing to a picture of serene normality within this untamed environment.

Nothing moved that could not be expected to; there were no sounds that had not been there on a dozen previous occasions. There was nothing that could be a cause for alarm or suspicion. But nevertheless, something felt wrong.

The man stood staring into the jungle for more than a minute before finally moving on. He was a firm believer in the power of protective paranoia; just because he couldn't see something didn't mean it wasn't there. He had been living with the constant threat of discovery and death for two years now, and his intuition had been honed to a fine edge. He moved slowly, checking each step and looking constantly around, his ears alert for any slight sounds that might tip him off. His hand did not stray from his side where the stunner rested easily on his hip.

The feeling of being watched increased as he walked. There were eyes out there studying his every movement, of that fact he grew more and more certain. But for what purpose? So far, the unseen observer had made no threatening moves—but the very fact that he *was* in hiding meant that his intentions would not stand up to open examination. That was not good.

As the pirate walked, his suspicions grew. The whole purpose of his coming up here had seemed funny from the start. "Check out the power feed at generating station number four," his boss had told him. "It's acting up at odd moments, almost as if someone was playing with it."

The request had seemed strange at the time. "I don't know much about the generators," he'd answered. "Wouldn't it be better to send someone from the work crews?"

"I think it may be one of them doing it," the boss had responded. Then, leaning forward, he added quietly, "We may have an infiltrator on the base, someone trying to sabotage our work. I trust you; I'd prefer that you have a look and let me know what you find out. Go the topside route so no one sees you."

There'd been no way to argue with that and so, reluctantly, he'd taken the assignment. It made sense in a way, though he had to smile despite himself at the irony of the situation. But now, as he walked carefully through the jungle toward the generating station, the conversation took on a much more sinister aspect. What if the boss suspected *him* of being the infiltrator? What if he had been sent up here to be executed as a traitor to the organization? Alone and isolated up here, he made a perfect target. Could this be a setup?

But what would be the point of that? If they suspected him of betraying them they could just as easily have killed him down in the base, without bothering to go through with this ambush. The boss held life and death over his subordinates—and had killed people in the past for less serious offenses. Why the charade this time?

None of it made much sense, and the man could not arrive at any answers. All he had was the unshakeable conviction that he was indeed being followed and watched.

On impulse, he stopped dead. As his ears strained to pick up some indication of his follower, a chill went up his spine.

There it was, at the very limits of his hearing: the faint *swish* of another body moving through the jungle in time to his own rhythm, coming to a stop just a second too late to avoid detection. It was impossible to tell in which direction the sound had been; it was gone again almost the same instant he heard it. But he had heard it; there was no doubt at all in his mind now.

That question, at least, was settled—but it brought a new one to mind: What to do now? Should he try to go back to the elevator tube, back down to the base and the safety of his fellow pirates? If his fears about his boss were correct, though, he would only be running straight into the arms of the enemy. Should he continue on his intended path to generating station four and hope to find some sanctuary there? But the unseen watcher had been waiting for him to come up; perhaps there was a trap waiting there ahead of him, with the watcher following to make sure he didn't deviate.

The options forward and back seemed pretty dismal, and simply standing where he was left him too exposed. The only recourse was to break from the path completely, head off sideways in an unexpected direction and hope to catch his follower by surprise.

Being righthanded, his first impulse was to break to the right. Instead, to avoid predictability, he ran to the left at about a seventy-degree angle to his original path. He made no attempt to maintain an unsuspecting air; stopping in the middle of his journey would have already alerted his enemy of his suspicions. Instead, he threw caution to the winds and ran through the jungle, pushing aside the brush that whipped at his face and ripped at his clothes.

The noise that he made as he crashed through the forest was loud in his own ears, as were his deep gasps for breath; nevertheless, the sounds behind him were unmistakable now—the sounds of someone, or some group of people, running after him before he could escape completely.

The barrel of his stun-gun beat against the man's leg with every stride he took, but he did not dare slow down yet to unholster it; he had a momentary advantage of speed and surprise, and he wanted to keep it. For all he knew, there could be five people behind him, all armed with blasters. He had to find himself a secure position before trying to pick off his pursuers.

Farther off to his left he heard the sound of rushing water, and a plan began to form in his mind. A small river ran nearby, cascading over a cliff and down to this level in a beautiful waterfall. The man recalled an outcropping of rock over which the water tumbled; he could hide in the grotto behind the waterfall and pick off his pursuer as he approached. While far from perfect, the plan offered more hope than merely running blindly through the jungle—and any hope was something to grasp at.

He altered course slightly, and soon he could see the cliffs rising into view over the treetops. With an extra burst of speed he dashed out across the small clearing between the trees and the cliffs, knowing full well he was dreadfully exposed for several seconds. He could feel the spray from the cascading water hit his face with sudden coolness—and then abruptly he was behind it, running around the side of the falls and into the small grotto in back.

He finally stopped, bending over and gasping desperately for breath. There was a stitch in his left side that felt like a knife stabbing through his ribs; he made an effort to will the muscles there to relax, and after a few moments the pain eased enough to let him move around some more. He drew his stunner from his belt and settled into a defensive posture, awaiting further developments.

In the next few quiet seconds he willed his mind back to the clear coldness it would need for the fight to follow. Actually, he was rather satisfied with the position in which he found himself; it was far more favorable than anything he might have dared hope for. The waterfall in front of him would at least partially obscure him from the view of any pursuers, while giving him a clear shot at anyone coming into the clearing. Even if his enemy stayed in the shelter of the trees at the edge of the jungle, he would be at the extreme limits of blaster range. The cliff behind him was solid; as a veteran of many fights, he knew well the advantage of a firm wall at his back. He crouched in the semi-darkness of his hollow, getting progressively damper, and waited.

The stillness descended once more on the scene. Whoever was following him must have realized the situation and halted just out of sight, still within the jungle, waiting at the edge of the clearing for him to make his move. The game of patience began again.

This was eerie, the man thought. He knew someone was

after him, but he had not had a single glimpse of his pursuer. It was a silent and deadly game of hide-and-seek—without rules and without free bases.

Tiring at last of the silent battle of wills, the pirate called out, "I know you're there. Why don't you show yourself? Or don't you have the guts for a showdown?"

A moment went by while the other considered his words. Then a voice came out of the jungle—a voice that sounded vaguely familiar, yet the pirate couldn't quite place it. "An interesting choice of words," the unseen watcher said. "In a way, you're right. By your definition, I don't have the guts. But I think it's time for a showdown, after all." And with that, he stepped forward.

Behind the waterfall, the pirate's jaw dropped. The man coming toward him was a duplicate of himself, complete in every detail. The walk, the clothing, the mannerisms—everything was identical to himself. He now knew why the voice sounded familiar—it was his own voice, one he certainly had not expected to hear from someone else.

At first he was too amazed to do anything but stare at the figure approaching him. Belatedly he realized that the other *him* was armed with a blaster, and was walking within easy range. Whatever the purpose of this apparition, it could mean him no good at all; he mustn't let it get closer. "That's far enough," he said, taking careful aim with his stunner.

The other man kept coming forward. There was a smile on his face.

Perspiration was beading on the pirate's forehead. He pulled the trigger of his stun-gun and heard the satisfying hum of its paralyzing beam.

The other man's smile broadened. He kept on walking.

The pirate knew he could not have missed; he was too good a shot. Perhaps the setting had been faulty. He checked his weapon quickly and saw that it had been set on four. His lookalike should have collapsed on the ground and been unconscious for two hours at that setting; instead, he was still walking relentlessly toward the waterfall.

There was little time left for playing games; the pirate could not spend the effort wondering what had gone wrong. He set the dial of his stunner all the way up to ten—instantly lethal—and fired again.

And again, nothing happened.

The double advanced to within fifteen meters of the waterfall and stopped there. He seemed strangely reluctant to come much closer, but he had little need to; his weapon would be quite effective within that range.

The blaster spoke in a deceptively quiet hum, but there was nothing deceptive about the charge of dazzling energy that streaked from the barrel. There was a whiff of ozone where the beam passed through air, and when it hit the waterfall it caused a cloud of scalding steam to boil upward. Some, but not all, of the beam's energy was dissipated in the water; the rest passed through and struck the pirate along the right side of the torso. The man fell to the ground and lay still.

The double watched the body lying motionless on the ground behind the waterfall for a few moments, then fired his blaster again. This time he directed its beam upward, at the projecting lip of the overhang down which the water cascaded. He kept the beam at a steady level until the rock, unable to withstand the continual energy bombardment, began to crumble away. A minor rockslide ensued, burying the original pirate beneath a pile of rubble. The body was totally hidden from view.

Observing his handiwork and deeming it good, the double silently tucked the blaster into its holser, turned, and walked confidently back to the pirate base.

"On the whole," Lady A said to her admiral, "you've done a most creditable job."

Admiral Shen Tzu smiled and touched the fingertips of both hands together in front of him to form an arch over his chest. "You'll pardon me I'm sure, milady, if I choose not to fully savor that remark. I've learned that compliments beginning with 'on the whole' usually have a substantial 'but' attached."

The two conspirators were alone in Admiral Shen's office, buried deep within the complex of the pirate base, seated opposite one another across the admiral's desk. Even a casual observer could have told that the two people were neither friends nor equals. Lady A had neither, nor did she wish any.

Lady A was not a large woman, of only medium height and build, but she nonetheless dominated any group she was in. She had a classically beautiful body behind which lay a soul of ice. She projected an air of calculated superiority, and coldly cultivated the impression that she was distinct from those who worked for her. She was dressed meticulously in a black cat suit with a tight-fitting hood and boots, and a tool belt around her waist. Tucked into the belt was a coiled whip, and none of her subordinates could be quite sure whether it was intended to be functional or merely ornamental.

As she looked across the desktop at her underling, she reviewed his qualifications in her mind as though he were merely another entry in a computer file. She was constantly revising and updating her opinions of her subordinates; she refused to tolerate inefficiency, and the moment anyone ceased to do his job the way she wanted it done, she got rid of him and found someone else who could.

Admiral Shen, though, was still high on her list of favored employees. He was a big, beefy man with multiple chins and a large belly. He had a long thin mustache that drooped well down past his chins, and braided forelocks on either side of his face. His hands were fat, his fingers like sausages, and he had a deep, booming laugh. He laughed often, this big man, but Lady A did not hold that against him. She judged a man by his performance, not his outward characteristics; she had read Shen's soul, and found him more than satisfactory.

One of Shen's weaknesses was a love of affectation. He was currently playing the role of a Mongol warlord, dressed in a long black coat trimmed with sable over baggy black velvet pants whose cuffs were tucked into embroidered red leather boots. He had a pointed leather cap, trimmed with white fur, on his head, and a scimitar—whose handle was really a disguised blaster—at his belt. An enormous gold medallion covered most of his chest like a shield.

The decor of his office matched his presumed persona. The walls and ceiling were draped with a red brocade fabric to resemble a Mongol tent. His desk was carved ebony with brass fittings. Oriental rugs covered the floor, and a profusion of silk pillows was scattered about the room. Shen and Lady A were seated on two of the office's camel-saddle chairs, which were more striking than comfortable.

Shen's extravagances might become tedious once Lady A's regime was firmly established over the Empire—but until then, his military expertise made him indispensable to her cause.

Perhaps Shen realized that as well. He was more flippant with her than she usually allowed subordinates to become. She decided to let his remark remain at face value. *Let him have his little jests for now,* she thought.

"The 'but' in this case is tolerable—so long as you learn

your lesson from it and see that the mistake isn't repeated. One of your ships, the *Lucinda,* was captured last week when it tried an abortive raid on a Navy decoy ship."

Shen shrugged his massive shoulders. "We're in a war. We have to expect casualties from time to time. A ship or two is hardly a catastrophe—unlike what happened to Ling." Shen shivered slightly. "That could have really been fatal if you'd actually implemented Operation Annihilate. We'd have been counting on those ships, and we'd have been slaughtered."

The incident to which he alluded had occurred several months earlier. Operation Annihilate had been ready to go into action, awaiting only the word from Lady A—or the mysterious C—to unleash it. The conspiracy's forces had gathered in the depths of interstellar space, waiting at several strategic points to descend upon Earth and capture the heart of the Empire in one bold stroke. The cue was to be the assassination of Emperor Stanley Ten and Crown Princess Edna during the Princess's wedding at Bloodstar Hall. With the two best claimants to the Throne dead, the Imperial Navy would be demoralized—and the subsequent bickering over succession would have allowed a strong outside force—namely the ships of the conspiracy—to sweep in and assume command.

That, at least, had been the theory. In actuality, the assassinations that were to have triggered the plan never came about, thanks to the superhuman efforts of some agents of the Service of the Empire. Their last-second interference saved the Emperor's and Princess's lives, causing Lady A to postpone Operation Annihilate.

But, at that same time, her conspiracy suffered another blow when the Imperial Navy raided one of the pirates' space bases run by Captain Ling, destroying or capturing all the ships waiting there to take part in the attack. Even Lady A, who claimed to know so much of the government's inner workings, had been surprised by the raid, leaving her to wonder whether her own organization's security had been breached; but when more time passed and none of the other bases were hit, she and C came to the conclusion that this one raid had been a fluke. Either the Imperial Navy or the Service of the Empire must have learned of the base through outside sources and acted against it on an impromptu basis. C had said he'd be checking out the details further. But for now, Ling was dead and any mistakes he'd made to reveal his location to the Empire had died with him.

Lady A was never one to dwell on past failures, except to make them object lessons for the future. "The loss of the *Lucinda* doesn't trouble me greatly," she said. "As you yourself pointed out, a few losses are inevitable. But aboard the *Lucinda,* the Navy found the body of Karla Jost—a woman who was exiled to Gastonia twelve years ago and who, as far as the Empire's official files went, was still there. Up until that time, the enforcement arms of the Empire had not suspected our Gastonian operations; now they do. Karla Jost was supposed to remain here with you. What was she doing on the *Lucinda?*"

If the implied charges of malfeasance bothered Shen, he did not let his feelings show. "She was going to be one of my wing commanders," he explained coolly. "Yet she hadn't been aboard a ship, except to come here from Gastonia, in a dozen years. I don't know about you, milady, but I don't want to put someone in a position of command until they've proven they can handle it. Jost was on a shakedown cruise, to regain her spacelegs and get the feel of command. It was only bad luck that *her* ship was the one the Navy snatched."

"Bad luck is the excuse of incompetent planners."

Shen smiled disarmingly. Not even Lady A could force him to lose his composure. "Quite so, but we've all had our share of it, eh? What about your government contacts? Couldn't they have hushed the matter before it reached SOTE's ears?"

Lady A frowned. "Unfortunately, by the time it came through official channels there was little we could do. There is a point of no return, after which an attempted coverup only makes matters worse rather than better. Covering up would have meant too many corpses, too many transferred personnel, too many falsified records—and if anyone had caught wind of *that,* they might realize how well organized our forces are. We decided it best to leave SOTE with the impression we're more fallible, to lull them into a false sense of security. In fact, we're working on a plan to turn the error to our advantage."

She stopped abruptly. "But that's not your concern. Whether we can profit by our mistake is immaterial; the fact remains that the mistake should never have been made in the first place." She did not have to say more. Her words implied strongly enough that Shen was to avoid such occurrences in the future. If he was not smart enough to read the implication, she would soon have a new admiral.

"I agree," Shen said amiably. "But here we run into a problem of morale. That first false alarm dashed everyone's hopes; sitting here on a jungle world, parsecs away from civilization, with nothing to do all day but polish the ships' noses is having a bad psychological effect on my people. We can't make the mistake of giving them too much time to think; who knows what dangers that might lead to? I must give them something to do. I'd rather send them out on their occasional piratical jaunts and risk losing a ship every so often than have them sit around and grumble and grow discontented. That's no way to win a war, milady."

Lady A nodded slowly. However insubordinate Shen might be, he knew his job. "I am not asking you to abandon your raids; you're your own master there. But I do ask that you pick your targets more carefully. And for your sake—for all our sakes—don't use so many ex-criminals. If they're caught, they can give away the scope of our endeavor."

Shen smiled. "You need both cons and piracy to make a conspiracy."

There was a pause of two full beats before Lady A said, "I will not dignify that with a response."

"I didn't think you would. Would you care for an inspection tour instead?"

Lady A agreed, and followed her admiral around the base, giving it a thorough examination. Shen's comment about bad luck happening to all of them had hit her harder than she would ever have admitted. Although the Service of the Empire had stumbled across the conspiracy very late in the game—too late, she was sure, to stop it effectively—they had scored a few lucky successes lately against her... too many. They had not yet even scratched the frost on the tip of the iceberg, but they were becoming annoying. The Service and its agents were like an insect bite, an itch she couldn't scratch—hardly fatal, but they did distract her and take some of her concentration away from more important matters.

She dismissed the thought from her mind. Plans were afoot to deal with SOTE, to use the very cleverness of its own agents against itself. All would be taken care of in good time, and Operation Annihilate would soon be in action once more. She did not bother telling Shen any of this, however; it was never a good policy to let an inferior know any more than he needed to operate efficiently.

2

Luna Base

Luna Base was the central command headquarters of the Imperial Navy. At the very formation of the Empire of Earth, the decision had been made that the control center of the Empire's armed forces should be located far from any inhabited regions; that way, in case of attack, the populace around the base could not be held hostage for the base itself. The population of Earth at that time had been close to four and a half billion, and there simply were no suitable land areas left that were far enough from inhabited regions. Locating the base underwater would have posed additional complications—chiefly in terms of communications and readiness of ships for instant takeoff—and so that possibility was discarded as well. Since Earth was to be the seat of imperial government, military headquarters had to be nearby—leaving as the only two alternatives either the moon or a station in free space.

Each alternative had both its champions and its detractors. The lunar enthusiasts argued that a space station would be far too exposed to enemy attack; on the moon, they could be firmly entrenched and unassailable. The lunar soil, too, would provide the necessary materials for building both the base and the fleet; any orbiting station would have to import its materials from the moon anyway.

The proponents of an orbital headquarters countered with arguments about how much added mobility a space station would give the fleet. They spoke of more efficient communications between Earth and an orbiting station than between Earth and a lunar base. Their most telling point was that battleships built at an orbital base could be much larger than those built on the moon, because they need not be designed to cope with gravitational conditions. Ships based on the moon would have to take off and land against a gravity of approximately one-sixth gee; if they were made too large, they'd be unwieldy. Ships constructed in space, with no need to land on the surface of a planet, faced no such restrictions.

The debate between the two factions raged for more than three years. The argument grew so heated that even now, centuries after the original squabble, there were families who still did not speak to one another because their ancestors had been on opposite sides of the dispute. Finally, in July of 2228, Emperor Stanley One settled the matter by taking the best of both proposals. The strategical headquarters and command center would be on the moon, buried deep below the surface and impregnable to all but the most concentrated thermonuclear attack. The orbiting station would be constructed for the superdreadnaught class of spaceship, anything too large to land on the moon itself; there would be comparatively few of those, but they would be the elite of the fleet.

Over the centuries, the balance swung slowly in favor of Luna Base. ORB, as the space station came to be known, was used today primarily as a shipyard and drydock, secondarily as a center for research and testing of space weapons and armor. Most other naval command functions were absorbed by the ever-growing lunar facility.

Luna Base was a huge, sprawling complex, far outstripping its modest beginnings. There were seldom less than five hundred ships sitting on its landing field at any given time, ranging in size from scouts to cruisers. It was located in the Mare Moscoviense on the lunar farside, with the body of the moon itself shielding the base's delicate communications net from the harsh volume of Earth's own radio broadcast signals. Enormous receivers, some kilometers across, listened to the universe, keeping track of all interstellar traffic, military and civilian, throughout the Empire. This deluge of incoming information was interpreted by the Navy's own computer system and eventually stored in the Empire's Primary Computer Complex.

Luna Base served other functions as well. The Naval Training Academy was located there, off to one side of the Mare. The Imperial Marines' special low-grav training center was off in a small crater just to the west of the base. There, too, were housed the thousands of personnel permanently billeted at the base, plus the hundreds more who were there awaiting reassignment to new ships.

Despite the best of intentions, human population had built up around the base anyway. It was inevitable; a project this big, employing this many people, needed administrators to keep it running and services to fulfill its needs. All told, nearly a hundred thousand people could be found at Luna Base at any given instant.

At this particular moment, four very special people were wandering down the labyrinthine corridors of Level 147. They were dressed in the bright orange coveralls of maintenance crew, but the security strips across the front of their chests gave them instant access to most rooms within the complex. The corridors were swarming with people, as they always were at this level, but no one paid particular attention to the four short, solidly built figures.

The four had planned it that way, and had worn orange uniforms specifically so they wouldn't be noticed. They made their livings by remaining anonymous; it could be tragic if their faces were widely known.

They talked among themselves at a normal conversational level; amid the din of the random conversations around them, they stood little chance of being overheard.

"I think we're lost," said one of the women to the man walking beside her. "Are you sure you got the instructions right?"

"Absolutely, and we've followed them to the letter," replied the man, who was her husband. "We left elevator tube number four at Level 147, kept the red wall on our right and followed the blue line on the floor. The room has got to be around here somewhere." The man made a motion to touch the brim of his hat, and then realized he wasn't wearing it at the moment.

"Well, something isn't right," his wife said. "We're looking for Meeting Room 147-16, and the room numbers are going down, not up. There's number ten, and beyond it is nine. We must be going in the wrong direction. I think we should stop someone and ask."

"Some superagents we'd be then," laughed the second man from behind them. "This was supposed to be a secret meeting, remember?"

"Well, it won't be *any* kind of a meeting if we don't get there," said the fourth member of the group, another woman. "If we don't do something soon, we'll only end up more lost than we are."

"Don't worry," the first man said lightly. "I've been dropping breadcrumbs behind us. If the birds don't eat them—ah, there it is, on the other side! Meeting Room 147-16. Once again I've delivered you to the promised land."

"I think that stint as a preacher addled his brains," his wife confided to the other two. "Now he thinks he's Moses."

The group cut across the busy traffic moving steadily past them and made it to the other side of the corridor, where the sign on the door indicated that was the room they were seeking. The first man reached for the button that would admit them, then hesitated. "Are you sure he wants to see Vonnie and me, too?" he asked. "We've never met him and . . ."

"He asked for you both specifically. You're not exactly what anyone would call a security risk."

Shrugging his shoulders, the first man pressed the button and the door to Meeting Room 147-16 slid silently open in front of them. Together, the four orange-clad figures entered the chamber.

It was hard for them to see anything at first. The room itself was dimly lit except for the far wall, which appeared to be a picture window overlooking the sunlit surface of Mare Moscoviense. The view was actually a triscreen projection; six hundred meters below the lunar surface, all they could have seen through a real window would be solid rock. The window effect did, however, help prevent claustrophobia in people who had to work constantly underground.

As their eyes became accustomed to the lighting, they could make out more details of the room. A dim blue light radiated down from the ceiling tiles; the three walls other than the one with the "window" contained computer projection screens; any information stored in the Navy's computers could be instantly called up and displayed on those screens—or, if it was preferred, conferees within the room could sketch their own illustrations via computer controls. In the center of the room was an enormous table, around which were clustered more than a score of chairs. The top surface was again an enormous computer projection screen, on which could be simulated entire space battles and war games.

Aside from themselves, the only other person in the room was a man standing at the far end of the long table. He wore a conservative gray jumpsuit, which normally would have allowed him to blend nicely into any crowd; here at Luna Base, however, where uniforms were the rule, the man stood out as quite an exception. He was close to fifty and totally bald—but even in the semi-darkness of this room, the fire of intelligence could be seen burning brightly behind his eyes.

This man was Zander von Wilmenhorst, and he was one of perhaps half a dozen people whose slightest actions could alter the destiny of the Empire of Earth. He was most widely known as the Grand Duke of Sector Four, that ten-degree sliver of an imaginary sphere surrounding Earth and extending toward infinity. Von Wilmenhorst was the hereditary ruler of all worlds lying within the boundaries of his sector, subject only to the Emperor himself—and since his sector was one of the most thoroughly explored and populated, he held a considerable amount of influence in galactic affairs.

But there were thirty-five other grand dukes, all his equal in rank; what set him particularly apart from the rest was the fact that he was also the Head of the Service of the Empire— that vast Imperial intelligence network that kept the Empire free of corruption and discontent. Being the supreme leader of SOTE—though that fact was known to a comparative handful, and most of those within the organization itself—was his primary responsibility; it made him a key advisor to the Emperor on matters of policy and internal security.

The Service of the Empire was not a spying agency, though many of its agents did work under cover; nor was it a police agency, though the targets of its attention were usually lawbreakers. The purpose of SOTE was, quite simply, to assure the safety of the Empire against all threats. It was loyal exclusively to whoever occupied the Throne, and did its utmost to ensure the stability of that person's reign. The Service was charged with the task of weeding out treason wherever it might occur and whatever the cost. The agents of SOTE were the most able, most conscientious people in the Galaxy, and their record of success spoke for itself.

Von Wilmenhorst, in turn, eyed the four people who had entered the room. Of all the loyal, talented people at his disposal, these four were his top choices. Together, they made two of the best undercover teams he'd ever seen; time and again they produced results that took his breath away.

The way they had multiplied was most gratifying indeed. He had started out with two: the brother-sister team of Jules and Yvette d'Alembert, circus performers from the high-gravity world of DesPlaines. In addition to bodies in prime physical condition, they also possessed minds that could act with lightning speed. They'd been his top agents. Jules d'Alembert was the only person currently alive who'd made a perfect score on the thousand-point test of ability given to all Service personnel; Yvette was barely a point behind at 999. Together they had helped smash a ring of traitors that had been building for sixty years, and had gone on to crack numerous other difficult cases as well.

Only a few months ago both had gotten married—Jules to his childhood sweetheart Yvonne Roumenier, and Yvette to a young nobleman, Pias Bavol, from the high-gravity Gypsy planet of Newforest. Both Pias and Vonnie were now in the Service as well, working with their spouses. Instead of one super team, the Head now had two—a double-barreled threat against the enemies of the Empire.

"Come in, please," the Head said. "You're right on time. I trust the directions I gave you were adequate."

Pias Bavol was a bit shy at meeting the Head for the first time—but as always, he covered his shyness with a light-hearted exterior. "The directions were perfect, sir. Despite the doubts of unnamed others who thought we were lost, I guided us safely here."

The Head laughed. "I know the feeling well. I got lost myself on my first few visits. Luna Base grew in a very irregular manner, and nothing is ever quite where you'd expect it to be. Sorry to have you meet me here rather than in Headquarters on Earth, but I've been involved for the past few weeks in security briefings with the Navy brass, and I couldn't get away." He looked pointedly at Jules and Yvette. "Aren't you two going to introduce me to your spouses?"

Brother and sister blushed. They had both conferred with the Head on so many occasions that it was difficult to remember that Vonnie and Pias had never met him. It was Yvette who finally took the initiative. "Vonnie d'Alembert, Pias Bavol, this is our boss, Grand Duke Zander von Wilmenhorst."

The two introductees were suitably impressed, but the Head put them quickly at ease. "Yvonne, I'd like to say that you're more beautiful and charming than Jules described, but I'm afraid that would be impossible; you'll have to settle for *as* beautiful and charming. And as for you, Pias," the Head went on, turning to Yvette's husband and looking him straight in the eyes, "I could never adequately thank you for helping save my daughter's life on Sanctuary."

Pias shrugged. "It was something I just sort of fell into," he explained with uncharacteristic modesty.

"And lucky for all of us that you did," the Head added.

"Amen," Yvette smiled at her husband.

The Head waved an arm at the chairs around the central table. "Please be seated and make yourselves comfortable. If you'd like some refreshment, you'll find that each place at the table has its own order box. Just punch in your request and it will arrive in a few seconds, compliments of the Imperial Navy."

Jules and Yvette were mad for orange juice, and each ordered a large glass. Yvonne preferred hot tea and a small buttered roll. Pias ordered a glass of *acolya,* a wine peculiar to his own homeworld of Newforest—and was pleasantly surprised to find that the Navy kept it in stock. Their orders arrived up a small tube within the table in less than a minute—a tribute to the Navy's efficiency.

When everyone was comfortably settled, the Head grew more serious. "As I'm sure you assumed, I didn't ask you here merely for a pleasant afternoon's conversation. There's work to do."

"Isn't there always?" Jules said.

The Head merely nodded and continued his explanation. "As Pias and Yvette found out at the time of Princess Edna's wedding, there seems to be a link between the conspiracy masterminded by C and Lady A, and at least some of the space piracy that is plaguing the Empire. We took care of Captain Ling and his crew, but we discovered that they were building a navy of their own. It wasn't until just a couple of months ago that I learned the Navy had been conducting its own investigation for almost three years and had not thought to tell us about it." Von Wilmenhorst shook his head. "Sometimes I think we may be our own worst enemies, with interservice rivalries and the lack of communication between branches of government. If they'd bothered to let us know . . ."

He paused and placed his hands face down on the tabletop. "Well, that's a problem for me, not for you. What matters now is that we've opened the channels of communication between us again and some surprising developments are coming out. The most important of them—and the reason for my calling you in—is a person named Karla Jost."

He punched a couple of buttons on his console and a face appeared on the screen in the center of the table. It was a middle-aged woman with mouse-brown hair, a two-centimeter long scar over her left eyebrow and a square, firmly set jaw. There was a steely look about her eyes that marked her unquestionably as a dangerous woman. "I'd hate to meet her in a dark alley," Vonnie commented.

"You won't have to—she's dead," the Head told them. "But the puzzle she represents is far more of a threat than she ever was."

The Head leaned back in his chair once more and began a recitation of facts. "Karla Jost was in and out of trouble ever since she was a teenager. She had a prison record that read like a short novel. About fourteen years ago she threw in her lot with a pirate gang, and rapidly rose to a position of leadership within it. It was her gang that made the famous raid on Taratuil—do you remember anything about that?"

The four agents had to search their memories for a moment. Thirteen years ago, the planet Taratuil was at the outermost limits of the Empire. It was a newly settled world, with a population of only about five thousand people. Seeing it as a weak target, a pirate gang swooped down on it and, with their superior arms, forced the locals to submit to their rule. The Navy, when it learned what had happened, moved into action—but with the pirates holding the citizens hostage, the government had to move carefully. Finally, after almost a month, a combined action by the Navy, SOTE and the Imperial Marines freed the planet and captured the pirate gang.

When he saw that his agents recalled the incident, the Head continued on. "The top two leaders of that gang were executed after a brief trial, as were eleven of the gang members who were convicted of committing atrocities. The remainder of the pirates—Karla Jost included—were exiled to Gastonia for life. The matter should have ended there—but it didn't.

"Just a few days ago, the Navy put out a decoy ship to trap a pirate group it had been chasing for some time. The pirates took the bait and, after quite a fight, the Navy captured the outlaw ship. More than half the pirates were killed in the battle—and when the Navy went about the routine task of identifying the bodies, they found that one of the women was Karla Jost.

"Quite naturally, they contacted us to tell us that they'd found an escapee, and that we no longer had to worry about her. The problem was that we *hadn't* been worried about her—all our records indicated that Karla Jost had never left Gastonia."

The implication was not lost on any of the agents, but it was left to Vonnie to voice the obvious. "Then someone spirited Jost off the planet without our knowledge, and she ended up with the pirates."

As the Head nodded, Yvette continued her sister-in-law's line of reasoning. "And where there's one escapee, there might be more. I presume you suspect an organized attempt to get the better talent off Gastonia and into a treasonous conspiracy."

"It sounds like a plan I've heard somewhere before," Jules drawled with no little irony.

Indeed it was. Lady A's conspiracy had already attempted a similar maneuver, hiding some of the Galaxy's most notorious criminals on a world called Sanctuary. Jules and Yvette had broken up that plot—and, in the process, they learned of Lady A's existence for the first time. It was also on Sanctuary that they met and teamed up with Pias, who had gone there on a private mission of revenge against one of the criminal refugees.

The Head nodded soberly. "It has Lady A's touch, no doubt about it. And as you can well imagine, we're a lot more concerned with these possible escapees than we were about ordinary criminals. Each of the exiles on Gastonia was sent there for one specific crime: treason. We have a planet populated by traitors, every one of whom has some reason for hating the Empire—and many of whom, like Karla Jost, are dangerous people. If Lady A and her cohorts are looking for help, they couldn't go to a better spot.

"As soon as I discovered that, I sent for you. While you were on your way here, I developed a preliminary theory. We already know from the raid on Ling's base that the conspiracy was amassing ships. We can tell from what little wreckage remains of the munitions plant Jules and Vonnie destroyed on Slag that the conspiracy was manufacturing weapons at an enormous rate. If what we fear about Gastonia is true, we now know where the conspiracy is getting some of its manpower."

The Head sat up straight in his chair and ran a hand lightly over his smooth-shaven scalp. "The thing that concerns me the most is that it's all starting to come together. Ships, weapons, manpower—and in the background, a pair of strategists who seem to know every move we make, while we know next to nothing about them. It's going to be soon, I can feel it coming. And in just four months . . ."

He didn't have to complete the thought; each of his agents knew exactly what he meant. In four months, Emperor Stanley Ten would reach his seventieth birthday—and he had already announced his intention of abdicating at that time in favor of his daughter. Crown Princess Edna would then assume the title Empress Stanley Eleven, becoming the supreme ruler of the Empire of Earth and its trillions of inhabitants. Edna Stanley was a powerful and resourceful woman, a fitting offspring of her noble lineage; but she was only in her mid-twenties, and lacked the depth of experience she might need to cope with a crisis of this magnitude. That, apparently, was what the conspirators were counting on, too.

With his point made silently, the Head shifted topics slightly. "We can't afford to sit around and wait for developments. Jules and Yvonne, I want you to go to Gastonia and find out what's going wrong. If anything's amiss there it's a particular embarrassment to us; the Service is supposed to be responsible for the disposition of traitors. If there are any of *our* people involved in this conspiracy, I want them weeded out."

"No more than we do," Jules said. His jaw was clenched tight; loyalty to the Empire and to the Service was virtually an inborn trait of the d'Alembert family. The thought of anyone betraying the organization to which he was so devoted was most repulsive to him, and the Head almost pitied any turncoats that Jules encountered. Almost.

"What about us?" Yvette asked.

The Head turned his attention to the Bavol couple. "Yes, you two have a little different assignment. Originally I'd thought to let you work with Jules and Yvonne, so that the case might be cracked twice as fast. But something else came up that might put your talents to better use elsewhere. Some of our people down in Computer Analysis, after performing their arcane rituals with their machines, came to the conclusion that a joint operation between SOTE and the Navy to wipe out the pirates might be a good idea. Piracy has usually been the Navy's territory, and I know that Naval Intelligence has an ongoing undercover operation; but now that the link has been found between the pirates and this conspiracy, we do have a vested interest in this aspect of the operation. I proposed a mission to Captain Nacorn of NI, and he's pledged his department's cooperation. Since the two of you helped us crack Ling's outfit—however accidental it was—you're the Service's top experts on pirate catching. How do you feel about the idea?"

"We go where the work is," Yvette said pragmatically. "If the pirates are part of Lady A's plans, it's our job to smash them."

"Good!" the Head exclaimed, a dash of gusto in his voice. "I knew you'd feel that way. This will give us a two-pronged attack on the problem. Jules and Yvonne will work from the Gastonia end, sealing off that escape route, while Pias and Yvette will go to work on the pirates. As always, you'll have carte blanche; when agents produce results as spectacularly as you do, it would be presumptuous—not to mention foolish—of me to tell them how to do their jobs."

He took a couple of bookreels from his jacket pocket and handed one to each of the teams. "Here is the background information you'll each need, as well as my number here at the base should you need to reach me with any questions. I'll trust you to do your usual superb jobs—within, I hope, four months."

He did not have to emphasize the date. The four agents had already dealt with Lady A, and knew how serious a threat she could pose to a newly crowned empress. They could also sense the process quickening, the pace of the conspiracy accelerating as time went on. It was a feeling they did not like—and it promised to get worse before it got better.

3

The Road to Gastonia

Had Jules and Vonnie been less dedicated agents, it would have been a simple matter to have themselves exiled to Gastonia. The Service's Documentation Department would have been happy to build for them a record of treasonous activities as long as they wished. The record would then be fed into the Empire's computer banks, along with the trial judgment that these two traitors be exiled to Gastonia. Jules and Vonnie would be imprisoned and, within a week, they would be on their way to the prison world. It would be an easy, fast and convenient way to reach their destination.

Jules had, in fact, used that procedure before on the planet Chandakha when he wanted to be put in prison to check out the procedures of a criminal mob that was murdering thousands of people every year. But in that case he had been dealing with a small, local organization with no way of tapping into SOTE's files to see how valid the fraudulent records were. Lady A's conspiracy was far bigger, spanning perhaps the entire Galaxy, and was much more organized than the Chandakha gang could have dreamed of becoming.

There was little doubt that C and Lady A had some informational sources from within the highest levels of SOTE. They knew who the Head was and they were intimately acquainted with the Service's innermost workings. The Head had been trying to trace down the leaks within the Service for the past several months, without any success; but in the meantime, Jules and Vonnie could not completely trust their safety to their own side.

On their last assignment, they had asked SOTE to provide them with some false documentation to fool members of this conspiracy. They had thought it might take a week or two for the conspirators to check out the sources and discover they were faked; instead, it took only a day—and that slip nearly cost the d'Alemberts their lives. They would not underestimate the opposition again; they'd find a method of getting to Gastonia on their own, without the aid of SOTE.

There was only one way of being sent to Gastonia: commit treason and be sentenced for it.

The situation was a little more complex than that, of course. The very worst traitors were executed rather than sent into exile. That was the fate that awaited C and Lady A when they were finally brought to justice. It was only the lesser traitors who were spared execution and banished to the harsh world of Gastonia.

The practice of exiling people to Gastonia rather than killing every convicted traitor began under the short, unhappy reign of Empress Stanley Five, more commonly known as "Mad Stephanie." Whether she was any madder than some of the other Stanley rulers is a matter of some dispute; her nickname derived from her fanatical knack for smelling treason on every breeze and spotting traitors in every crowd. This obsession did have a basis in fact; when she was thirty-six her younger brother Edmund made a power play for the Throne, killing her father (then-Emperor Stanley Four) and very nearly killing her. Only the supreme loyalty of the Navy—primarily in the person of Fleet Admiral Simms—prevented the revolt's success. After several weeks of turmoil, the rebels admitted defeat, and Stephanie ascended to the Throne with a vengeance.

Prince Edmund and Grand Duke Gaspard of Sector Nineteen, the principal architects of the revolution, were publicly tortured and executed. Seven hundred and twenty-eight naval officers were court-martialed and shot. Stephanie combed the entire peerage; any noble who could not prove a record of unimpeachable loyalty was apt to find himself facing charges of treason—and, since Stephanie's will was the ultimate law, a trial was but an automatic prelude to death.

When, after a year, Stephanie showed no signs of abating her purges, all the Empire—including her closest advisors—began to worry. At the rate she was going, there would soon be none of the nobility left—and she was already beginning to accuse the more influential commoners as well. To prevent a further bloodbath, the Imperial advisors finally convinced their empress to banish the lesser offenders to the newly discovered planet of Gastonia at the outermost limits of Sector Twenty. The death penalty, while still the official punishment for treason, became reserved only for those who opposed their sovereign on a grand scale. In Stephanie's eyes, there were still plenty of those to go around—but thousands of people escaped execution and were "merely" banished for life.

As Stephanie's tyrannies grew more obsessive, the plots to depose her became very real indeed. The Service of the Empire, founded by Stephanie's grandmother Empress Stanley Three, had its work cut out for it, becoming little more than a terrorist police squad. Even SOTE could not keep the lid on all the revolutions, however, and Stephanie—along with most of her family—was finally assassinated in 2299, six long years after the start of her bloody reign. Only her youngest son Edward survived, and became Emperor Stanley Six. To his credit, he pardoned most of the prisoners who had been unjustly exiled to Gastonia—but he kept the possibility of banishment open for future cases, and so it had remained down to the present day.

Jules and Yvonne thus found themselves having to tread a fine line. They had to commit treason; ordinary criminals were dealt with on a local level, and usually assigned to planetary prisons. The treason they committed had to be serious enough to rank them above the level of the common crook—but not so serious that they would die for it.

After a couple of long brainstorming sessions between them, the d'Alemberts decided that they stood the best chance of being noticed on one of the younger pioneer worlds. They took the names of Ernst and Florence Brecht, ostensibly raised in a backwoods community on the very crowded planet Promontory. This identity was carefully selected; since Promontory was so crowded, and since its backwoods area was so primitive, a great many people existed without adequate documentation.

The fact that the Brechts had no birth certificates, no marriage license—indeed, no records of any sort—would not be considered unusual.

Also, because of its overcrowded condition, Promontory was a focal point of the Empire's emigration drive. Whenever there were new planets opened, the Empire subsidized migration from the crowded worlds to the newer ones. The population of the Empire kept moving and spreading; theoretically, there was no end in sight.

Thus it was that, one afternoon, Ernst and Florence Brecht showed up at the emigration office in Tor, capital city of Promontory, and volunteered to emigrate to the new planet Islandia. The recruiting officer was delighted with this young couple, in such fine physical condition, and did not delve too deeply into their background. He had a quota to fill, and this couple satisfied all the necessary conditions. Within three days, the Brechts were aboard a spaceship bound for Islandia.

The planet Islandia was so named because more than ninety percent of its surface area was covered by water. These vast oceans were dotted by thousands of small islands, many of them still unexplored. The islands were a biologist's paradise, since many species of animals had evolved separately on each of the islands, making it an ideal laboratory for testing theories of parallel evolution. In addition, the sea life was rich and varied; most of the colonists' food and materials came from the oceans.

All the inhabited islands so far were located in the equatorial regions, making Islandia a tropical paradise. Life there was easy and relaxed. At present there were only about fifteen thousand people on the planet—though as word of its delights spread through the Empire there would undoubtedly be a large influx of tourists and settlers looking for the good life.

Jules and Yvonne settled right in, and for the first two weeks they were model citizens. Jules took a job as a dispatcher for a small fleet of fishing boats; Yvonne worked in a factory that processed *lecthit,* a native sea plant similar to kelp. They rented a small, modest apartment and kept very much to themselves. On a new colony like Islandia, that was all they needed to establish their identities.

They spent all their waking time away from their jobs studying the structure of life on Islandia, analyzing it with their expert eyes and calculating its weak points to a fine degree.

Although the planet's population was spread out over more than twenty islands, the administration required to serve its fifteen thousand people was minimal and was concentrated on Bantor, the largest inhabited island. The entire police force for all of Islandia was a squad of thirty-six officers, only one-third of whom were on duty at any one time—and of those on duty, only half remained at the central police station while the rest patrolled around the islands in cruising air cars. The local SOTE office was merely a formality, with only two agents assigned to it, keeping regular business hours rather than around-the-clock protection.

"It's a lucky thing this planet isn't more valuable," Vonnie commented, shaking her head in wonderment. "A baby could take it over."

"Isn't it nice to know we'll be performing a worthwhile service?" Jules agreed. "They'll be much more careful after we get finished with them."

The first step of their plan was to obtain weapons. The local sporting goods shops carried a wide assortment of stun-guns and stun-rifles for hunters. The settings on these weapons available to the general public only went up as high as three—a half hour stun; with the specialized training in weaponry that the d'Alemberts had received, however, it was easy enough to modify the guns they bought to deliver a number four stun, sufficient to knock a victim unconscious for two hours. They had the knowledge, had they wished, to give their stunners a lethal capacity as well; but they specifically wanted to avoid killing anyone during their little coup. The d'Alemberts had a great respect for innocent human life, and didn't want to kill anyone just to achieve their aims. Besides, committing a murder during their crime could very well lead to execution rather than banishment to Gastonia. A two-hour stun would serve their purposes well enough.

With their weapons properly modified and concealed, the d'Alemberts walked brazenly into the local SOTE office late one afternoon. The building SOTE rented on Islandia was small, consisting of a storefront reception area, two separate offices for the agents, and a locked room at the back where emergency equipment was kept. Jules and Vonnie looked around and saw, as they'd expected, that they were the only "customers" in the office.

The receptionist—a local employee rather than a SOTE

agent—came up to greet them at the front counter. "Can I help you?" he asked.

"Yes," Jules said hesitantly. "We . . . that is, my wife and I . . . we think we overheard some people plotting against the Empire. This *is* the proper place to report that, isn't it?"

The man's eyes went wide. In the short time he'd been working here, the only problems SOTE had had to deal with were immigration forms, visas and routine security checks of police applicants and nominees for the still-forming local nobility. Nothing as exciting as treason had ever even been intimated on this sleepy young planet.

"It certainly is," he said, unable to keep the quiver of excitement out of his voice. "You just wait a minute and I'll get someone here to talk to you about it." Returning to his desk, he buzzed the intercom for both agents, explaining the situation in a few crisp words. Within seconds, both SOTE agents came out of their offices to greet the young couple.

The men introduced themselves and began asking for particulars. Jules and Yvonne looked nervously to either side. "Are you sure we're alone here?" Vonnie asked. "I'm afraid these people might kill us if they found out we were talking to SOTE."

"We're quite alone, I assure you," the chief agent said in soothing tones.

That was all the d'Alemberts had been waiting for. In one simultaneous gesture they pulled out their concealed stunners and gave the three startled men a two-hour nap.

Vonnie clucked sympathetically as she stood over the unconscious bodies. "This'll look bad on their efficiency reports," she said. "But they'll probably be better agents in the future because of it."

They locked the front door to prevent other people from wandering in, then dragged the three stunned men into one of the offices and tied them up securely. That accomplished, they broke into the locked back room and stole all the weapons stored there. This SOTE station was not as fully stocked as would be expected on a larger world; there were two suits of battle armor—both of which were too tall to comfortably fit the d'Alemberts' DesPlainian body shapes—and some hand weapons, including six blasters. a dozen stunners and extra power packs for each. There were no high-powers or mobile field pieces, nor any indication of special Service spacecraft or attack vehicles. SOTE had not been expecting much trouble on Islandia—which was why the d'Alemberts had chosen it as their target. There was a subetheric communicator set against one wall; Jules blew it apart with one of the captured blasters. It simply wouldn't do to let any calls for help go off-planet before the d'Alemberts were ready for them.

With Phase One successfully completed, they drove to the police station and began Phase Two. The tactics they had used on the SOTE people worked equally well here; instead of treason, Jules announced that he had overheard some neighbors discussing a drug smuggling operation.

The only difficulty here was that there were six police to be dealt with at the station, as opposed to three men at SOTE headquarters. The d'Alemberts could only draw three of them out to hear their story, while the rest were attending their routine chores throughout the building. The agents had to settle for those three at once, and then spread out through the station to take care of the others. The operation did not take very long; the policemen were all natives of worlds with a standard gravitational field of one gee, and as such they were no match for the stronger, faster DesPlainians. Jules and Yvonne picked off the officers one by one before their victims even realized anything was wrong.

With the station now secure, they used the dispatcher's radio to call in the patrol craft one at a time on a variety of pretexts. Within five hours, all the on-duty police—plus three who had been off-duty and came into the station to begin their shifts— were in the d'Alemberts' custody. With scarcely any effort at all, the SOTE agents had immobilized all the armed forces on this world that could conceivably be directed against them.

Swiftly they transported their prisoners from the SOTE building to the police station as well. The jail cells were a perfect place for their captives, so they could eliminate the unpleasant bonds on hands and feet. The d'Alemberts said very little as they escorted their prisoners into cells, but they treated their captives with as much courtesy as the situation allowed, and never spoke harshly to them. They wanted the people to remember later that they had been exceedingly polite and non-violent.

While Vonnie stayed behind at the police station—both to keep an eye on their current prisoners and to catch any more police officers who reported in for work—Jules went out alone to pay a call on the Duke of Islandia. Duke Phillip had only been appointed ruler of this world by the Emperor eight months ago, as a reward for his many and valuable services to the Crown. He had not even begun work on his ducal palace; his official residence was merely a house slightly larger than normal size, set apart from the main portion of the city on a parcel of land covering less than two hectares and surrounded by a simple stone wall. Three bodyguards was the extent of the security force the Duke had for himself and his family. Jules d'Alembert could have cracked through tougher defenses blindfolded.

It was now midevening, and Jules knew that the Duke and his family would be at home either reading, working on late reports, watching the trivision, experiencing the sensable, or preparing for bed. It was a good time to catch them unprepared.

Parking his car a short distance from the wall, Jules got a running start and easily vaulted over the barrier. He sprinted toward the house at a pace that would have made many athletes envious, but which seemed only moderate to him. He was scarcely even breathing hard as he made it to the side of the house and began disconnecting the simple burglar alarm the Duke had installed to protect his home.

Jules entered the house through a window he forced open, into a darkened room on the ground floor. He made his way through the room to the hall door and, stunner in hand, began his exploration of the rest of the building. The house was not large, and within a minute he had made his first encounter: the Duke's teenage daughter. The girl received a taste of Jules's stunner before she even had time to cry out in alarm; she dropped silently to the floor and Jules continued his prowl through the house.

He found people scattered around in ones, twos and threes—never in a group so large that he couldn't handle them quickly and efficiently. Family members, servants and bodyguards all fell before the buzzing of his stun-gun. Jules finally confronted the Duke himself in the study, with one final bodyguard. Jules stunned the guard and turned toward the Duke. The man was obviously frightened for his life, but held firm despite his fears.

"What do you want from me?" Duke Phillip asked.

"Your job," Jules said in a matter-of-fact tone. "I've always wanted to be a duke, and I figure I've got as much right to the title as you do, since neither of us was born to it." In point of fact, Jules d'Alembert was of a far more noble lineage than the man he faced. His father, Etienne d'Alembert, was the current duke of DesPlaines, and Jules was sixth in line to inherit the title after his older brother Robert, Robert's three children, and his sister Yvette.

But it was Ernst Brecht speaking now, not the young lord from DesPlaines. Duke Phillip, staring down the muzzle of the stun-gun, might have been frightened but he wasn't cowed. "You'll never get away with it," he said. "The police... SOTE..."

"Interesting that you should mention them," Jules smiled. "I already attended to those details before coming here, *tovarishch*. They won't give me any trouble."

"Do you think the Emperor will sit still for..."

Jules dismissed that with a wave of his hand. "The Emperor is old and far away. He won't care what happens on some obscure little colony. What does it matter to him which of us is duke, just as long as he gets his taxes on time?" He pointed his gun resolutely at the Duke once more. "Now, please be so kind as to write your abdication letter. I'll dictate it for you."

"And if I refuse?"

"Then I'll just have to shoot you and forge it myself. No one but historians will ever have the chance to verify it, and by then it will be too late."

The Duke set his jaw stubbornly. "You'd only kill me after I wrote it, anyway. Why should I give you the satisfaction?"

"Please. I'm not a bloodthirsty man. No one has yet been permanently injured and if you behave yourself, no one will be. You have my word as a duke on that." Jules smiled. "Once you sign over the planet to me, I'll have no need to kill you. I may have to imprison you for a few months until the general populace adjusts to the idea of my reign, but once that happens you'll be free to go. I have nothing against you at all—you merely have something I want. Now, write as I say."

Duke Phillip looked over this strange man holding him at gunpoint, trying to evaluate him. Jules had been unfailingly polite, if single-minded. Perhaps he was only a madman; perhaps he would keep his word. In any event, Duke Phillip saw little alternative but to comply with this man's wishes for now and trust to the future to correct the situation. Slowly he took a piece of paper from the drawer of his desk and prepared to copy down what he was told.

Jules paced pompously around the room as he dictated the resignation letter. "I, Phillip Masson, former Duke of the planet Islandia, do from this day forward renounce and abjure forever any and all claim I may have to ranks and titles bestowed upon me, and to any lands ceded to me by Imperial statute; and furthermore, I hereby name Ernst Brecht to be my legal successor to all aforesaid ranks, titles and lands, including the right of inheritance to all his descendents. There. I think that should cover it well enough. Sign it, date it and stamp it with the official seal."

Jules knew, of course, that the document would be proved illegal on several counts, the most obvious being that it had been made under duress and was not legally binding. But more than everything else he had done, this paper would assure his and Vonnie's trial on charges of treason against the Throne rather than merely planetary charges of assault and kidnaping. It was strictly illegal for any nobleman to abdicate his authority without first making written petition to the Throne—and even when permission was granted, it was totally illegal for the abdicator to name his own successor. The laws of inheritance were strictly laid out in the Stanley Doctrine; if a noble, for some reason, wished to disinherit his legitimate heirs, his only recourse was to deed his title back to the Throne and allow the Emperor to appoint the successor.

By violating these basic tenets of Imperial law, Jules was rising above common criminality—he was thumbing his nose at the Empire, usurping its authority and declaring himself above it. That was treason, pure and simple—and the Empire was always eager to prosecute for treason even above any other crimes a criminal might have committed. In ruling a dominion so large and diverse, even the faintest hints of treason had to be thoroughly and publicly quashed.

When the document was completed, Jules looked it over to make certain it was in order, then forced Duke Phillip to accompany him to his groundcar—leaving behind the bodyguards, servants and family. They would come around in a short while, hardly the worse for wear—and they were scarcely important to the d'Alemberts' plan.

Jules drove to the planet's major radio station, where the Duke's authority and Jules's gun allowed them to interrupt the broadcast to read the resignation letter over the air. Jules then made a short speech to "his people," filled with platitudes about how wonderful life would become under his regime. From the radio station, Jules took the Duke back to the jailhouse, where Yvonne greeted them cheerily and escorted the Duke to a private cell of his own.

Two hours later a ship rose from the Islandia spaceport into the sky. Jules and Yvonne could see it from the police building, and smiled. The captain of the ship was undoubtedly concerned about this coup, and wanted to get his ship away from any possible danger while he still had the chance. He had no way of knowing that the coup consisted of only two people, and he didn't want his cargo confiscated or his crew detained. Once out in space, he would broadcast a distress signal that would let the Empire know what had happened here. The d'Alemberts had waited to stage their coup until there were several ships in port, so they could be sure that at least one captain would panic and leave to spread the word.

With that accomplished, they settled back to await results.

Around them, the world of Islandia was in a turmoil. This was the most dramatic event in the planet's short history, and everyone was talking and wondering what would happen next. Most people were roused to anger—Duke Phillip was very popular on this world—but they were unable to direct their rage constructively. With the Duke, the police and SOTE all imprisoned, there were no leaders capable of welding the people into an effective force to fight back—nor were the citizens' weapons any match for the artillery the d'Alemberts had captured from SOTE and the police. The people stewed and did nothing.

For Jules and Yvonne, time dragged by in a slow routine. The police station became their headquarters, and they did not leave; instead, they had spouses of the police officers bring food and supplies in to them, to assure that everyone would be fed adequately. This also served the function of letting the outside world know that all the prisoners were being well-treated; time and again, the visitors to the station would report back that no one had been hurt, and that everyone was in high spirits despite the awkward circumstances.

The d'Alemberts spent a lot of time talking to their captives, always being polite and even friendly. Jules ordered in a local tailor and had himself measured for a military uniform of his own outrageous design. Occasionally, on a whim, he would issue edicts as "Duke Ernst," passing them outside to the throng of news reporters who had gathered outside the building, waiting for any tidbit to pass along to their public. Ernst declared his and his wife's birthdays to be public holidays, abolished taxes, raised the speed limit for groundcars, instituted a curfew and, in general, rewrote sections of the local ordinances. He had no power to enforce anything, and he knew it; he merely wanted to make Duke Ernst look as though he were serious about ruling the world.

The siege lasted three days. Vonnie, who had spent some time monitoring communications on the police subcom unit, overheard fragments of a conversation which allowed her to deduce that a special SOTE assault squad was on its way from the nearby planet Appeny. After so many days of forced inactivity, the d'Alemberts were glad that something was finally going to happen.

They knew the assault was to begin when the reporters were cleared away from the building. Standard SOTE procedure for taking an occupied edifice was to try using tirascaline first; tirascaline was one of the strongest sleeping gases ever developed, and it would harmlessly knock out criminals and hostages alike, allowing SOTE to come in peacefully and mop up. There were gas masks in the police station the d'Alemberts could have worn to avoid such a fate, but they didn't bother. They could have held the station for some time against a small army, but there would have been no point to doing so; they wanted to be captured, and the less effort all around, the better.

They waited alone together in the front hall of the police station. "I don't think we'll get to see each other much for a while," Jules said. "I'll need something to tide me over."

They kissed passionately for several minutes until they smelled the sickly sweet aroma of tirascaline—and within seconds they were lying unconscious on the floor.

They awoke in prison in separate cells, but their time of imprisonment was short. The Empire believed in giving traitors a speedy trial, and in making as big a spectacle of it as possible to deter others from the same path. The case against Ernst and Florence Brecht was clearcut, and the imperial prosecutor finished in one day.

Jules insisted on defending both himself and his wife. He made no attempt to deny the facts, and his closing statement was basically an arrogant diatribe on why he should be a duke, and why the Emperor should be dismissed as an old fogey who was no longer competent to run a galaxy, and who should be ignored. It was neither apologetic nor conciliatory, and helped settle any doubts about the verdict.

The Brechts were found guilty of treason. While every treason verdict carried an automatic death penalty with it, clemency was granted because of the Brechts' consideration of their prisoners, and their sentence was commuted to life exile on Gastonia.

Although outwardly they acted stunned, inwardly the d'Alemberts were much relieved. Taking over an entire world had been the easy part of their assignment; the hard part lay ahead of them on the cold, forbidding exile world of Gastonia.

4
The Paradise

Pias and Yvette Bavol faced a somewhat different problem—how to work their way into the pirates' base without being obvious about their intentions. It was a problem that Pias attacked with his usual good humor.

"How does an ordinary honest citizen become a pirate?" he mused aloud as he and Yvette were discussing their strategy. "It would be gauche to run an ad: 'Situation wanted: pirate. Formerly free-lance, now seeks association with others. Good shot, good fighter, no piloting experience. Prefers administrative position.'"

"You never know," his wife laughed. "You might get some interesting offers." She cleared her throat and grew serious again. "But they must get new recruits from somewhere. We could make the rounds of the spaceport bars and underground hangouts until we hit some contacts."

Pias made a face. "I had my fill of those places when I was hunting Rowe Carnery. Three years of low dives can build up a toxic reaction. There has to be another way." He paused and smiled at his wife. "Besides, my love, you should know by now that that's not really my style. I prefer something with flash and elegance. Let the mountain come to Mohammed; I'll be more valuable to them if they have to seek me out."

"I don't think they're *that* desperate for manpower; there are plenty of cheap blasterbats for hire on any planet in the Galaxy. The only people they seek out are their victims."

Pias snapped his fingers and pointed at her triumphantly. "Then that's what I shall be. I'll make myself such a great target they won't be able to resist me."

"You can't be serious."

"Why not? It worked for us before, didn't it? We smashed Ling's gang after they captured the ship we were on."

"We were *very* lucky," Yvette reminded him. "We almost didn't make it out alive."

"That's because we stumbled into the situation accidentally. This time we'll be planning the program in advance, so we can take the variables into account."

"But our job is to infiltrate the pirates, to join their organization and destroy it from the inside. You can't do that if you're a victim."

"With my boyish charm, I'm sure I can reason the situation out with them."

"Your 'boyish charm' didn't work on Ling—and I'd like to see you reason with anyone after you've been chucked out an airlock with no spacesuit."

"Mere details," Pias said with an expansive gesture. "They can be worked out more conclusively once the broader plan is decided."

Though she loved her husband very much, Yvette would be the first to say that there were times he vexed her considerably. One of those times was now. She was still more used to working with her brother, and Jules had always preferred the direct approach. *Search and destroy* had been his motto; on the few occasions when they'd been forced to let the opposition find them, such as on Algonia during the Banion case, Jules was always much happier after the waiting was over and he could go into action. With Pias, she suspected, this was all much more of a great game; he seemed to enjoy the setting up of ruses as much for their own sake as for their ultimate end.

Still, she could hardly fault his performance. Even though he didn't have the family tradition in the Service that the d'Alemberts had, Yvette knew he was dedicated to their job. And she had to admit, his methods got results. She had doubted him before in their last mission, on Purity, but he had succeeded there, where her more direct attempts could not.

Yvette sighed. She would go along with his plans, if only to keep a check on some of his more extravagant ideas. But she still wished he were less *unorthodox*.

Pias's plan was to offer the pirates a target so irresistible that they would have to make a try for it. "Pirates go for money," he reasoned. "We'll have to offer them one of the richest ships in the Galaxy to guarantee their attack."

"Money alone isn't enough," Yvette countered. "Some of the richest people in the Empire travel on the big liners all the time without worrying about safety."

Pias thought that over. "Liners don't have a high enough concentration of wealth," he decided. "You have a few rich people and a lot more ordinary ones who are traveling on business or who have saved up for years for a luxury vacation. A big liner is a hard target, because it takes more manpower to overrun it—and for the small percentage of really rich people, it's not worth the effort.

"From what I've heard of pirates, they prefer either a cargo ship with a load of freight that can be resold at high profit margins or else the smaller private or chartered ships with enough people to hold for ransom."

"I know," Yvette exclaimed. "We can start a cargo company, specializing in rare and expensive merchandise, risky loads that other companies refuse to handle. That should offer a tempting package for pirates."

Pias thought the matter over, then shook his head. "No, not good enough. For one thing, how likely is it that we would form such a company? Neither you nor I can pilot a spacecraft, and there isn't enough time to learn if we want to crack this case before the Princess's coronation. Nor is it very likely that the nonflying owners of such a company would waste their time flying on every one of their flights—and if we're not along, we don't get a chance to meet the pirates.

"Besides," he added with a grin, "it's not flashy enough. It gives the pirates no incentive to deal with us directly."

Yvette's patience with her husband was momentarily pushed beyond the exasperation point. "Then what *is* flashy enough for you, your majesty?"

Seeing that he'd upset her, Pias backed off a bit from his assumed stance of grandeur. "Actually, I was thinking in terms of a gambling ship. If there's one thing I do know, it's that."

Yvette's irritation dissipated as she considered the idea. Pias had spent three years posing as an easy-going professional gambler while he sought revenge on Rowe Carnery, the man who'd murdered his former fiancée. It was a role perfectly suited to Pias's eccentric temperament—and one that added to the aura of mystery about him that Yvette had found so fascinating at the time.

Pias watched her reaction and saw that she was calming down, so he proceeded to outline his ideas. "Not just an ordinary gambling ship, either; if we want to attract the top money to act as pirate bait, we'll have to give them something worth coming to. The most glamorous spacegoing casino ever conceived, an interstellar vessel overflowing with decadence and luxuries."

Some of Pias's enthusiasm was now beginning to rub off on Yvette—as he'd been sure it would. "An exclusive pleasure palace," she said, eyes beginning to glow as the idea caught fire within her mind. "The more exclusive we make it, the more people will be clamoring to get in—and the more select our clientele. Admission by invitation only, with a basic two thousand ruble fee at the door."

"Fifty ruble minimum bets," Pias went on. "And a strict house policy of no credit. Everything will be on a cash basis—which will ensure our having plenty of rubles to lure the pirates."

"We'll bill ourselves as being a hundred percent safe, completely pirate-proof. Not only will that help our image with potential customers, but it will be a gauntlet in the pirates' faces. If we keep shouting loud enough about how impossible it is for them to take us, their own egos will eventually make them come to us."

"Is it possible to be completely safe?" Pias wondered. "And would we really want to be even if it were?"

"Yes to both. As long as the pirates don't simply blast our ship out of the skies—which would hardly be profitable for them—I can find us a crew to repel any possible boarding party. And if we want them to deal with us as equals, and take us into their plans, they have to respect us first. By beating them at their own game, they'll have to come to terms with us."

Such was the genesis of the *Paradise*, the most lavish vessel of its kind ever conceived and built in the history of the Empire.

It was not meant to compete with the large luxury liners; those were intended to impress their passengers with their size and stateliness. Even drawing upon the fortunes of the d'Alembert family and the Circus of the Galaxy, the Bavols could not have afforded such a spacegoing behemoth. The *Paradise* would be a smaller, but no less impressive, spaceship.

The competition they would face ranged from dreadful to very good indeed. Gambling ships had begun to grow popular thirty years earlier, their popularity coinciding with the rise of a moral movement on many worlds against the "sin" of gambling. The antibetters, as they were called, persuaded many planetary and local governments to forbid gambling—a maneuver which produced an effect directly counter to what the reformers had wanted. People who'd previously had only a mild interest in gambling suddenly became obsessed; the lure of the forbidden was as strong as ever in the human spirit.

The antibetters petitioned the Emperor to ban gambling throughout the Empire, but Stanley Ten would have none of that. He was, by that time, fifteen years into his reign and well aware of the limits of any power. A government that tried to forbid basic human drives would quickly lose all sympathy; trying to enforce unenforceable laws only made it laughable. The need to test one's luck at games of chance was as old as humanity, and would never be eradicated. The Emperor chose instead to take no position, and that was that. The antibetters had no power to persuade him to do anything.

As a result, while gambling was illegal on many planets within the Empire, it was not illegal in interstellar space, the region between the star systems where only Imperial law was in effect. Gamblers and entrepreneurs were quick to take advantage of this loophole, and the concept of the gambling ship—a spaceship traveling between the stars for the sole purpose of providing its customers with a legal casino—was born.

Most gambling ships catered to citizens of ordinary means and were tawdry affairs—small vessels with unpainted walls, holding perhaps twenty-five to fifty guests, with meager living and dining accommodations. The more a customer was willing to pay, the better his chances of finding something aesthetically pleasing.

The best of the gambling ships to date held upwards of a hundred guests at a level of comfort equivalent to that of a good hotel, and cost a thousand rubles for a one-week "cruise."

No one had built anything more extravagant because there didn't seem to be a market for it; the *very* rich gambler could always afford to go to Vesa to indulge his hobby. In that self-styled "Playground of the Galaxy" he could find luxury and indulgence to suit the most decadent tastes.

Pias and Yvette, of course, did not care whether there was a long-term market for such a gambling ship or not; they were not in this as a profit-making venture. For the few months they needed their operation to work, they could *create* a market. People would try anything at first if it was hard to get and promised them something original. All they'd have to do was build a mystique, and the rest would take care of itself.

They would have preferred to build the *Paradise* from scratch, their own design from beginning to end—but that would have taken six months just by itself, and they couldn't spare the time. Instead, they bought an older gambling ship that was still in good condition, brought it into a spacedock and had it completely refitted, inside and out. They had work crews operating around the clock to get the job completed as quickly as possible, and still it took more than a month before the *Paradise* was ready for its maiden voyage. Money was no object; the Bavols threw rubles around like confetti. But when they were done, not even the *Paradise's* former skipper would have recognized her.

From the outside, the *Paradise* looked like an electronic genius's Christmas tree ornament. It was onion-shaped, and its silvery hull was polished so that it reflected like an enormous funhouse mirror. Few people ever saw the hull itself, though, for virtually the entire outer surface of the vessel was covered with a myriad of flashing laser light displays of all colors. So dazzling was its appearance that, in the depths of space, it was visible to the naked eye almost a million kilometers away. "Any pirate who can't find *that*," Pias remarked, "is no threat to anybody."

Inside, too, the Bavols had been equally innovative. The ship had originally been designed with 107 passenger cabins of reasonably comfortable size, but the SOTE agents decided that cramped quarters were not the image they wanted to project to their luxury-minded customers. The amount of space within the ship was obviously limited by the external hull, but they could create the *illusion* of vast spaces inside. Forty of the passenger cabins were ripped out, and the rest expanded proportionately to give a roomier feel. Many walls were torn out of the public sections of the ship as well. In place of the three smaller dining rooms, Pias had them all combined into one magnificent banquet hall. The smaller gambling rooms were also consolidated into larger casinos, giving even those people who were not gambling at the moment a chance to mingle with the crowd and sample the vicarious excitement. Pias left only three of the original small gambling rooms untouched; they would serve to host the special high-stakes card games that were an invariable feature of such cruises.

In the exact center of the ship, instead of more casino room, Pias had the walls ripped out to construct a two-story tall entrance hall. In the middle of the floor stood a fountain in which a larger-than-life sized gold statue of a woman wore a gown of raindrop filaments; water trickled down the individual wires that composed the gown, producing a shimmering effect in the ever-changing light that illuminated the fountain. The entire room served no purpose but to create the appearance of lavish waste space; and since interstellar vessels were notoriously economical in that regard, it could only create an impression of extravagance in the customers' minds.

Yvette had charge of the actual decorating within the ship, and decided on a style she called "early precious." All the colors were pastels, leaning heavily on cupid pink. There were no bare walls anywhere; the interior surfaces of both the public areas and the passengers' cabins had all been wallpapered, then covered over with thick velvet curtains looped over elaborate gold wall sconces. The effect was to soften the hard lines of naked bulkheads and again preserve the illusion of open spaces.

The chairs and lounges were all of real wood, with pink flocked velvet upholstery; the gambling tables were all covered with pink tablecloths, and large crystal chandeliers hung from the ceiling in the casinos. The thick plush carpeting was pure white, with small touches of red scattered lightly throughout. In the corners of the room, tall potted plants covered with red, pink and white blossoms reached upward toward the ceiling.

Pias and Yvette had had a long talk about the services the *Paradise* should provide its patrons. Elegant casinos and gourmet food were not enough; if the *Paradise* was to project the image of a rich people's playground, there would have to be "special services" available, too. The morality was not appealing to either of them—both had been raised in stern, strait-laced cultures—but they knew that their own feelings did not matter in this issue. Excessive prudery would detract from their vessel's image and ruin all they had worked so hard to build. For the sake of the Empire, they would have to put aside their own personal prejudices.

The task of procuring the more exotic supplies fell to Yvette, since she would be the official "hostess" of the ship. The liquor was the easiest to obtain; nearly all of it could be bought through legal channels except for a few specialty items which had to be smuggled off planets that discouraged the export of native substances. As for the paid companions, she spent almost two weeks scouting talent, finally selecting ten beautiful young women and agreeing to pay them on a salary-plus-commission basis; to be on the safe side, she also hired five handsome men for any of the women guests who felt inclined to use the ship's special services. The drugs were the hardest of all to track down, but Yvette had enough previous experience to ask the right questions in the right places and was able to pick up a variety of illegal substances to suit the tastes of the very rich and the very bored.

While Yvette was rounding up her supplies, Pias had the job of attracting customers to this unique enterprise. During the three years he had spent as "Pias Nav," a professional gambler, he had learned the customs of the gambling world from top to bottom. The richest customers, he knew, did not always frequent the most expensive clubs; certain spots were more popular than others for the type of clientele he was striving for.

Pias and Yvette had chosen the *Paradise*'s cruise route very carefully. It would travel the quadrangle between the planets Egon, Bromberg, Hsoli and Kuragana. All four planets were prosperous, all had thriving illegal gambling operations because gambling had been officially forbidden there—and all four lay within the most heavily infested area of pirate activity in this sector of the Galaxy.

Pias visited all four of the planets in turn, soliciting business in an almost casual way. On each world, he would first spend a couple of days locating the casinos where the best action could be found. He would then spend another few days observing who the most important gamblers were. He made friends with dealers, croupiers and "hostesses," pumping them most discreetly to learn the latest scuttlebutt. His trained eye was sizing up everyone in the house, and it seldom took him more than an hour to ascertain which people would be of interest to him and which could be ignored.

Once he'd chosen his quarries, his plan of attack was carefully calculated. A few select words about the wonders of the new gambling ship; a hint that the maiden voyage might already be filled up; and a card he would hesitantly slip to an interested listener, a card bearing only a subcom number to be called for a "ticket to Paradise." Pias refused to answer any questions about the ship in person, giving his prospective clients the impression he had already let out too much as it was. If they wanted to know more, he told them, they would have to call the number and set up a screening appointment. Then he moved on—usually without even giving his name.

By the time Pias had made the rounds of all four planets and returned to Egon, where work on the *Paradise* was being completed, the clamor for tickets was surprising even to him. Yvette was going slightly crazy trying to process all the applications by herself while doing her own job as well; Pias promptly stepped in and relieved her of this responsibility.

People he had talked to were unable to resist telling their friends about this unique excursion, and the friends, in turn, had told even more people. Applications were even coming in from outside the four planets where Pias had done his recruiting. As a result he could afford to be quite selective, often rejecting people on seemingly trivial grounds. With each rejection he sadistically sent along a full-color trioptic brochure showing all the wonders the *Paradise* had to offer—and with each rejection, the demand seemed to double.

Looking up from a stack of applications one evening, Pias told his wife, "You know, if the pirates don't hit us on the first couple of trips, we may actually make a profit on this whole deal. Even including all meals in the package, we've got a high enough basic fee; with the house percentages of the take, plus our share of the money on the special services, we could end up doing quite well for ourselves."

"Mon Dieu, I think you're starting to like this."

"Just thinking about job security. We've got to catch Lady A and her crew sometime—and if there aren't any more plots, SOTE may put us out to pasture. I'm too old to learn brain surgery—I have to have something to fall back on."

As Yvette had promised, she was responsible for obtaining the crew—a crew that would never be overrun by pirates, no matter how well armed the outlaws were, no matter how badly they outnumbered the ship's complement. Fortunately, this was the easiest part of the entire operation. Yvette merely called for members of her family.

The Family d'Alembert was unique in human history. Throughout the Empire the family was renowned as the principal performers in the Circus of the Galaxy—aerialists, acrobats, jugglers, animal tamers, magicians, clowns, wrestlers . . . the whole gamut of thrilling entertainment. The d'Alembert clan was synonymous with the Circus—more than a thousand of them, constantly on tour throughout the inhabited planets, playing to packed houses wherever they went.

But that was only the surface appearance of this truly incredible family. Beneath the glittery facade, the Circus was also one of the most valuable weapons in SOTE's arsenal against treason. This was a fact that was known to only a handful of people outside the d'Alembert family itself—that handful being the Imperial family, the Head of SOTE, and his daughter/second-in-command. So secret was the Circus's connection with SOTE that no mention had ever been made of it in writing and no records of its activities had ever been put on file, lest some enemy gain access to SOTE's computer and learn the truth. The d'Alemberts were not even on the Empire's payroll; through a complicated system of maneuvering, the Circus's taxes were rebated to the d'Alemberts—and so successful was the show that that money was more than sufficient to fund the family's activities for the Service.

Yvette had at her disposal dozens of relatives to help staff the *Paradise*. All the members of her prolific family were from the high-gravity world of DesPlaines—and as such, they were the products of generations of forced evolution. Their reflexes were three times quicker, their bones three times stronger and their muscles three times more powerful than those of normal humans. DesPlainians in general were in great demand in any job requiring speed and strength.

Added to that, though, was the d'Alembert family's longstanding tradition of physical perfection. They were circus performers, their bodies well-oiled machines of classic efficiency. The d'Alemberts were DesPlainians-plus; and that extra margin of ability was sometimes the only advantage the Service had in its eternal struggle against the forces of chaos.

With the exception of those men and women Yvette had

hired exclusively for their physical charms, each of *Paradise*'s crewpeople—from the captain down to the lowliest galley boy—was a member of her talented family. Each was skilled enough to perform his appointed task—and in a fight, there was simply no comparison.

Pias's only objection at first was on the subject of croupiers and dealers. He wanted to put professionals in those positions, to guard against any card sharps that might slip past even his thorough scrutiny. But Yvette put his mind to rest in that regard; all the people she assigned to work the tables were protégés of her Uncle Marcel, the Circus's magician. Not only were they adept at sleight of hand themselves, but their trained eyes could spot any trickster in a moment. They gave Pias a free show, and the Newforester left shaking his head . . . but convinced that no cheats would manage to evade the *Paradise*'s security.

Finally, after seven long weeks of preparation, the *Paradise* was ready to begin its historic maiden voyage. Pias made it a gala celebration, hosting an enormous party for the press and public alike. He made a short, exciting speech about the thrills of the excursion they were about to undertake, and of the many marvels that awaited the *Paradise*'s passengers. He announced that the first four voyages were completely booked, and then asked for questions. Many of the inquiries dealt with him personally. Who was this mysterious entrepreneur who had appeared out of nowhere to start this daring project? Pias, who had assumed the pseudonym of "Brian Sangers," had a great deal of fun dropping misleading and totally invented clues about his shady past—much of which he stole shamelessly from the bookreels he had read so avidly as a child. Finally, a d'Alembert, who'd been planted in the audience as a member of the press, asked the question the Bavols had been wanting raised all along. "With all the money and valuables that will be on board your ship, aren't you afraid you might become a target for pirates?"

"Not at all," Pias replied with a casual toss of his hand. "As you might have guessed from what I've told you of my background, I'm familiar with many aspects of violence in space. I have devised a security system that makes the *Paradise* as immune to pirate attack as an Imperial battle cruiser. Our patrons will be as safe aboard this ship as they would be in their own homes. Safer, in fact; in your own home you always have to worry about burglars, and there will be no burglars aboard the *Paradise*."

With that provocative little tidbit of information thrown to them, the reporters leaped on the subject of security. They wanted to know whether the *Paradise* had its own heavy space artillery to ward off attackers. Pias smiled as he replied, "You all know it's a violation of Imperial law for any private vessel to travel armed through interstellar space."

The reporters did not consider that an answer, and kept pressing for more details. Pias was delighted by their attention and milked it for all it was worth, while saying nothing in the process. Finally he called a halt to this line of interrogation.

"Please, everyone—if I give you all the details of my security system, the pirates will know them, too. Any successful gambler will tell you the value of keeping something in reserve. That's all I intend to say on the subject."

The next morning, all the newsrolls were filled with the story of this mysterious Brian Sangers, his incredible gambling ship—and his reputed "secret weapon" against pirates that made his ship all but invincible. The Bavols read the reports and smiled. They had thrown a challenge directly into the pirates' faces; the next move was up to the other side.

Two days later, the *Paradise* left orbit around the planet Egon on the first leg of its initial voyage. The passengers were looking forward to fun and thrills; Pias and Yvette were hoping to supply them with even more thrills than they'd bargained for.

5

————— Traitor's World —————

Gastonia:

A planet the same size as Earth, circling a yellow dwarf star similar to Sol; a planet with one large moon and three smaller ones; a planet with a breathable oxygen atmosphere and an axial tilt of twenty-one degrees, providing the standard seasons; a planet with a large abundance of water; a planet with a flourishing population of native plants and animals; a planet composed of mountains and plains, of oceans and barren wastes; in short, a planet not too dissimilar in many respects from Mankind's original homeworld.

There was, however, one crucial difference. Gastonia circled its sun at a mean distance of 220 million kilometers. Being 1.4 times farther from its primary, it received only half the amount of radiation that the Earth did. Gastonia was a cold world, harsh and forbidding to people attuned to warmer climates. Its rivers and lakes were frozen over for large portions of its long year; only the complex tidal actions of the four moons insured that the oceans themselves remained fluid and ever-churning. In midsummer at the equator the temperature could sometimes reach up as high as twenty-five degrees Celsius—but that was hardly a time for rejoicing. Such temperature extremes from the normal climate range only served to increase the furious wind currents, bringing storms that made Earth's Asian monsoons look like spring showers.

This, then, was the world that "Mad Stephanie" had chosen as the permanent home of those who opposed her regime. It was a habitable if not a happy place; there were plenty of native plants and animals to serve as the settlers' food, and a guaranteed water supply from the frequent snowfalls. The Empire supplied the basics of human comfort, but little else; by opposing the Empire, these traitors had turned their backs on what the Empire could provide, and now they were paying the consequences.

As the SOTE prison ship carrying the d'Alemberts to their new home approached Gastonia, Jules and Yvonne were allowed a few quick peeks at the exile world. The planet appeared very bright from space, with lots of cloud cover through which there were tantalizing glimpses of blue ocean and white, snow-covered land. During the landing, though, they were sent back to their cells and not allowed out until the ship had touched down.

The ship landed at the single small spaceport on the entire planet, inside the walled administrative garrison the Empire maintained to keep an eye on its prisoners. Gastonia was one of the two inhabited planets in the Galaxy that was not ruled over by its own duke, the other such planet being Earth; like Earth, it was considered the personal property of the Emperor himself, and subject to his direct supervision. The Emperor appointed a Governor to run the world, and the Governor, in turn, selected his own staff and reported to the Emperor at intervals through SOTE.

The d'Alemberts were ushered unceremoniously off the ship and into the garrison, where they underwent a thorough ID scan to make certain these were the same two prisoners who'd been convicted on Islandia. When that was finished, they were treated to a complete physical examination, certifying their health upon arrival. The administrative center maintained the medical facilities on Gastonia and needed files on all the incoming prisoners before any problems developed.

Check-in procedure completed, each of them was dressed in a warm thermal uniform consisting of a shirt and slacks, thick leather boots and a heavy fur parka. A guard escorted them to a door, handed them each a fistful of small brass coins, and pressed the button that opened the portal. "Go through here and walk quickly to the other end. The door will open for you there. Enjoy your new home."

"Wait a minute," Yvonne said. "Where are we supposed to live? What will we eat? How do we meet the other prisoners? What . . . ?"

"There'll be someone outside to meet you," the guard said brusquely. "There usually is; they can tell the difference between an incoming prison ship and a regular supply ship."

The guard was not in a talkative mood. She shoved her two prisoners roughly through the door and slammed it shut behind them. The door closed with a solid bang of finality and the agents could hear a hissing as it sealed itself tight. There was no knob or button to open it from this side. Unless they wanted to stay here for the rest of their lives, they would have to move forward.

They were in a bare, iron corridor fifteen meters long. Lighting panels overhead gave but feeble illumination. At the far end was another door. That was their only alternative. Jules shrugged. "No point in staying here," he said, and led his wife to the door at the other end.

The corridor itself was chilly, but they were unprepared for the shock of freezing air that blasted them as they opened the far door. They closed their eyes and covered their faces with their hands to protect them from the stinging cold of Gastonia's weather. They realized that the fur parkas, which they had thought were quite warm inside the garrison, would be scant protection here on this frozen planet.

After a few seconds of adjustment, they moved out through the doorway, and the door closed automatically behind them. There was no way to open it from this side; they were now irrevocably committed to life on Gastonia and all that implied. "I hope we know what we're doing," Yvonne muttered under her breath; Jules beside her nodded imperceptibly. Self-doubt could hardly be avoided under these circumstances, but at the same time they knew that they had risked their very lives before on longer gambles and come out successfully. No one, after all, had promised them a job without hazards.

Behind them, the blank iron wall rose ten meters high, towering well above their heads. The administrative garrison had been built with its back to a series of mountains to forestall attacks from the rear. The high wall prevented attacks from the front. As far as the official records went, there had never been a successful escape from Gastonia in its more than one hundred and fifty year history as a prison world. Yet somehow a woman named Karla Jost had managed it without anyone's knowing—and how many others as well? That was what the d'Alemberts were here to find out—and to stop, by any means whatsoever.

"If you want a ride to the village," said a sour voice, "you'd better move along. I ain't got all day."

The d'Alemberts turned from their perusal of the garrison behind them to study the man who had spoken. He was an older man, possibly in his middle to late forties, with a bushy beard and a craggy, weather-lined face. He was dressed in a fur parka similar to their own, but his boots were fur-lined and wrapped tightly about shins and ankles. He stood beside a handmade sleigh that was harnessed to a large, powerful quadruped. The animal was covered by a thick coat of shaggy gray fur and sported two pairs of wicked-looking horns, but otherwise appeared quite placid as it stood hitched to the sleigh awaiting its master's orders.

"Who are you?" Vonnie asked.

"Name's Zolotin. I drive new arrivals to the village—unless you prefer to walk."

"How far is it?" Jules asked.

"Five kilometers. Make up your minds quick."

There was really little decision involved. Walking that distance on Gastonia when they were unaccustomed to the severe climate would have been almost suicidal. "We'll ride, thank you," Jules said, starting toward the back of the sleigh.

Zolotin moved to interpose his body between Jules and the sleigh. "Fare's fifteen slugs apiece."

"Huh? Oh." Jules looked down at the coins he'd been holding since the guard gave them to him. All were of brass, of different sizes and shapes, but without any markings to distinguish the denominations. "Which of these is what?" Jules asked the man.

Zolotin looked disdainfully at the collection in Jules's hand. "The small round ones is one, medium round ones is five, large round ones is ten, triangles is fifty, squares is a hundred. Hexagonals is a thousand, but you won't be seeing many of them for a while." He chuckled at his private little joke.

The d'Alemberts took a quick stock of their "wealth," and computed that they had nine hundred slugs between them. They had no idea what prices were like in the village, but thirty slugs did not seem an outrageous fee for "cab fare." Carefully they parceled out the indicated coins and paid Zolotin what he demanded. Only then did the man let them climb in the back of his sleigh and, with a crack of his small whip, he drove his animal forward.

"What kind of an animal is that?" Vonnie asked, hoping to start a conversation.

"It's called a yagi."

The yagi was plodding at a pace somewhat faster than Yvonne could have crawled. "Doesn't it move any faster than this?"

"Maybe if there was a fire behind it or a female yagi in front. Why? You in some kind of a hurry?"

Yvonne blushed. She was used to fast-paced environments; Gastonia was obviously a place where people conserved as much of their energy as possible just to keep warm. What reason could there be for hurrying around? No one was really going anywhere.

Seeing his wife's embarrassment, Jules stepped into the conversational gap. "I imagine there must be some kind of rules for living here."

"Sure," Zolotin said. "You do what the mayor tells you and you don't make no trouble. Most of all, you never ask anybody what their life was like before they came here. If you do those things, you'll probably live a while."

"Who is the mayor?" Jules asked. "One of the Governor's men?"

Zolotin gave a derisive snort. "The Governor don't have much to do with us, or us with him. Right now the mayor is a man named Kwame Tshombase. The farther you stay from him, the longer you'll live."

Perhaps that formula explained Zolotin's longevity in a world of cutthroat politics, which was the state of things on Gastonia if Jules read his remarks correctly. The d'Alemberts were not here to play things safe, however; if this Tshombase were in any position of power, he would probably be involved in the conspiracy they'd come to investigate. They would be tangling with the man sooner or later—but first it was wisest to learn the ground rules of this new world they were forced to inhabit.

"Where do we find a place to stay?" Vonnie asked. "The guards didn't tell us much at all."

"I'll take you to the Central Registry," Zolotin said. "They'll assign you quarters and a job. You both together?"

"We're married, yes."

Zolotin gave Vonnie a knowing leer. "A young, good-looking woman can earn big money fast. Sex ratio here's better than three-to-two male."

"I'm not that desperate, thank you!" Vonnie exclaimed.

The driver shrugged. "Suit yourself. But your value is higher now than it will be later. Hard work on Gastonia lowers your desirability and your price. In a couple of months, maybe nobody'll want you."

Yvonne spent the remainder of the ride in angry silence, leaving the rest of the interrogation to her husband. Zolotin was an infuriatingly taciturn man, seldom volunteering any information; Jules practically had to use a crowbar to pry loose any useful data. The yagi's slow pace, though, gave him plenty of time to ask questions and build up a picture of the society in which they would be living.

There were more than twenty thousand people living in "the village," as the local settlement was called. Most people worked at menial jobs—hunting wild animals, growing crops, working at crafts, tanning hides and constructing buildings being the chief occupations. The village was ruled by a mayor and his lieutenants, who achieved their positions of power by sheer brute force. The job of mayor was subject to change without notice. This was, after all, a planet populated by ambitious, scheming, violent people; little wonder the political situation was so volatile.

After a ride of almost an hour over a "road" that was merely an accumulation of tracks in the snow, the sleigh topped a hill and the d'Alemberts had their first glimpse of the village. It was much larger than they had expected. The Empire provided the inhabitants with some prefabricated dwellings, a basic minimum for survival, but the people themselves had enlarged on that by using native trees as timber and adding constructions of their own. Houses were laid out in irregular streets that wound narrowly up and around a group of low hills. Larger buildings, Zolotin told them, were bars, barracks, storehouses, and homes of the more affluent citizens—that is, the mayor and his gang.

Zolotin dropped them off in front of the Central Registry, where they would be required to check in and arrange for their future jobs and housing. The driver then rode off without a word of farewell, and they made no effort to thank him—he had made no move of friendship or courtesy, and they felt required to give none in return. He had taught them the first lesson of Gastonia: don't get involved with other people.

The d'Alemberts entered the Registry, and found the indoors scarcely warmer than the frigid climate outside. They were greeted by a sour-faced bearded man behind the counter who regarded them as an intrusion on his privacy. After taking their names, he informed them brusquely that they could have a hut of their own for four hundred slugs a month or they could live in the barracks for a hundred slugs apiece. Since they needed some privacy to talk out their ideas together, they opted for the hut.

"Cash in advance," the clerk said. Jules counted out four hundred slugs from their assembled change and handed it across the counter. "Not enough," the clerk said, looking at it with slight disdain.

"What do you mean?" Jules counted it again, aloud. "There's one hundred, two hundred, two-fifty, three, three-fifty, four hundred."

For the first time, the clerk smiled. "Zolotin taught you that, didn't he?"

Jules was starting to get a sinking feeling in his stomach. "Yes, why?"

"He does that to all the warmies," the clerk said, working hard now to suppress his laughter. "He taught you wrong—probably took about 150 slugs from you, if I know him." The clerk showed them the right way to figure the change, and he was right—Zolotin had taken 150 slugs apiece. Figured the new way, each of them had started with only 350—and now they had only enough money to pay their first month's rent in advance.

Zolotin had also taught them the second lesson of Gastonia: never trust anybody.

"What'll we do about food until we get our first pay?" Vonnie asked.

"You can apply for a loan," the clerk said, slipping back to his previous sour expression now that the joke was over. "Interest rate is twenty percent, compounded daily."

"I see," Jules said, and he did. They were rapidly learning the third lesson of Gastonia: money is everything. "We'll both need jobs, though, before we could pay back the loan. What have you got available?"

The clerk looked Jules up and down. "Have you ever done much hunting?"

Jules remembered his last hunting trip. It was on Ansegria, as part of Princess Edna's Progress—quite a different situation from the present one. "Yes," he said. "I'm pretty good."

The clerk sneered. "With a spear?"

Jules refused to be daunted. "I've never tried it that way, but I'll bet I'd still be smooth."

"Let's try you and see." The clerk led Jules out back to a yard where the outline of a small quadrupedal animal had been crudely chalked on a wall. The two men stood twenty meters away and the clerk handed Jules a long spear. The shaft was of a lightweight wood, the point of chipped stone held onto the haft by leather thongs. Jules suddenly realized how primitive the conditions on Gastonia were.

He hefted the weapon for a few seconds, allowing himself to become accustomed to its weight and balance, then suddenly hurled it—with the strength of a DesPlainian and the accuracy of a skilled aerialist—directly toward the target. The stone tip, dulled from repeated usage, did not stick in the target—but it did hit close to dead center before bouncing off. Jules looked at the clerk. *"Khorosho,* how's that?"

If the man was impressed by the newcomer's ability, he managed not to show it. "Head shots are best," was all he said. "Gut shots can spoil the meat."

"Sorry. Let me try again." Jules's second attempt did hit the target's head, though was not as well-placed as he would have liked. He knew his cousin Jean, the Circus's knife-thrower, would have been able to split the creature's eye five times out of five.

His performance, though, was good enough to convince the clerk that he could handle a hunter's job, and the man assigned him to the lowest-grade hunting position with a team scheduled to go out on a two-day hunt the next morning. Apparently good hunters were hard to find; even the lowest position as a hunter paid better than other professions—and since pay was based in part on how much he caught, Jules stood a chance to make good money indeed.

Vonnie would have liked to get a hunting job, too; it sounded much more interesting than any of the work available in town. But she knew that she and Jules should cover as wide a cross section of Gastonian society as possible in order to find out what they needed to know, so she ended up taking a menial job in one of the village's tanneries. Their combined salaries would be small, but they calculated that it would at least be enough to pay for their food and rent, with a little left over to repay the loan quickly, before it mounted out of all proportion. They straightened out all the financial arrangements and the clerk directed them to their new home.

After half an hour of wandering through the narrow, twisting streets they finally located the hut that was theirs. It turned out to be a prefabricated, one-room hovel, crude and lacking anything in the way of furniture. The "bed" was a pile of moldy furs thrown in one corner of the floor; all cooking would have to be done in the fireplace—but they had no kettle, no pots, no implements and no firewood. All would have to be purchased out of the small and dwindling supply of money they had borrowed—money they had thought would be needed only for food. As for personal hygiene, it soon became clear that they would have to share the communal lavatory facilities with their other neighbors along this street.

A lesser pair might have broken into tears at the turn their fortunes had taken. Instead, the d'Alemberts merely stood for several silent minutes in the center of their hut, gazing around themselves at the sorry conditions they would have to endure.

"Cherie," Jules said at last, "if I ever decide to commit treason for real, do me a favor—talk me out of it."

6

The Gastonian Way

They found a foodstall that was open and bought a few staples
to see themselves through the night. They were learning to
survive on Gastonia, though; they dickered over the price instead of merely paying what the seller asked, saving themselves
more than half of the initial demand. They also had to buy
firewood, since Jules had no axe with which to chop his own;
he did find a couple of long sticks, though, on which they
could roast their vegetables over the fire. It was not a con-
noisseur's meal, but they were both too ravenously hungry to
care. The strain of this first day on Gastonia had taken its toll
on even their superhuman bodies, and they went to bed immediately after dinner, making no attempt to explore the village
further. It was cold inside their hut despite the fire, and they
huddled together under the furs for warmth; *that* part, at least,
was far from objectionable.

Jules was up at dawn the next morning to report for work
with his hunting team. There would be half a dozen other men
on this particular expedition, all under the supervision of their
group leader, a man named Dusabi. All the others had been
on many hunts before and knew each other well—although it
was clear from some of the interchanges that they didn't all

57

like one another. Jules braced himself for the inevitable kidding he would take; a new man on a tough job was usually the butt of practical jokes, delivered in a spirit that could sometimes be cruel. Jules, as the warmest of all possible "warmies," was fair game.

Each man was given his own spear, with a different number of notches on the haft for identification; that way, they could tell which man had been responsible for which kill, and judge his pay accordingly. Then the group started out on foot away from the village and into the forest beyond. Some of the men sang as they marched, others chose not to.

Jules struck up a conversation with one man, a fellow named Bagheddes. Though the other man was reluctant to talk much with this brash newcomer, Jules did manage to pry some useful information out of him. This was a small hunting party, as such things went; that was because they would be staying near the village and hunting only small game—wolflike animals called sleekars that traveled in packs. It was not uncommon for some of the hunting parties to take as many as thirty men and be gone from the village for a week or more. The larger groups hunted bigger game, and usually took a sleigh and yagi with them to bring back their catch. The bigger parties were considered the choice assignments; pay and working conditions were much better there than in a small group like this. The men in this particular party either were not very good hunters or else were out of favor with the mayor and his gang.

They reached the forest after a two-hour walk, and spread out for the hunt. Group leader Dusabi stayed close by Jules, explaining the procedures of the hunt. The sleekars were animals about the size of large dogs with shaggy gray-brown fur, flat muzzles and sharp, rending claws. They traveled mostly in packs through the trees and were slightly out of their element on the ground—although with their sharp claws they could be fierce opponents if cornered. They had been known to drop out of trees and attack humans, though such attacks were rare; their usual prey was the small tree-dwelling rodents that lived all through the forest.

They'd been hunting for more than an hour without success before a cry from one of their fellow hunters drew their attention off to the right. Dusabi broke into a run in that direction, and Jules was right at his heels. Even before they reached the man who'd made the sighting, they spotted the pack of sleekars rushing through the treetops straight toward them. Jules was frankly astounded at how fast such large creatures could bound from branch to branch; the herd was almost upon him before he could stop and take hold of his spear, preparing to throw.

Beside him, Dusabi planted his feet, took careful aim and hurled his stone-tipped spear at his chosen target. The missile lodged cleanly in the beast's neck, and was thrown with such force that its tip went cleanly through the tissue and came out on the other side. The sleekar gave a brief scream that was abruptly cut off in a gurgle, and fell from its branch to land on the ground a few meters away from the men.

Jules's throw was no less accurate. As he was taking aim his quarry seemed to sense his intention. It turned suddenly and snarled at him, baring a mouthful of vicious fangs and leaping down directly toward him. Jules hurled his spear instinctively with all his DesPlainian strength—and the missile went straight into the beast's gaping mouth and completely through the back of the throat. The sleekar fell dead at his feet, while his spear lodged into a tree branch high above.

The pack continued its panicked stampede through the branches overhead, and within less than two minutes the entire confrontation between hunters and sleekars was over. Jules, after checking that the treetops were now safe once again, climbed up into the tree to retrieve his spear while Dusabi took count of this particular hunt. As Jules was climbing down again, the group leader announced the results. "Four kills: one for Ashai, one for Jeddman and two for me."

Jules stared at him, unbelieving. "You only killed one. That other one is mine."

"Your spear stuck in the tree," Dusabi said calmly. "You just finished getting it out."

"Sure it stuck in the tree—after it went clean through the throat. You were right beside me. You saw me kill it."

"Did I?"

Jules d'Alembert was normally a man of very even temper. An agent of his caliber could seldom afford to let his emotions control his actions because his life depended on every move he made. But he had suffered nothing but humiliation at the hands of these scum for the past two days, and he was tired of being pushed around. If the law of the jungle was all that applied here, he'd show these people he could roar with the loudest. It was time he earned a little respect.

Taking his spear, he walked over to where Dusabi was standing next to Jules's kill and, with full DesPlainian strength, jammed his spear through the dead sleekar's head. In the forest silence, the crunching of the skull carried to the ears of each hunter; brains and blood splattered on the ground and across the top of Jules's boots. Jules ignored that. He let go of the spear and it stood upright, while he focused his entire attention on Dusabi.

"My spear is in it now," Jules said in a cold fury, enunciating each syllable. "I claim the kill."

The other men in the party gathered in a circle around Jules and Dusabi as the duel of wills flared. For an instant it seemed the very air between the two would ionize from the charge of personality flowing back and forth. Finally, without taking his eyes from Jules's face, Dusabi took a step away. "Four kills," he repeated in an even tone. "One for Ashai, one for Jeddman, one for Brecht and one for me."

From that point onward, Jules was accepted as an equal in the party. People didn't necessarily like him any better—no one seemed very friendly to anyone else on Gastonia—but he was at least treated with the respect they gave someone who could hold his own in their company.

The four dead sleekars were lashed together with leather thongs and hung from a tree branch, to be gathered up tomorrow on their way back to the village. Dusabi sprinkled a greenish powder over the bodies, and at Jules's inquiry explained that it was a peppery substance that kept the local scavengers from becoming too interested in the hunters' catch.

They left that location well-marked and traveled onward. As Jules surmised, they would have to travel quite a distance before they could hope to find another pack of sleekars; such large carnivores needed a wide hunting area themselves to support their numbers, and the territories of various packs would not overlap. They stopped for a short midday meal; Jules had not known to bring his own food, but managed to get small portions from each of his colleagues with a promise to pay them back at the end of the hunt.

There was one more hunt later that day, and Jules again bagged a sleekar, one of the five killed in this encounter. He heard assorted mumblings of "beginner's luck," but paid them no attention. A worse problem to the group was a loud argument between Bagheddes and another man, Pajjar, over which of them had actually killed a given sleekar. By the time Dusabi and the rest of the men arrived at the scene, both hunters' spears were lodged in the carcass and each man was accusing the other of trying to steal credit for his kill. Dusabi examined the evidence and awarded the kill to Bagheddes, saying that Bagheddes's spear looked to be in the beast at a more believable angle, and that Pajjar's spear could have been stuck in afterward. This decision stopped the argument but did little to quell the animosity that raged between the two men. For the rest of the day there was a barrage of verbal sniping back and forth. Some of the men took sides in the dispute, others chose to remain completely neutral; discretion prompted Jules toward the latter path.

They camped that night in a small clearing and gathered branches for a fire. Dusabi assured Jules that there were nocturnal carnivores larger and more dangerous than the sleekars roaming the forest, and that a guard would be maintained at all times. As low man on the totem pole, Jules drew first watch, and accepted the responsibility silently. Several times during his turn he was startled by some loud, mysterious noises in the darkness nearby, but nothing came close enough to the circle of light to be identifiable. When Jules was relieved he was so worn out that he fell into a deep sleep until awakened at dawn for the next day's activities.

All morning they searched unsuccessfully for signs of more sleekar packs. Their lack of success, coupled with the continuing insult battle between Bagheddes and Pajjar, served to make the entire party edgy. Finally in midafternoon, just as Dusabi was ready to give the order to turn back and collect the previous day's catch, they found signs of sleekar activity in the area. They spread out once more in a hunting pattern, and this time Jules was confident enough to go off on his own.

When the stampede was launched and the hunt began, Jules downed another of the beasts with comparative ease. Hoisting the carcass over his shoulders, he started hauling it back toward the central rendezvous area when he heard a very human scream to his left. Without dropping his catch, he ran in that direction to see what was the matter.

He came upon a sight that brought him to a stop. Pajjar was bending over Bagheddes's lifeless body, his spear through his enemy's chest. He was stripping the clothing off the corpse, having already pawed through the dead man's knapsack. Jules let his sleekar fall to the ground as he leaped through the air to tackle the murderer and wrestle him to the ground. At the same time, he called out to the other hunters for help—but it wasn't needed. One punch was all it took to knock Pajjar unconscious.

Dusabi and the other men were on the scene within seconds, and the group leader could tell at a glance what had happened. He helped Jules off Pajjar's body and told him, "Tend to your own catch. I'll handle this."

He personally began stripping the body of all its valuables, including a small stone knife and a leather coin purse attached to the belt by a thong. Pajjar was just starting to come to as he finished; Dusabi bundled the plunder together and tossed it roughly at the murderer. "Here's the stuff," he growled, "and you'll get half-credit for that kill yesterday. But I don't ever want you in a group of mine again, understand?"

Jules could hardly believe what he heard. Gastonian society was actually rewarding Pajjar for murdering another man. He started after Dusabi to complain, but the group leader saw him coming, took him by the arm and led him aside. "Before you start lecturing me, warmie," he said coldly, "you'd better know I did that for your sake."

"Mine?"

Dusabi nodded. "You're a good hunter. I don't want to lose you. If Pajjar thought you were responsible for his losing what he'd earned he might slip a spear in your back sometime. This way he'll just curse you as a *doob* for a while and then forget about it."

"What about Bagheddes?"

The group leader shrugged. "Live bodies are more important than dead ones. There's too much work in the village."

Jules looked back at the body. Bagheddes had by this time been stripped completely naked by Pajjar and the other hunters; resources on Gastonia were too scarce to allow anything to be wasted. "Aren't we at least going to bury him?" he asked.

"Why bother? Plenty of scavengers around to finish him off. We've got to get our catch back into town before it starts going bad. Besides," the leader laughed ironically, "what are you going to dig a grave with—your bare hands?"

Jules was silent for the rest of the afternoon as the party gathered up its catches from the previous day and began the arduous task of hauling the sleekars back into the village. He was soberly pondering the new lesson he had learned about life on Gastonia: anything is forgiven if you can get away with it. Nothing, particularly here, succeeded like success.

They got back into town just before dusk. They were met by a party of workers who hauled the sleekar carcasses away for processing; Jules and the other hunters went down to the Central Registry to collect their wages. Jules was due a handsome bonus for his three kills, but when the money was counted out he found he'd gotten only half of what was owed him.

"Taxes," was the clerk's only answer when Jules complained. Jules swallowed his intended reply, and stomped out with his money.

By the time he finished paying back his colleagues for sharing their meals with him, he had only a third of what he'd earned. As he turned to go back to his and Yvonne's hut, Dusabi stopped him and told him of a much larger hunting expedition that would be leaving in three days. The wages on that trip would be higher, although, since they'd be hunting bigger game, the work would be harder and the risks greater. Dusabi was impressed enough with Jules's work to recommend him for that group, along with a promotion to the next higher grade. Jules said he was indeed interested in serving on that team, and told Dusabi to contact him if it became definite. Somehow, though, he could not bring himself to say "thank you" to the group leader, nor did Dusabi seem to expect it. "Please" and "thank you" were expressions seldom used on Gastonia.

Vonnie had already finished her work for the day and was waiting for him when he arrived home. Even as he rushed to embrace her, Jules was almost overpowered by the smell. His wife stank of tannery chemicals. "Phew!" he said after they kissed. "Let's hope you don't have to sneak up on anyone while we're here, unless he's upwind of you."

"You're not exactly a flower garden yourself, *mon cher*. Dead animals stink, too."

Briefly they filled each other in on what had happened to them since Jules's departure yesterday morning. Jules's re-

counting of Bagheddes's murder and the reactions to it left
Vonnie strangely silent for a long time. It was clear that she,
too, was wondering what sort of hellhole they had gotten themselves into.

By contrast to his, her own experiences had been rather
tame. Other than turning down propositions from every man
she encountered, her job was quite routine. She was a common
laborer, carrying piles of skins to and from the chemical vats.
She had not yet drawn her first salary payment, and was dis-
mayed to hear Jules's tale of the "taxes." "It doesn't look like
we'll get ahead very quickly here just being ordinary hard-
working citizens, does it?" she said.

"I think we'd better find some way to get ourselves into the
mayor's organization quickly," Jules agreed, "before we find
ourselves so buried in debts that we can't move effectively."

While Vonnie's two days had been unexciting, she had
managed to learn a great deal, and had done wonders toward
making their little hut into a more civilized place to live. She
had "liberated" a couple of candles from the tannery to provide
them with some light at night, and had bought a few small
kitchen implements to help make their meals more than a mere
spontaneous satisfaction of animal appetites. They had a pot
of hard-baked clay, while most of their utensils were of carved
bone. Gastonia, for all the harshness of its interactions, was
a society that let nothing go to waste. Of the animals killed by
hunters, for instance, the meat was eaten; the furs were worn;
leather was made into boots, belts, pouches and thongs; fats
were rendered down into tallow for candles; and bones were
carved into tools such as spoons, forks, knives and needles.
There was even one animal whose bones were so hard that
pieces of them could be used as nails in carpentry, allowing
the people of the village to build more elaborate structures than
the simple huts SOTE provided.

While Vonnie went to work the next day, Jules strolled
around the village, familiarizing himself with its layout. There
was one section of the town which was roped off apart from the
rest, and guarded at intervals by men wielding wicked-looking
bone machetes. Jules was turned away when he casually tried
to explore inside; he surmised that this was the area where the
mayor and his cohorts lived. He would make a more serious
attempt to get inside there when he knew more of what he was
looking for.

There were plenty of the one-room prefab huts; they were the predominant architectural feature in the village. There were also larger buildings: barracks to house those people who wanted to live more cheaply, who didn't mind sacrificing privacy, and who may even have preferred the close companionship and warmth of their fellow exiles. Other large structures were the manufacturing areas, where mass production of hides and tallow was performed. Pottery, stoneworking and bone-carving, Jules assumed, were cottage industries best done in the security of one's own home.

The only buildings that had any real color to them were the bars. Jules had expected to find such places, and was not disappointed. No matter where they were, human beings devoted a large portion of their invention and energy to distilling alcoholic spirits—and the more depressing the living conditions, the more important alcohol seemed to be. Gastonia was a natural haven for bars, and there were plenty of them. The villagers had learned, over the years, to make an astonishing array of beverages from local varieties of grains and fruits.

Jules had not expected to find the bars open during the day but, to his surprise, they were. Hunters between assignments, such as himself, could not be expected to stay home all day, and there was a minumum of other entertainment available in the village. People who were "self-employed"—potters, wood- and bone-carvers, and others who worked in the necessary crafts—would often take a little time off to drop around the local bar to see what was happening. And the mayor's lieutenants, who seemed to have little to do all day but swagger around and lord over the less fortunate, made a habit of hanging around the bars, gambling, drinking and making life miserable for everyone else.

Jules scouted the various places out. One of them in particular seemed to be a favorite haunt of the mayor's gang, although the action in there during the afternoon was a bit slow. Jules made himself a note to return there later with Vonnie, then returned home to fix dinner for his wife.

When Yvonne came home from work they had a quick meal and then went out. Vonnie was eager to see what they could stir up in the bar. "When all you do is haul hides around all day," she said, "*anything* is a welcome change. I hope we get a break in this case soon—I know our job is dangerous, but hazardous duty should not include being bored to death."

Once inside the bar—a dimly lit establishment known simply as "Sasha's"—they ordered a couple of mild drinks and went over to a pair of stools in one quiet corner to observe events. They had long since learned the knack of nursing a single drink all evening; like all DesPlainians, they were allergic to alcohol and found the taste utterly disgusting. They forced themselves to drink, though, as just one more of the sacrifices they made in the service of their Emperor.

As they watched people's interactions and eavesdropped on random conversations, they slowly gained more of a feel for the social life in the village. As was true in all human society, status levels had formed based on such factors as occupation, income and personal character. People in the routine, menial jobs—such as Vonnie—were considered on the lowest rung of the ladder, while hunters ranked fairly high. A top-notch hunter, in fact, could become a minor celebrity. The top spots in the village were occupied by the mayor and his minions, plus a few of the classier ladies who had chosen to be courtesans.

As the d'Alemberts watched, it became clear that there was one loudmouthed braggart named Voorhes who was much taken with his own self-importance at being the number three man in the mayor's administration. After a whispered consultation between them, the two SOTE agents got up from their seats and approached the man. "Gospodin Voorhes?" Jules asked with what he hoped was the proper degree of reverence.

Voorhes looked them both over. The only clothing the d'Alemberts had was the outfits they'd been given just before leaving the walled garrison—much too well-made to pass as native wear. It marked them instantly as warmies to the local populace. They would buy new clothes as soon as they could spare the money, but until then they could expect little but scorn from the more established people.

"What do you want?" Voorhes asked brusquely, wanting as little to do with these newcomers as possible.

"We were hoping you could help us get a job with the mayor. We've been hearing you say how important you are to him, and we were wondering..."

"How long have you warmies been in the village?"

"Four days now, sir."

Voorhes gave them a sneer. "Four whole days, and you'd like to work for the mayor. I've been here ten years, and I had to work hard to make it. Get out of my sight before I take it into my head to beat some respect into you."

He started to turn away, had a second thought and turned to face Vonnie. "You. You're not bad-looking. The mayor might just be willing to give you a very special job. Of course, I'd have to try you out first, just to make sure you're good enough."

"Oh, I'm good enough," Vonnie said, her voice as cold as the weather outside. "In fact, I'm more than good enough. I'm entirely too good for either you or your boss."

"Sassy little jamtart, aren't you?" Voorhes said with a lazy grin. "We'll have to teach you a lesson in Gastonian manners." He reached out one meaty hand to grab Vonnie's arm and pull her toward him.

But Vonnie was no longer there. As the man reached for her she sidestepped adroitly, grabbed his extended arm, and flipped him through the air in a single motion that looked positively effortless—and it was effortless, for someone with the strength of a DesPlainian in perfect physical condition. The bar's other patrons cleared hastily out of the way, and Voorhes landed with a solid thud on the hard stone floor.

The man shook his head and rose slowly to his feet, still not completely convinced that a mere woman had been able to toss him so easily. He was angry, though, at being made to look a fool in front of the people he'd just been bragging to. He was not going to let that happen again. With a snarl, he braced his feet firmly and reached for Yvonne a second time.

The agent dodged again, but this time—instead of flipping Voorhes through the air—she twisted his arm around behind his back, so high that his hand was well up between the shoulder blades. As the man cried out in pain, she used the side of her flattened left hand to give a hard backhand chop to his mid-section, right at kidney level. Her victim exhaled sharply, and she hooked a foot around his to trip him. As he fell to the floor, she fell on top of him, her knee pressed with just enough force on his windpipe to prevent his making any sudden moves.

When the fight started, Jules backed away to give his wife more room to work. He knew that Vonnie was perfectly capable of handling a lout like Voorhes without any assistance from him; he was more concerned with the rest of the spectators. He was going to make certain this was a fair fight.

Most of the bar's patrons were grinning as they watched Yvonne handle Voorhes as though he were a sack of flour. They had endured endless hours of his pompous boasts, without the courage to stand up to him; now they were all reaping vicarious revenge on the bully. But some of Voorhes's underlings were less than pleased about the way their boss was being treated. They knew what a temper he had, and they were more than a little afraid that he would take out his aggressions over this humiliation on them. Three of them started forward to tackle this presumptuous young lady who had so badly embarrassed Voorhes.

Although Vonnie could probably have taken care of four louts as easily as one, Jules could see no reason why he should let his wife have all the fun. As the first of the trio passed by him, he reached out and grabbed the man's wrist in an unbreakable grip. With a quick turn, he flipped the man around so that he went crashing into the other two, and all three would-be rescuers ended up in a tangled heap on the floor. The rest of the crowd roared with laughter as the threesome scrambled around on the floor, cursing madly as they tried to extricate themselves from one another.

But the laughter stopped abruptly as the front door swung open and a man entered the bar. He was a big black man, easily over two meters tall, with shoulders almost as wide as the doorframe. The bulky furs he wore made him seem like some wild creature of the forest. His thick eyebrows arched over brooding, intelligent eyes, and his black beard held only a few discrete touches of gray.

Neither Jules nor Yvonne needed a formal introduction. This man could only be Kwame Tshombase, the mayor of the village.

No one moved as Tshombase's head turned and his eyes scanned the scene with a penetrating stare. This was a man accustomed to power and the knowledge of what he could do with it. The mayor's eyes rested on the helpless form of Voorhes lying on the floor at Yvonne's mercy. "What's going on here?" he asked. Although his tone was conversational, his deep, booming voice carried its authority to every corner of the room.

Jules was not cowed by Tshombase's power. Stepping forward, he bowed his head slightly as a minimal acknowledgement and said, "My wife and I wanted to work for you, sir.

We asked Gospodin Voorhes about the possibility, and he saw fit to assault my wife instead. Since we were sure you would not want your officers to appear so uncouth in public, we took it upon ourselves to reprimand him and his friends on your behalf."

There was a hint of a smile at the corners of Tshombase's mouth, but none of it crept into his voice as he told Yvonne, "Release him."

Vonnie glanced over at her husband, and Jules gave a short nod. Reluctantly she stood up, releasing her hold on Voorhes, and backed two steps away. The mayor's lieutenant choked and coughed a bit and got woozily to his knees, but could get no higher for another minute or so.

Tshombase looked back at Jules. "I do not hire warmies, no matter how good they are in a fight. They simply don't have the experience to make themselves useful to me. Try again in a couple of years."

He then turned to his number three man. "I'll have a talk with you in my office tomorrow morning," was all he said. Without further ceremony, he turned and walked out the door as abruptly as he'd entered.

Later that evening, after the d'Alemberts had returned home, they discussed the situation between themselves. Both were disappointed that their prowess had not led to a job offer; they knew they had to penetrate the organization somehow if they were to find out how people were getting off the planet.

"We could try taking Tshombase in a fight," Yvonne suggested. "By beating him we could take over the whole operation, and start in at the top."

Jules shook his head. "It won't work. You have to be more than just a good fighter to rule a village like this. Didn't you see Tshombase's eyes? He's no dummy. You need a full-scale organization behind you. If we knocked off Tshombase, we wouldn't be able to control his men; the village would split into a dozen different factions as each of his officers carved out his own chunk of territory. We'd have to work slowly, behind the scenes, and build up our own organization, to be prepared to step into the power vacuum as soon as Tshombase's out of the way. That kind of work takes time—months at a minimum, years more than likely."

"We haven't got months, or years," Vonnie sighed dejectedly.

"Exactly. Which is why we'll have to find some other way." Jules paced about the small room, pounding his left palm with his right fist. "Somehow, on this crazy planet, there must be some method of working our way into the system quickly enough to find what we need."

But they were unable to think of it that night.

7

Pirate Raid

If Pias and Yvette Bavol had founded their ship, the *Paradise*, as a purely commercial venture, they would probably have been delighted with the results. The passengers were all quite rich, and more than happy to spend their money in such luxurious settings. They praised the rooms and the furnishings. They gambled their rubles away at a prodigious rate, with the house raking in a generous percentage of the pot. The men and women Yvette had hired as "escorts" were doing a bang-up business, and the owners of the *Paradise* got their cut of that. Money was coming in so well that Pias calculated it would only take a year, at this rate, to recoup their initial investment and begin to show a profit.

Nevertheless, they were depressed. The d'Alembert family considered its money and its entrepreneurial talents merely as a means to an end—the end being the safety and security of the Empire and the Imperial family. In this particular case, they were not achieving the results they'd hoped for.

The *Paradise* had started out from Egon to the planet Bromberg, where they picked up some more passengers for their quadrangle cruise through the chosen four star systems. Despite the fact that they had the best subspace detection system money could buy, they detected only one other ship near them during the run—a large, ponderous freighter that posed no threat whatsoever. On the second leg of their journey, from Bromberg to Hsoli, and on the third leg from Hsoli to Kuragana there was not the slightest trace of company. Their alarms went off on the journey from Kuragana back to Egon as a small fast ship pulled up to them, but it turned out to be a false alarm—merely a private vessel that had lost its bearings and was needing some help returning to port.

Even the normally ebullient Pias was becoming discouraged. "Maybe we're not being obvious enough," he complained to his wife. "Maybe we ought to paint a sign on the side: 'First Interstellar Pirate Bank. Withdrawals Encouraged.'"

"They may be sizing us up. We did put a heavy emphasis on how unbeatable our defenses were; they may want to see a little more how we operate before trying anything. We've only made one complete circuit so far. Now that our first passengers are getting off, they'll spread the word about what a fantastic time they had—and what a rich haul this could be. The largest part of a SOTE agent's job is waiting, I'm afraid."

"But how much longer can we afford to wait? The Coronation is only two months away."

Yvette reached across to ruffle his light brown hair. "At least you seem to be enjoying yourself while we're waiting. You've got a casino all your own to play with. The pirates are just a little out of touch, that's all; as soon as they learn about us, they'll be here. Besides—don't you have some old Gypsy proverb or other to console you?"

"Sure." Pias gave her a mock laugh. "'Patience is good, but quick hands are better.' In other words, all things come to he who waits—but he who takes gets them first."

The *Paradise* made a second complete circuit of the four planets, and still there was no sign of trouble. The entire crew was rapidly losing spirit. As was true of all d'Alemberts, they longed for quick action, and the waiting was a strain on their nerves.

At last, on their third run from Egon to Bromberg, the *Paradise*'s pilot encountered an unidentified reading on their detection screens. The object was matching their course precisely, and was not emitting any of the standard recognition signals. All in all, it was a prime suspect for a pirate craft.

Ever since the first voyage, Pias had scheduled "pirate attack

drills" for the passengers at irregular intervals. As he explained
to them, it was just so they would know what to do in case of
an emergency. Rather than alarm people, he pretended that this
was just another drill. As they had done on previous occasions,
the guests filed obediently to their comfortable rooms and
locked themselves in, expecting the "all clear" buzzer to sound
in a minute. This time, however, they were destined to wait
a bit longer.

When the monitors showed that all the non-d'Alemberts
were safely in their quarters, Yvette activated the internal security system. Heavy metal doors slammed down in front of
all the passenger cabins, making it impossible for anyone to
get in or out without at least a heavy-duty blaster and five
uninterrupted minutes of burning through the shield. This
would keep the pirates from bothering any of the ship's
guests—and it would also keep the passengers out of the line
of fire, giving the d'Alemberts free rein to act as necessary.

At first, the *Paradise* made the standard maneuver for a
ship that suspected it was about to come under pirate attack:
it dropped out of subspace into the real universe and began
sending out a distress signal to the nearest Navy base. This was
necessary because a ship within subspace could not generate
a subcom signal; they would have to be in normal space to call
for help. Also, the theory was that by dropping into normal
space—thereby slowing their speed considerably—there was
always the chance that the pirate ship would overshoot them
and then be unable to find them again.

The pirates, of course, knew this trick as well, and were
quite prepared for it. The instant the *Paradise* slipped back into
regular space the pirate ship did the same, staying right beside
its prey and not giving it a chance to escape. Simultaneously,
the outlaw vessel sent out a jamming signal to prevent the
Paradise's distress call from being understood. All this worked
exactly according to the pirates' plan.

Unfortunately for them, nothing else did.

The next phase of the attack was supposed to be a shot from
the pirate ship to destroy its target's engines, thus making it
incapable of further flight. But that was not possible this time.
The *Paradise*'s engines, located at the bottom of the onion-
shaped bulb, retracted into the body of the ship. The *Paradise*
could not fly in that configuration—but neither could it be
incapacitated unless the pirates were willing to blast large

chunks out of the vessel itself and risk losing a sizeable percentage of their potential loot.

The pirate captain decided not to do that. The *Paradise* was immobilized, which was all he thought he needed; if the ship extended its engines again for an escape attempt, his gunners could destroy the drive components then. In the meantime, he ordered his boarding party into action.

Forty pirates, each clad in heavy battle armor, jetted across the gulf of space between the two ships, bringing with them a boarding hatch. This was an auxiliary compartment that could be sealed on the outside of the *Paradise*, thus allowing the pirates to cut through the hull without letting the air escape. This was not a humanitarian gesture prompted by concern for the welfare of the passengers and crew of the *Paradise;* the pirates knew that many of the passengers were wealthy people, and there was always the possibility of obtaining extra money by holding them for ransom.

When the pirates reached their objective, however, they discovered that the boarding hatch was quite unnecessary. The *Paradise*'s outer hatch was standing ajar, an open invitation for them to enter. This disturbed the leader of the boarding party sufficiently for him to radio back to his own ship for further instructions. His captain, a man of great bluster and little imagination, told him to proceed with the attack as planned. If the *Paradise*'s crew were foolish enough to let the pirates in, they deserved what they got.

The *Paradise*'s main airlock would not accommodate all forty pirates at once. Fearing that this might be a trap to break them into smaller groups, the attack leader had the boarding hatch fastened to the ship anyway, so they could all go through the inner lock at once. They waited the required three minutes for the pressure to equalize between the airlock and the rest of the ship, then pushed through the inner lock, prepared for battle.

They found themselves facing an empty corridor—something that had never happened before. The airlock confrontation was normally the crucial battle, because the crew of the victim ship was hoping to stop the invaders at the bottleneck as they came out of the lock. To let the pirates simply walk in unopposed did not seem like sound battle tactics. Nevertheless, the leader urged his fighters to be cautious as they spread out through the ship in search of their victims.

They had crossed several intersecting corridors without seeing any sign of life, and had fanned out to cover more territory when, without warning, the ultragrav was turned up in the hallways. Suddenly, the pirates found themselves battling the crushing forces of more than two gees.

Space armor is heavy stuff; it has to be, to protect its wearer from the blaster beams he can expect to take in a pitched battle. It is usually used under zero gravity conditions. (This is another reason why the pirate vessel tries to destroy the engines of its prey—to knock out the equipment for generating artificial gravity.) In freefall, a man in battle armor is well-nigh invincible.

The pirates had encountered a standard one-gee field when they entered the *Paradise*. This was uncomfortable, but hardly catastrophic. The armor could be managed under such conditions, and the protection it gave more than made up for the slight loss of maneuverability.

But now the gravitational pull was more than twice what they expected. Some of the pirates, caught in an off-balance position by the sudden switch in gravity, fell to the floor and had trouble getting to their feet again; like turtles on their backs, they kicked around awkwardly in their cumbersome suits. Other pirates staggered, and had to brace themselves against the walls to keep from keeling over like their fellows. Given enough time, they could have adjusted to the situation and helped their comrades to their feet again as well; but, of course, the d'Alemberts were not about to give them enough time.

The instant the ultragrav was turned on, an army of d'Alemberts appeared as if from nowhere, descending on the hapless pirates. They too were clad in full battle armor—but there was a difference. In this two-gee field, even with the heavy armor on, the DesPlainians still only weighed about the same as they normally did on their own home planet. They could move about with perfect ease and breathtaking speed. In comparison, the pirates were stodgy and awkward, stumbling around like drunks on an icy sidewalk.

There was no contest. The d'Alemberts had blasters of their own, but scarcely needed them. They closed rapidly with their foes, locked in personal combat. The pirates were so slow-moving that generally the d'Alemberts would have a pirate's helmet off before the invader could raise his weapon and fire in self-defense. A gentle "tap" from an armored fist was more than sufficient to render each pirate unconscious and past caring about the outcome of the fight. The *Paradise* suffered no major damage at all, merely a few minor burns on the walls where some stray blaster beams went awry. None of the defending crewmembers was in any way hurt.

While the fight was going on inside the *Paradise,* an even more surprising development was taking place aboard the pirate vessel. Even as the attack force had been jetting over to the *Paradise,* a small group of d'Alemberts with a boarding hatch of their own was surreptitiously swimming over to the outlaw ship. They took a long, roundabout route so that the pirate captain did not even think to look for them; they approached his ship from the side facing away from the *Paradise,* and the captain had no inkling of their presence until they actually blew open his inner hatch and began taking over his ship.

This was an unheard-of maneuver. Never in the history of commercial space travel had a "victim" ship ever launched a counterattack against a bandit. The crew of the target vessel normally had enough trouble defending their own craft; they should have neither the resources nor the presence of mind to strike back at their tormentors.

The *Paradise,* however, had been designed first and foremost to deal with pirates; gambling was at best a secondary consideration. Its crew were all well-trained professionals, and they had their plans laid out well in advance of this encounter. They were here to smash the pirate threat thoroughly, and that was what they were going to do.

The fight aboard the outlaw ship was no better matched than the one aboard the *Paradise.* The pirate vessel was manned only by a skeleton crew; all its fighters had gone across to do business on the other ship. Those left behind had not expected a fight. They were not in their battle armor, and they did not have their weapons readily at hand. They were waiting casually, as they'd done plenty of times before, to hear from their comrades that the other ship had been taken and there was lots of booty for all. There were only ten d'Alemberts in the attack force, but that was quite enough.

Before the bandit captain could give the order to flee, his ship had been overrun and his crew was unconscious from the effects of the d'Alemberts' stunners. The captain himself fared little better. Three DesPlainians broke into the bridge, where he had hastily barricaded himself, and captured him without a fight. The captain was a pitiful sight as he pleaded desperately for mercy from his captors—mercy he would never have shown them had their places been reversed.

With the situation now well in hand, the d'Alemberts turned off the pirates' jammer and calmly sent out their subcom call to the Navy. At the same time, aboard the *Paradise*, Pias released his passengers from their rooms and casually explained that there had been a *real* pirate attack this time, but that his defense system was all he had promised it would be. The bandits had been defeated, and the Navy would come soon to take them away. The cruise would then continue on as it had been doing—but he did apologize that there would probably be a one-day delay in reaching the next port.

Some of the passengers were upset that they had been kept in the dark about the raid until it was all over, but most of them were quite relieved. Few ships had ever dealt with a pirate attack so successfully, and the security they gained from that knowledge more than made up for the uncertainties they had felt during the raid itself. They knew they were safe in the *Paradise*—a claim few other nonmilitary ships could make.

The Navy officers who came to the "rescue" were quite astounded at what the crew of the *Paradise* had done. Pias did not tell them that this had been a SOTE operation from beginning to end; there was no point in blowing his cover. Nor, despite strong pleas from the captain of the naval destroyer, did Pias explain exactly how he had managed to turn the tables on his attackers. He simply presented the capture to the Navy as a *fait accompli* and let them worry what to do about it from there. He had a ship to run, after all, and it was already behind schedule.

"The best part," Yvette said later, when they were alone in their own cabin, "is that none of the pirates got away to tell their cronies how we did it. The same trick would work again if we have to do it."

"We shouldn't have to, though," Pias replied. "We've just made the point we wanted to make—we're no pushovers, despite the ship's frivolous appearance. From now on, the pirates will respect us—and me in particular, since I'm supposedly the brains of the outfit. Now we move into Phase Two, before they decide to regroup and try another attack."

Yvette scowled. This was the part of the plan she didn't like. It would separate them as a team and make coordinated effort difficult, if not impossible. Each would be on his own from this point until they could actually smash the pirate organization. Yvette recognized the necessity for acting this way, but there was no rule that said she had to enjoy it.

Thus it was that Yvette left the *Paradise* when it reached Bromberg and, operating under the name Mila Farese, set about the process of betraying her husband, and selling him out to the pirate chief.

8

A Proper Gastonian

Time on Gastonia had an unpleasant tendency to lapse into a monotonous pattern. The days dragged by for Jules and Yvonne, stacking one atop another in an accumulation of weeks, and—aside from learning how to survive on their new world with more than a minimum of comfort—they had the dreadful feeling that nothing was being accomplished.

Jules was gaining himself quite a reputation as a hunter, being successful on all the hunts in which he participated. After a month on Gastonia, during which he'd been on three major expeditions, he was making top money for a mere spearman. It was only a matter of time before he'd be promoted to an assistant hunt leader, in charge of coordinating a subgroup within the expedition. He was accepted by the other hunters as a friend and comrade, and became a trusted member of their circle. But despite the fact that they would talk to him more freely, he could not find out anything about a conspiracy on Gastonia. The ordinary run of villagers did not know about such things.

Vonnie was able to confirm that from her own experience. Work in the tanning plant was far less glamorous than hunting, and there was less room for advancement without several years of apprenticeship learning the secrets of the craft. Nevertheless, Vonnie's strength, her devotion to her job, and her willingness to shoulder even the dirtiest tasks without complaint—a rare quality on Gastonia—brought her into favor with the plant's managers. She occasionally received incentive bonuses, and was appointed shop warden over the other workers in her department. Some of the people who'd been there longer than she had were jealous of her rapid advancement, feeling their seniority should have been taken into account, but she got along with most of her co-workers and there were few problems. As Jules had found with the hunters, though, the ordinary citizens did not appear to know about a conspiracy to take some people off the planet.

Because Jules spent much of his time away from the village on hunting expeditions—once for six days at a time—the task of learning the ins and outs of Gastonian society fell largely to his wife. Vonnie was a shrewd observer, and paid particular attention to the finely spun webs of power within the village. Kwame Tshombase was, of course, the ultimate boss, and his word was law—but he could not be everywhere at once, and he relied on a series of lieutenants to keep the peace. Within the broad limits established by Tshombase, each of these lieutenants was a petty tyrant within his own fiefdom. The infighting and jockeying for favored positions among the lieutenants could sometimes become fierce and bloody—a phenomenon their boss seemed to encourage. Perhaps it amused him to watch his underlings squabbling among themselves—but more likely he recognized the principle that if they were busy fighting each other, they would not have the time or energy to think of overthrowing him.

But even Tshombase's men could not wield all the authority in the village. There were always cracks between the jurisdictions, and in these cracks the scavengers gathered. Petty bureaucrats held sway over their own minor territories; bullies and ruffians terrorized the less agressive members of the community; and always in the background were muffled plots and dreams to build a rival organization, depose Tshombase and take over control of the village. For some, this was only idle speculation—but Yvonne had little doubt that there were a few laying serious plans in that direction.

One night, while Jules was away on a hunting trip, she awoke to hear a strange noise. At first, in the moment of half-wakefulness before coming fully alert, it was only a dull buzz-

ing sound—but something told her that this sound had no right
to be here on Gastonia. As she came to complete consciousness
the sound was already receding. It had come from above, and
was definitely mechanical. To Vonnie's sharp ears, it sounded
exactly like a copter flying overhead.

Wrapping her body in furs, she leaped off the bed and ran
to the door to check out this development. The cold night wind
hit her like an icy fist as she threw open the door and peered
out into the night. But there was nothing to see in the sky
except the dark, oppressive gray of storm clouds swirling the
third snowstorm of the week down upon the village. The humming sound was now at the very limits of audibility, and in
another second was gone altogether. If it was a copter, it had
gone on its way in a hurry.

Yvonne was in a thoughtful mood as she closed the door
and returned to snuggle deeply into the bed furs. A copter was
almost as out of place here as a palm tree. It certainly could
not belong to any of the exiles. The residents of the village
had only wood, stone and bone implements; they totally lacked
the capacity to work in metals, let alone construct anything as
sophisticated as a copter. The vehicle could, of course, belong
to the Governor or his staff; perhaps the guards conducted
systematic surveys of the area by air, or perhaps there was
some special mission that Vonnie couldn't even guess at. But
if it were part of a regular survey, why do it at night in a
snowstorm? They'd be unlikely to see much under those conditions.

There were no easy answers to the puzzle, although she had
the definite feeling that the copter pilot had wanted to remain
as secretive as possible. She finally fell alseep once more with
the knowledge that there were still facets of life on Gastonia
that were eluding her grasp.

The complexities increased dramatically two days later.
Jules was still away on his hunt, not expected back for another
couple of days, so, instead of going straight home after work,
Yvonne took one of her long exploratory walks through the
village. She was learning her way around the town quite well,
and had not gotten lost once in the past two weeks. It was an
accomplishment in which she took no little pride.

Suddenly she heard an outcry of several male voices, including one man yelling distinctly, "There she is! Don't let her
get away!"

Vonnie whirled defensively, thinking at first someone might

be after her. After a second, though, it was clear that the cries were coming from the next street over, past this row of shanty houses, and that the sound of running footsteps was paralleling her path rather than coming toward her. Ever curious, the SOTE agent broke into a run herself, dashing between the houses to see what was happening in the next street.

As she emerged on the new street, she saw a fleeing form thirty meters away being pursued by half a dozen men—and one of the pursuers she recognized instantly as Voorhes, the man she'd fought in the bar several weeks ago. Rumors had spread shortly after that incident that Voorhes had been demoted by Tshombase after the fight—though whether the reason was for unseemly brawling in public or for being unable to defeat a woman was never made clear. Vonnie suspected it was the latter, and she'd made a point to avoid contact with Voorhes since then. Life on Gastonia was dangerous enough without making enemies—especially when there were no laws against murder.

One of Voorhes's men reached out and grabbed the fugitive's arm. As the figure was spun back facing Vonnie's direction, the DesPlainian could see with some surprise that it was a very young girl, clad in lighter furs than the men. The man who had initially grabbed her held her long enough for Voorhes to catch up. The bully gave his captive a vicious backhand slap across the face that sent the poor girl reeling backward into a snowbank.

There was no question where Vonnie's sympathies lay. For all she knew, the girl could be a thief and a murderer, and Voorhes might be perfectly justified in hunting her down with his friends. But having seen Voorhes in action before, and knowing something of his reputation, the SOTE agent was willing to bet there was more innocence on the girl's side of the slate than on his. Running at top speed, now, she hurried to the fugitive's rescue.

The six men had been so intent in their pursuit of the girl that Vonnie's attack from the rear was a complete surprise. Launching herself in a low trajectory, Vonnie dove at the legs of the nearest man. She hit him right in the back of his knees with the full force of her seventy-two kilogram weight, and he fell forward with a surprised grunt. Vonnie came down with him and was tangled in his flailing limbs for an instant; but she used her momentum to help her roll forward, and she was extricated and back in action before any of the other men could act.

Scrambling to her feet, the battling DesPlainian turned toward the next man. He had heard his friend cry out and was swiveling to face her when Vonnie caught him squarely in the stomach with a punch delivered at full DesPlainian strength. The man doubled over, offering his face as a target too tempting to resist; Yvonne gave him a solid uppercut that literally knocked the man off his feet. He crashed to the ground a meter away and sprawled unconscious on the snow.

The few seconds she had spent on these two men gave the other four a chance to prepare themselves for the fight. Each was armed with a long stone knife—crude, perhaps, in terms of modern-day weaponry, but quite capable of slitting open a careless opponent. As Voorhes looked at Yvonne, wondering why anyone should attack him here, a dawning light of recognition appeared in his eyes. Yvonne had undoubtedly starred in numerous retribution fantasies dreamed by Voorhes in the past few weeks; it didn't matter to him now *why* she was here. The mere fact that she was facing him alone, unarmed, while he had three friends, all with knives—that fact was quite sufficient for him.

Vonnie took but a second to give the situation a quick scan and plan her moves. Although she had never been a circus performer like her husband, she had undergone a thorough training at the Service Academy in the techniques of unarmed combat, and had scored a respectable 989 overall in the thousand-point test—and those in addition to her being a native-born DesPlainian. Under those circumstances, four to one was an even match.

The nearest man came charging at her like an enraged bull, knife held outward in a very obvious posture. Vonnie had to resist the urge to shout "Olé!" as she daintily sidestepped him, grabbed his outstretched arm, and twisted it back with a severe yank. The man's arm had been stiff, and there was a quite audible crack as the SOTE agent jerked it around. The man screamed and, in his agony, dropped his knife. With a quick, sweeping gesture, Yvonne plucked the blade out of midair before it had fallen halfway to the ground. As her attacker fell writhing to the snow, she spun to deal with the other three.

The man next closest to her had hoped to take advantage of her preoccupation with his friend. While Vonnie had been busy in one direction, he came lunging at her from another, his blade slashing quickly through the air. She barely had time to turn around before he was upon her. He'd brought his blade up to aim at her face, but her very act of turning caused his swipe to miss by several centimeters. As his arm came up, she ducked under him and slipped around behind him.

She wanted to use her knife to slash at him, but realized that would be almost useless. Everyone on Gastonia dressed in heavy furs, and unless she could be certain of scoring a direct hit the most she would probably accomplish with her crude weapon was to cut open the coat's sleeve. Worse yet, there was the chance that the edge of her blade might snag on her enemy's coat and be torn from her grasp as he pulled away from her again.

Rather than risk losing her weapon, Yvonne decided to stick with her already successful tactics of hand combat. As she came around behind her attacker she jabbed her elbow backward into his side, right at kidney level. The man howled and instinctively grabbed at his side, leaving his defenses open. Vonnie promptly took advantage of the lapse, stepping around to the man's other side and delivering two more punches that dropped him to the ground, where he lay moaning in pain.

Even as he fell, however, Vonnie was tackled from behind by Voorhes's last remaining accomplice. The impact of his body against hers knocked her down into the snow. He landed on top of her, jarring her slightly—but coming as she did from a three-gee world, the fall seemed both slow and trivial. She had time to twist around slightly and get into a better position for landing—and a better position to defend herself.

Finding himself momentarily in a superior position, the man raised his knife to bring it stabbing down at the woman's throat. Vonnie quickly reached up and blocked the motion with her forearm, simultaneously squirming to roll over and try to get on top. With a sudden convulsion she arched her body upward, catching her assailant by surprise and tossing him off. Yvonne rolled on top of him and, with one quick stroke, brought her knife down hard at the base of his throat, just above the collar bone. The man made a soft gurgling sound as his body jerked spasmodically for a few seconds, then lay still. Yvonne had not a trace of sympathy for him. He would gladly have done the same to her—and he was already a convicted traitor, anyway. She merely supplied the death sentence.

Even before the dead man's body had stopped moving, she had rolled off it again and was getting to her feet to deal with Voorhes himself. But the leader of the pack was not waiting around to be beaten or killed. Having seen Yvonne dispose of his five comrades, and having himself been the victim of her abilities once before, the cowardly traitor decided that discretion, at this point, would be the better part of his valor. Turning tail, he ran off down the street, totally abandoning both his friends and the girl who had been the original object of his attentions.

Vonnie got to her feet and started after him, but one boot hit a patch of icy snow and she slipped to her knees. By the time she stood up again, Voorhes had better than a twenty-five meter lead. With her superior speed she could probably have caught him had she really tried, but she could see no point in it now. The village was small enough that she would certainly run into Voorhes again sometime, and any unfinished business could be dealt with then. In the meantime, she turned back to look at the girl who'd been the cause of the fracas.

The girl lay in the snowbank where she'd fallen after Voorhes slapped her, cowering away from Yvonne and whimpering with pain and fear. Yvonne tossed her knife aside and approached the girl slowly with open hands. "Don't worry," she said quietly. "I won't hurt you. I only want to help."

The fugitive's face was unfamiliar, and as Vonnie studied it more closely she realized with a start that the girl was no more than thirteen years old—far too young to have been sent to Gastonia as a traitor. She started to wonder how the girl had gotten here, and then realized how simple the answer must be. The girl would have gotten here the same way almost any thirteen-year-old got anywhere—by being born there.

Gastonia had first been settled by exiles a hundred and fifty years ago. Many of the people sent here were still comparatively young and of child-bearing age. It was only natural, once she thought about it, that the exiles would begin building up a "native population" of their own, children born here who had never lived anywhere else. If she and Jules had indeed been doomed to spend the rest of their lives on this planet, they would undoubtedly have had a number of children here. The idea only seemed strange because the rest of the Empire thought of Gastonia purely as a prison, not as a colonized world in its own right.

Vonnie realized, too, that she had not seen any children in the village since her arrival. *Where are they?* she wondered. *After a century and a half, there must be great-great-grand-children of the original exiles living somewhere on this enormous snowball. But they're certainly not in the village; I'd stake my life that all the people here are traitors sent to this prison. Where do the natives live?*

She put her questions aside for a moment to examine the girl more closely. The fugitive's face was covered with welts and bruises, and she held her left arm cradled delicately in her right. Vonnie reached inside the girl's furs to probe with her delicate fingers, and confirmed her suspicions that the girl had suffered a shoulder separation. That, plus the bruises, meant the girl would need medical attention.

"How are you feeling?" Vonnie asked. "Would you be able to walk for a while?"

"My shoulder hurts," the girl said in a pitiful little voice. She tried to stand, but was too dazed. She'd been able to flee from her captors because adrenaline was being pumped through her body, pushing away the shock of the pain. Now that the crisis was over, she was far too stunned to be much help to herself.

"Don't worry," Vonnie said as the girl continued her struggle to get up. "I can carry you. You don't look all that heavy."

Bending down, she picked up the girl and cradled her in her arms. The girl only weighed forty kilos, so the two of them together on Gastonia weighed only half of what Vonnie alone weighed on DesPlaines. The SOTE agent had little trouble carrying her timid passenger.

There were no doctors in the village itself. Vonnie had learned that the little bit of medical services provided were dispensed from a special gate back at the walled garrison. It would be a walk of about five kilometers; Jules and Yvonne had been unwilling to risk it when they first arrived, being unaccustomed to the harsh climate, but now she thought nothing of such a jaunt, even carrying the wounded girl. Walking would be preferable to hiring that old pirate Zolotin's carriage—and, as Vonnie remembered its speed, probably faster, too.

"What's your name?" she asked the girl as she started carrying her along the road out of the village to the hills where the garrison was located.

"Katanya." The girl's voice was faint, and sounded very far away.

"You're not from the village, are you?"

The girl's eyes widened like a frightened fawn. She twisted in Vonnie's arms, trying suddenly to escape, but the Des-Plainian held her firmly. "Relax, I'm just taking you to a doctor to help you get better. I'm your friend—or at least, I'd like to be if you'll let me. My name is Florence Brecht."

Slowly, over the course of the long walk, Vonnie dragged the girl out of herself, prompted her to explain the true situation on Gastonia. It was a portrait that was not only fascinating, but also a little frightening in its implications, and gave the SOTE woman a great deal to think about.

Gastonian society was divided into two cultures that had very little to do with one another. There were the people in the village, the criminal element, the exiles who came to Gastonia from all over the Galaxy. As hardened and tough as they were, they were still too soft to face life on their own in the Gastonian wilderness, so they banded together among their own kind not far from the outpost that kept watch over them. The garrison gave them medical attention and a modicum of supplies—at least enough to keep them going. These were people used to the comforts of civilization, and under these harsh conditions they feared to wander too far away.

The first native Gastonians had been born over a century ago. They'd never known ease, or warmth, or a life based on mechanized labor. For them, the bleak and barren forests and plains, covered with snow the year around, ravaged by bitter storms and chilled by freezing winds—for them, all these things were the norm. They could not understand their parents' complaints about the life they had lost, and they frankly disbelieved some of the stories of the marvels on other worlds. Gastonia was the only world they knew, and they adjusted to it readily.

Between parents and children, exiles and natives, there grew a gap that could never be bridged. Even though they knew they were here for the rest of their lives, the exiles from the Empire could not forget their past. In their own small ways they clung to the pattern of Imperial civilization, borrowing—and sometimes perverting—the social institutions that existed on the other worlds. The children could not understand the need for

anachronisms that flew in the very face of survival on this
forbidding world. To them, there were simpler ways of existing
without these elaborate and pointless rituals. There were constant disputes between the generations over how things should
be done.

Finally, when enough members of the native generation had
reached an age when they could take care of themselves, the
formal split developed. The nativeborn people left the village
and went off to form their own culture—one that, to them,
made more sense than their parents'. They cooperated with
nature on Gastonia rather than fighting aggressively against it;
they found an ecological niche as hunters and nomads. Their
numbers grew as they adapted to this world more and more
over the years; they now numbered well over a hundred thousand people, divided into hundreds of small tribes that ranged
over the continent.

More and more exiles came, but they, like their predeces-
sors, were tied to the ways of the civilization they'd known
before coming here. After a while, though, it became painfully
obvious that any children they had would follow the pattern
of the first children, and leave when they were old enough.
Rather than let each generation of newborns make the same
mistakes over again, a pact was arranged between the villagers
and the nomadic tribes: any children born in the village would
be given over to the tribes whenever one of them passed by
that way. It was hard for any parent to simply hand his child
to a stranger and never see it again, but everyone in the village
knew that the child would have a better and a freer life than
they themselves could ever hope for.

In general, the contacts between the villagers and the tribes
were few and reasonably pleasant—but every so often, someone would get out of hand. In this case, it was Voorhes and
his rowdy friends. There was currently a shortage of available
females in the village, and this half dozen had decided to do
something about it. Learning that one tribe had been camping
nearby, they staged a raid to kidnap some of the women. The
only one they had managed to catch was Katanya, who was
too small and weak to fight off all six. She had resisted furiously, and been beaten unconscious for her efforts. She was
back in the village when she came to; she managed to break
free of her bonds and run away, but one of the men saw her

and started the chase. Vonnie had ended it, and Katanya was very grateful.

The implications of all this were enormous. There were many thousands of good, decent people living here on this hostile prison planet, condemned to a primitive existence because of something their parents—or, in some cases, even their great-grandparents—did. Yvonne had never been a strong believer in visiting the sins of the fathers upon the children; she preferred to let people's actions stand or fall on their own merits. The native Gastonians must know of the Empire's existence from their dealings with the villagers. What did they think, she wondered, of a government that totally ignored their existence and left them to the mercies of this harsh world solely because of their ancestors' crimes?

One thing was certain: Vonnie planned to have a long talk with Jules about this, and to stress in her report to the Head that something should be done about this blatantly unfair situation.

She did not discuss the matter with Katanya, though; in her identity as Florence Brecht, she had no authority to do anything about the problem. She merely questioned the girl as an interested newcomer to Gastonia, and filed the answers away for future reference.

They came at last to the great wall around the garrison, the Empire's only official presence on this planet. Vonnie had to walk almost a kilometer along the wall's perimeter before she found what she'd been told was there—the "dispensary" door, the only opening in the wall through which any of the exiled traitors could pass. Vonnie opened the door and stepped inside with the wounded girl.

The room was small and dimly lit. There were a couple of booths in which patients could sit facing a trivision screen. There was another door on the opposite side of the room leading to the interior of the garrison, but there was no knob or any other way for a patient to open it from this side.

A mechanized voice blared out of a hidden speaker in the walls. "Take a seat before the screen, and state your name and medical problem."

Vonnie placed Katanya in one chair and then sat down in the adjacent one. The screen before her lit up to show a very bored looking nurse seated at a desk. "My name is Florence

Brecht," Vonnie said. "I don't have a problem myself, but I brought someone who does."

The nurse looked at her screen and saw the image of the injured girl. "What's her name?"

"Katanya. No last name."

The nurse punched that into her computer and waited for a response. "The records don't show any prisoner by that name."

"That's because she isn't a prisoner. She was born here, and both her parents were born here. She's a native Gastonian, so she's not on your records. But she is in need of medical help. She's got a dislocated shoulder and multiple facial bruises and lacerations."

The nurse seemed a bit flustered for a moment, wondering what to do, but finally the healer's instincts in her won out over the bureaucrat. "Have her lean back in the chair as comfortably as possible and place both her arms on the armrests. I'll do an analysis."

Katanya did as requested, and watched on the screen as the nurse inside the garrison pressed a number of control buttons. The chair was a passive body sensor, capable of examining a person in it from scalp to sole, taking readings on the major bodily systems. It was, Vonnie realized, a most ingenious system. It allowed doctors to make diagnoses of their criminal patients without having to be physically present—and without allowing prisoners the opportunity to seize a doctor and use him as a hostage in a potential escape attempt.

The sensor system confirmed Vonnie's amateur diagnosis. "Florence Brecht must leave the diagnostic chamber," the nurse said, "at which time the girl Katanya will be allowed to enter the dispensary for treatment."

"I'd like to wait outside for her," Vonnie said. "About how long will the treatment take?"

"Two hours," replied the nurse.

Yvonne told her new friend to trust the people here, that they would help her, and that she herself would be waiting outside if anything went wrong. Then she left the room and waited outside the wall in the cold evening air. The sun was setting by this time, but the area was not dark; the expanse of land immediately around the wall was lit as bright as day to prevent any sneak attacks at night by groups of exiles.

She had no way of telling how much time had elapsed, but

it did seem less than two hours later when Katanya emerged again from the dispensary. Her arm was in a sling and the worst cuts on her face had been bandaged, but she appeared to be in much better shape than when she'd entered. Her eyes were more alert and she was able to walk without assistance.

She approached Vonnie with a sincere expression of gratitude on her face. "Thank you very much for all you've done for me," she said. "I won't be going back to the village with you, though. I have to return to my own people before they leave the area—and maybe stop them from launching a vendetta against the village for my kidnaping."

Vonnie watched the girl walk away until she vanished into the darkness beyond the well-lit area around the wall. Then, with a shrug, the DesPlainian began to make her own way home. It would be a rough walk in the dark, and there was a small danger of her being attacked by some wild animal, but she had been on Gastonia long enough to think she could face up to any ordinary dangers the planet could offer.

She speculated as she walked, though, that every time she thought she understood Gastonia, something new always popped up like a jack-in-the-box to surprise her.

I wonder, she thought, *what new surprises are waiting ahead for us.*

9

The Blizzard

The next night, as Vonnie was walking home from work, a voice called to her from out of the shadows. "Gospozha Brecht."

Vonnie was instantly suspicious. Vendettas were entirely too common a phenomenon on Gastonia, and she had beaten Voorhes twice. It would not be one millimeter above the man's moral level to have her waylaid in some alley. "Yes?" she asked warily.

"I'd like to talk with you for a moment." The voice was barely audible, the man behind it obviously trying to remain secret.

"Come out and talk, then. I won't stop you."

"You'll have to step into the shadows with me. I have my reasons."

"I'll just bet you do."

As she peered into the shadows between the buildings, she could see the outlines of the man's form. He was of medium height and build, far too small to be Voorhes—but that did not necessarily mean he wasn't sent by Voorhes. Almost as though reading her mind, the man said, "Voorhes has nothing to do with this. I just want to talk with you."

"I suppose you have that notarized in writing."

Out of the corners of her eyes, Vonnie could see two men edging slowly toward her from opposite sides. She braced herself for a fight, but pretended for a moment not to notice them as the man in the shadows said, "Five minutes of your time is all I ask."

"Oh? And what about them?" She pointed suddenly at the men approaching her.

As soon as they were aware she'd seen them, they stopped their advance and looked into the shadows for guidance. The man who'd spoken gave a sharp laugh and said, "Smooth, boys, you can go. I can handle this myself." Then, to Yvonne, he continued, "They're just my bodyguards—follow me everywhere. Sometimes they get a little overeager. What do you say?"

Vonnie watched the two men retreat again, and decided to take a chance. "*Khorosho*," she said, walking forward into the shadows. "I'll talk. But only five minutes."

Up close, the man was no one she recognized—but with twenty thousand people in the village, that wasn't peculiar. His face was badly pitted from acne in his youth, and there was a long knife-scar down the right side of his face.

"The word I hear," he said softly, "is that you and Voorhes don't get along."

"We've had a few run-ins," Vonnie admitted.

"I also hear," the man continued smoothly, "that Tshombase turned you down for a job."

Vonnie shrugged, but said nothing.

"Let me be blunt, then. I'm not as bigoted as Tshombase is. I'm looking for good people no matter how long they've been here. From what they tell me, you handle yourself pretty well. How would you like a job with me?"

"Doing what?"

The other gave a brief laugh. His laughs were harsh and unpleasant; Vonnie didn't like them at all.

"Let's just say I'm not happy with his administration, and I think it's time we had a change of government. A clever lady like yourself could rise high in a new regime."

So—when she least expected it, here came an offer to join in the midst of intravillage politics. Vonnie reminded herself that all the exiles here had been convicted of treason, and therefore had a predilection for games of intrigue and treachery.

The plot to overthrow Tshombase would be a dangerous one at best—but if it succeeded, they would be inside the village's power structure and able to unwrap the mystery surrounding the escapes from Gastonia. Time was definitely running out before the Emperor's abdication and Edna's ascension to the Throne; Vonnie knew that she and Jules would have to do something to force some action.

"I'd have to talk it over with my husband," she said after a moment's hesitation. "He and I work together as a team. You'll either have us both or not at all."

"Agreed."

"He's off on a hunt right now. He's supposed to be back tomorrow night. We'll discuss it then and let you know."

"*Khorosho.*" The man nodded and began retreating down the alleyway.

"Wait," Vonnie called. "What's your name? How do I get in touch with you again?"

"You don't," the man said. "I'll contact you." And he turned a corner and disappeared.

Vonnie debated with herself whether she should tail him, but decided against it. If she should be seen following him he wouldn't trust her, and this promising opportunity would be lost forever. He wanted her on his side; he'd keep his promise and contact her again.

Bundling herself against the wind, she headed for home. There was a bad storm heading in from the west—and that was the direction where Jules's group had headed. Vonnie hoped her husband would be safe out there, unprotected from the weather.

The storm hit the hunting party in late afternoon, when the teams were scattered out to search for wallowers. A more prudent hunt leader, seeing the signs of impending trouble, might not have split up his men with such a gale coming in; but the leader of this expedition was edgy. They had only caught one wallower in four days of hunting—not a very impressive record. The men under him were grumbling that the small catch would mean less money for them, and they were taking their discontent out both on each other and on him. He looked at the sky and saw the storm clouds gathering, but his mind—hoping to get in at least one more try this afternoon before heading back to the village tomorrow—allowed him to miscalculate its effects. He estimated it would be a weaker storm than it was, and that it was traveling too slowly to reach them before nightfall. He decided to press his luck and try for one more hunt. The men grumbled; they too could see the approaching storm—but like their leader, they were hoping they could catch at least one more wallower before the end of the expedition.

The country through which they were traveling was a frozen marsh, a terrain ideally suited to the wallowers. These were large mooselike creatures with enormous sets of antlers and broad paddle feet to help them in their half-swimming movement through the mixture of mud and ice that comprised the marsh. Jules's team consisted of himself and two other men, Phillips and Li. Like the other teams, they had been sent out to look for wallowers—and if they saw any, they were to herd them into the center of the large circle encompassed by the hunters, where the group as a whole would bring down the large creatures.

The storm struck them without warning. One moment they were facing a chilly breeze, typical of almost any afternoon on Gastonia—and the next, they were in the midst of a raging blizzard, pelted by hailstones the size of marbles and blinded by the fury of the driving gale that blasted them with a curtain of sleet. The sky grew dark as the sun was totally obscured by the thick black storm clouds, and there was an ominous rumbling overhead.

"Stay together!" Jules yelled, hoping to make himself heard above the rush of the wind. "Grab hands, or we'll be separated."

He wasn't sure, at first, that the other men had even heard him—but then, out of the snow, Li grabbed his hand and Jules held on tightly with an acrobat's grip that was virtually unbreakable. On the other side, he could barely make out Phillips grabbing Li's hand. The three of them formed a chain, with Jules in the lead.

"We must try to get back to camp," Jules bellowed. Beside him, Li nodded agreement but Phillips, only slightly more than a meter away, made no reaction—the storm was so loud he hadn't heard. Nevertheless, Jules started off in the direction of the camp; Li would tend to the job of pulling Phillips along.

They stumbled off through the storm back the way they had come. The hail had given way quickly to snow, but it was scarcely a relief. The freezing gale went right through the men's furs, chilling them to the bone. Jules had to squint to keep the wind out of his eyes, and tiny snowflakes were sticking to the lashes, making it even more difficult to see where he was going. The stinging cold made his eyes water, and the tears froze on his cheeks. He kept his gaze steadfastly glued to the ground in front of him; lifting his head too straight only made the effects of the wind that much worse.

Their previous footprints were all but obliterated from the storm, and Jules had nothing but his own inborn sense of direction to tell him whether he was going the right way. At this point he wasn't even sure it mattered; there would be little protection even in camp against a storm this severe. He knew, though, that in a situation like this he had to keep moving; to stand still, to give in to the blizzard, would be to invite a lonely, frigid death. Jules had too many things left to do in his life before surrendering it that easily.

The ground beneath him was covered by a layer of snow, which in turn was covered by a thin crust of ice. The men's boots made a crunching sound as they trudged step after weary step into the teeth of the gale. Jules's eyes were closed almost completely now—but even had they been wide open, it's doubtful he would have seen the edge of the marsh, covered over as it was with the same layer of frost as the snow.

With one step, instead of his boot sinking through snow to solid ground, it broke through the ice layer and sank thigh-deep into the freezing mud of the fen. Jules toppled off balance and stumbled forward deeper into the mire, but years of training made him keep his grip on Li's wrist. As a result he yanked the other two men with him into the frigid slush of the marsh.

The iciness was a shock to his system, but Jules did not panic. He had been warned of the dangers that dwelled in the marsh—the animals that swam beneath the surface, feeding on one another and on the occasional land creature that was lured into the mud. Most of them would not attack anything the size of a man, but Jules had no intention of placing temptation in their path. He wanted to get out as quickly as possible.

He thrashed around for a few seconds, trying to get his feet planted firmly on the bottom. The two men behind him were not helping matters. The sudden fall into the fen had frightened them, and they were acting on sheer instinct, flailing helplessly about with their arms and distracting Jules from the concentration he needed to think his way out.

The coldness seeped right through his skin, numbing the muscle tissue beneath. Jules was beginning to lose all feeling below the waist; even if there weren't any creatures living in the marsh he would still want to get out of it quickly to avoid the possibility of frostbite.

He regained his sense of direction and tried to walk back toward the shore. The muck around him clung to his legs, holding him back; each step was like walking through molasses. His leg muscles, born to resist the pull of a three-gravity planet, were up to the task as he dragged his two companions along with him; a lesser man might not have made it.

In four steps he was back at the edge of solid ground. Li, still confused but less panicky, was right behind him, and Phillips still clung at the end of the train. Jules grabbed at the ground, trying for a handhold, and found a large rock to serve as anchor. He started to pull himself up when suddenly the load behind him seemed lighter. At the same moment, there was a scream that pierced even the roar of the wind.

Phillips had let go of Li's wrist and was now standing hip-deep in the frigid marsh. "I can't move!" he shouted. "Something's got me!" Jules could not see anything attacking Phillips from where he was, and he knew that any sensation below the man's waist would be faint at most. Perhaps it was true that some marsh creature had attacked him, or perhaps his leg was merely tangled in some underwater plant. It was impossible to tell.

The important thing was that Phillips believed he'd been attacked. He started beating at the mud around him frantically in an attempt to chase off whatever creature it might be and, at the same time, thrashing about wildly in an attempt to break free of its grip. All his actions accomplished was to make him lose his balance in the slippery mud. He fell forward onto his face, and for a moment he was completely submerged. He lifted himself out of the muck once more, sputtering for breath, but his brief immersion only served to panic him further. He was twisting and shaking his right leg, trying to free it from whatever obstacle had snagged it. His screams of terror alternated with his gasping for air.

Jules wanted to help, but there was little he could do. He dared not let go of his rock, or he himself would slip back into the marsh; if there was indeed a creature attacking Phillips, it might decide to go after Jules and Li next. The DesPlainian could only watch helplessly as his terrified companion struggled wildly in the mud behind him. Three more times Phillips fell, and each time he managed to come back up for air—though it was for a shorter duration each time. And once more Phillips sunk below the mud. This time he didn't come up. A hand splashed around, breaking the surface of the mire and waving about, then it too disappeared. There were a few bubbles, and then all was still.

Jules pulled himself the rest of the way onto land, with Li dragging along behind him. The SOTE agent was feeling sick over his inability to save his comrade's life. He barely knew Phillips, just a nodding acquaintance, but even so Jules would have liked to help him. The fact that Phillips had been sent here for treason against the Empire was small consolation; no one, Jules felt, deserved to die that way.

He forced the thought from his mind. There were two of them still alive, and the storm had not abated in the slightest. His legs felt a million parsecs away, both numb and tired from the ordeal in the marsh, but he didn't dare rest; at the rate the snow was falling now, he could be covered up completely in just a couple of minutes. They would have to keep moving once more.

He pulled Li unceremoniously to his feet. The other hunter complained that he was too tired, but Jules refused to listen. He had lost one companion because he'd been unable to act; he was not going to lose a second. Roughly he yanked on Li's arm, and the man had no choice but to stagger along behind him.

The blizzard was swirling around them, mocking them, making it impossible to see more than half a meter in front of them. Jules kept his eyes to the ground, both to keep the driving snow out and to prevent another misstep into the marsh. He had no idea where they were headed, nor did he care. His chief concern was to keep them in motion, to keep the blood circulating, to prevent frostbite if at all possible. He didn't know how long a storm could last on Gastonia, but he knew it wouldn't be forever; if he and Li could weather the worst of the blizzard, they could orient themselves when the air was calmer and find their way back to the village somehow.

His toes could have been completely gone for all he could feel them, and even his feet were only vague rumors below his ankles. His leg muscles were accustomed to pushing him around at three times the current gravitational level, but even so they were protesting this mistreatment. Mud and ice were caked on his pants; the wet material was shrinking against his thighs, biting them with a chill that threatened to deaden all sensation. And still he forced himself onward, placing one foot before the other in an endless series of plodding steps.

The minutes dragged by and became an hour, then two. The blizzard continued to rage, stinging like needles against their skin. Each individual snowflake seemed to hit with the impact of a cannonball, and for all the protection their coats gave them they might as well have been naked. Li, being from a normal gravity planet, was having a much harder time keeping up with the pace Jules had set; he stumbled several times and the DesPlainian had to yank him bodily to his feet. But despite Li's panting, despite his protests, despite his repeated pleas to stop for a rest, Jules pressed relentlessly on, fighting his own fatigue with a superhuman effort.

Finally Li collapsed behind him, and no amount of shaking him or slapping his face could revive him. Jules stood over the other man's body for a moment, clenching his fists with hopeless frustration. A quick memory flashed through his mind, the image of Phillips sinking into the marsh for the last time while Jules had to stand by helplessly and watch his comrade die. He did not want to let it happen again.

Bending over awkwardly in his heavy furs, he lifted Li up and draped him over his shoulders like a stole. The combined weight was still less than Jules was used to back home, but nonetheless it was an added strain on the DesPlainian's already overtaxed muscles. The snow was piled waist deep in some places, resisting his every effort to move, but Jules plowed ahead with the typical d'Alembert stubbornness and a refusal to surrender.

As quickly as it had come, the blizzard stopped—and so numbed were Jules's senses that he continued slogging along for a couple of minutes before he even realized it. The snow stopped falling, and the wind died to nothing, leaving behind a silence so profound that it became a ringing in Jules's ears, the dying echo of what once had been. The sky overhead was still dark with clouds, but over on the western horizon the clouds were parting and the red rays of the setting sun pierced the gloom. The air was crisp and cold, and perfectly clear with a visibility extending for kilometers. Jules put down his burden for a moment and just stood, exhilarating in the clean, fresh air.

After the initial surge of triumph at surviving the storm, he returned to more practical matters. He and Li were separated from the main hunting party, without supplies or transportation back to the village. The storm might not be completely over; this could be merely a temporary lull before the full fury returned. Night would be upon them soon as well. He had best make preparations accordingly.

When he turned around to scout the immediate area, he saw it. There, high up on the top of a hill, its walls reflecting the dying sunset rays, was a large house. It was nothing spectacular as houses go—but on Gastonia, anything that was neither a prefab hut nor a crude wooden shack could be considered a mansion. It was three stories tall, with walls of brick, stone and timber, and it stood imperiously on its hilltop looking down on the valley in which Jules stood, as though it knew it was the grandest edifice on this world outside the Governor's garrison.

Such a house should not be here, not this far from both the village and the garrison. Despite his physical fatigue, Jules felt a surge of renewed energy charging through his body. He and Vonnie had come to Gastonia looking for something that was not quite right, and this house in the wilderness certainly fit that description. He would have to investigate it more closely— and he would never have a better cover story than the truth, that he was a hunter lost in the storm and needing help.

He picked Li up once more and started off toward the house. The strangely clear air after the storm had a deceptive effect, and the building turned out to be farther away than it looked at first. Jules found he had to trudge nearly two kilometers before it seemed appreciably closer. He kept walking, though, and the house appeared even more magical the nearer he came. In the long, fading shadows of twilight the windows lit up, and the house took on the aspects of some grand castle in a fairy tale.

There was a small stand of trees at the base of the hill, and from out of the shadows, before Jules could think to hide, came a guard. He was a tall man, wearing clothes that had obviously been made off-planet . . . and he carried a blaster. Jules noted that particular detail with a great deal of interest indeed.

"Stop!" the guard ordered. He did not have to reach for his weapon, confident that any normal Gastonian would not be armed well enough to fight him. "What are you doing here?"

"Looking for help," Jules said. "My comrade and I got trapped in the storm. He's badly hurt, and I'm not in such great shape myself."

"Why did you come here?"

"We got lost, separated from the rest of our hunting party. After the storm, I saw this house. It's pretty fancy; how did it get here, and how did you get that blaster?"

"I'll ask the questions around here," the guard said brusquely. "Come this way—and stay in front of me at all times."

Jules walked in the indicated direction, still carrying the unconscious Li. Fifty meters up the hill, behind a large boulder, was a guard station. Two other men were currently on duty there—and both of them had blasters, too. Jules decided to play the role of a rube, and gawked blatantly at the station's equipment, which consisted largely of an intercom back to the house and an infrared scanner to survey the valley at the bottom of the hill. *No wonder they spotted me so fast,* Jules thought. *They probably had their sights on me all the way across the valley.*

One of the other guards had noticed his staring, and took out his blaster in a threatening gesture. "Hey, you, stop looking where you ain't supposed to."

"Sorry." Jules quickly looked down at his feet in a gesture of abject apology. "I just never expected to see a setup like this here on Gastonia. Where'd you get it all, anyway?"

"Shut up!" The guard who'd brought him here gave Jules a hard backhand slap across the face. The agent's anger rose, but he kept it under control. This was not the time for a fight— not until he learned more about what was going on here, and what odds he had to face. "Didn't I tell you not to ask questions?" the guard continued.

Jules remained silent, and the three guards conferred among themselves about what to do with these interlopers. Finally one of them said, "We might as well call up to the house and find out what she wants to do with them."

Mention of the word "she" quickened Jules's pulse slightly. Could they be referring to Lady A? Was she here on Gastonia? Was he finally going to meet her face to face—and if so, how could he turn such a meeting to his advantage under these circumstances?

His hopes were dashed, though, when the woman to whom

these men owed allegiance replied over the intercom. Jules had heard Lady A's voice before, on a tape, and this voice, though strong, did not have the same tone of imperious command as the conspiracy's ringleader. There was something familiar about it, though; Jules would have sworn he'd heard it before, although the precise memory escaped him at the moment.

The chief guard explained to his boss how he had found the prisoners, and repeated Jules's story. The woman at the other end was silent for a moment, then said, "Bring them up to the house. I'd like to have a look at them."

The guard turned to Jules. "You heard what she said. Get moving."

Jules walked out the door of the station, still carrying Li on his shoulders, and marched up the steep hill to the big house. The guard followed a few steps behind him. Even had he wanted to make an escape attempt, Jules could not have dropped Li's body and turned to fight before the guard could have drawn his blaster and fired. Of course, Jules desired no such thing; at the moment he was delighted to be getting an escort into the house.

As he walked through the door, he was greeted by a sensation he hadn't felt since he'd arrived on Gastonia, a feeling he'd almost forgotten existed—warmth. This house was heated efficiently, and did not need to rely on the uneven heating of the crude fireplaces in most Gastonian dwellings. To Jules, who had now spent more than a month living under the cold Gastonian conditions, it was almost uncomfortable to be comfortable.

He was ushered into a room that could have passed for a wealthy salon on any civilized planet—comfortable furniture, carved wooden tables, circular carpets, indirect ceiling lighting, even a sensable set in one corner. Anywhere else, Jules would not have thought twice about the decor—but on Gastonia it was an anachronism for which he had to find an explanation.

A woman walked into the room from another hallway. She wore a red caftan covered with gold beadwork, silk slippers trimmed with fur and a dark blue fur-edged cape. But when Jules got a look at her face, his heart froze. Coming across the carpet toward him was Tanya Boros—former Dowager Duchess of Swingleton, former heir to all of Sector Twenty . . . and the only daughter of the infamous Banion the Bastard, pretender to the Throne until a couple of years ago, when the d'Alemberts thwarted his carefully laid conspiracy.

Although the harsh climate of Gastonia could age a person quickly, Tanya Boros looked as beautiful and young as ever. Her years of exile on this world had been gentle with her, and Jules was sure she could not have spent much time in the village. But life within this villa could not have been what Stanley Ten had had in mind when he commuted her death sentence to life imprisonment in exchange for her renunciation of all titles and a renewed vow of loyalty to the Empire.

Jules cursed himself as all kinds of a fool for not expecting to run into her here. It had been his actions that condemned her to this planet, and yet he had scarcely given her a thought in the intervening years. Partly it was because he'd been too busy with other things—but also, he knew, it was because there was a tendency to think of someone on Gastonia as already dead. Now he was learning how wrong that assumption was.

He had to think quickly. Tanya Boros had met him years ago as duClos, an ex-Puritan masseur and bodybuilder. He had moved with an athletic spring to his step and affected a prissy, supercilious tone, sneering at her nobility and insulting her to her face. He had been smooth-shaven save for a pencil-thin mustache and had spoken with a slightly nasal twang.

Since there were no shaving implements on Gastonia, his face—like that of every other male here—was half hidden by a thick growth of beard; that would help. He let his shoulders sag slightly under the load they were carrying, and he hunched in his neck so that his chin was almost even with his shoulders. He reminded himself to speak in a slow drawl. He wanted there to be as few clues as possible to remind her of anyone she might have known.

"What are you doing here?" she asked sharply. From her tone, she might still have been one of society's leading lights questioning a disobedient servant.

"Well, gospozha, I didn't mean to come," Jules said. He was putting on an act, creating a character as different from duClos as he could make it, staring abashedly at the floor and shuffling awkwardly from one foot to another. "Me and my friend here, we're just hunters from the village, and we got lost from the rest of our friends in the storm, and..."

"Look at me when you speak."

"Uh, yes, uh sorry, gospozha. Anyway, we was lost and my friend collapsed, so I started carrying him, and then the storm stopped and I saw your house up here, and I thought I might ask for some help, and I..."

"You *carried* him all the way up the hill?" Boros's eyes narrowed and she looked more closely at Jules.

The agent gave her a broad, toothy grin. "Why yes, gospozha, he ain't that particularly heavy. When you get used to draggin' wallowers around in the marsh, you don't think much of luggin' a little guy like him."

The woman was staring at him, now, examining his face closely—too closely for his comfort. "What did you say your name was?" she asked.

"Brecht, gospozha, Ernst Brecht. Can I put my friend down somewhere—he is startin' to get a mite heavy."

"No, you may not." She walked around him, observing him from all angles, then came back to face him again. "Tell me, Ernst Brecht, when were you last on Earth?"

"Oh, I ain't never been on Earth, gospozha. No, never been there in my life. How could I afford it? That's for the rich folks and the nobles."

"Then where could I have met you?" The question was only half directed at him; the other half was to herself.

"Don't know, gospozha. I'm sure I'd remember someone as pretty as you. Ever been to Islandia? That's where I come from."

"I've never even *heard* of Islandia."

"That's too bad, gospozha. It's a really nice place. I wish I was there right now—all bright and warm and sunshiny. I wish I'd never left. I sure wish now I'd never done them things . . ."

"Oh, shut up!" Boros snapped peevishly. Jules could tell she was emotionally as childish as ever—a fact he'd been relying on. She had little patience for anything that didn't play the game the way she wanted it played.

Turning to her henchman, she said, "This imbecile's no threat to us. Wait until it gets a little darker, then take him back in the copter. Drop him off near the rest of his friends and let him walk the rest of the way. Don't let them see you."

She turned back to Jules. "One thing you'd better keep in mind, Gospodin Brecht. I know everything important that goes on in the village. I have people keeping me informed. I don't want you to start talking about this house, is that clear? If you do, I will be very upset, and I may have to take steps to silence you permanently. Do you understand?"

Jules gulped noisily. "Yes, gospozha."

The guard who'd brought Jules in looked at Boros in amazement. "Why don't we just kill him now and be done with it?" he asked. "No one would miss him."

"I gave you your orders. Carry them out." Tanya Boros stalked huffily out of the room once more.

The guard was a bit perplexed, but he knew better than to disobey instructions from that woman. Taking Jules roughly by the arm, he said, "This way, snowslusher."

Jules was equally puzzled by Boros's action. Although she had never, to his knowledge, committed murder as part of her father's plot—she was much too lazy and self-indulgent to care about such things—he nonetheless did not believe such things were beyond her capabilities. If he'd been in her place, he'd have killed the trespasser in an instant. He'd been prepared to put up a fight immediately if it became necessary—but he was most thankful that it wasn't. He would rather have the opportunity to make more careful and detailed plans. He would not look past the molars on this particular gift horse.

But he was still worried as he was escorted out of the house. Tanya Boros might not have recognized him this time, but he knew they would meet again—and anything might happen then.

10

Betrayal

When Yvette left the *Paradise* on the planet Bromberg, she took with her a great deal of specialized equipment—including a miniaturized nondirectional subcom transmitter. The pirates' appetite had been whetted by their disastrous attack on the Bavols' vessel, but the interest would have to be maintained. Left to his own devices, the pirate leader might decide that the *Paradise* was not worth the effort for further forays. It was Yvette's job to convince him otherwise—and for that, she needed inside help.

Naval Intelligence had already managed to infiltrate the pirates' hierarchy with one of their own men, a Commander Paul Fortier. The Navy's spy had worked his way into the position of the pirate leader's chief lieutenant, and was sending back useful information at irregular intervals—whenever it was safe to broadcast—that had allowed the Navy to keep the pirate menace at least under control. The Navy had been on the verge of closing this gang down for good when Fortier sent word hinting at a larger organization extending throughout the Empire. The decision was made back at Headquarters to allow this gang to continue while Fortier probed deeper into the subject of the overall conspiracy. At about this time the Gastonian connection came to light, and now SOTE was involved as well. Yvette hoped to work with Fortier to smash this treasonous network before Edna's ascension to the Throne. There was not much time left.

Once she had set up her base of operations in a small hotel room on Bromberg, Yvette set about the tricky task of signaling Fortier. This was not easy, because the naval officer could not stand by his subcom unit waiting for calls. His communicator was probably well-concealed somewhere on or near the pirate base, recording all incoming messages. Whenever it was safe to do so, Fortier would play them back and learn what was expected of him. In this case, Yvette gave him instructions in a high-level code to rendezvous with her as soon as practical at The Black Hole Cafe on Bromberg at ten any evening. She described what she looked like and told him she'd seen his photo, so she could identify him.

With that accomplished, there was nothing to do but wait. As an important officer in the pirate force, Fortier would have more freedom of movement than most of the men—but even so, he could not come and go as he pleased. To avoid suspicion he would have to wait until there was a logical reason for him to go to Bromberg—either to sell some of the pirates' stolen goods, to buy supplies or to recruit more people for their band; then he would have to find a reason to slip away from his companions and meet her at the designated spot. It could be days or weeks before he showed up, but Yvette forced herself to be patient. She knew all too well the hazards of an agent working in the field, and she knew Fortier could not afford to hurry; it was his neck on the line, after all.

Yvette became a steady customer at The Black Hole Cafe, coming in regularly every night at eight-thirty and staying well past eleven. After the first week, the manager began setting aside a special table just for her, off in one dark corner where she could have the privacy she requested. Sometimes the cafe's staff wondered about this beautiful, mysterious woman who sat by herself and ate dinner, rebuffing the advances of the few men who tried, at first, to pick her up. Eventually no one bothered any more, and Yvette became as much a fixture in the cafe as the paint stains on the baseboards or the faded paper on the walls.

Finally, after more than three weeks of waiting, Yvette looked up one night to see Paul Fortier enter the cafe. He was a short, muscular man with black hair, brown eyes and a thin mustache. He wore an open-necked white shirt with a gray vest and pants, boots, and a short gray cape with red velvet appliqués. On his head was a small red skullcap. He glanced around the room a moment; then, seeing Yvette sitting in her corner, he came to her table and sat down.

"I understand the dinner for two is better than the a la carte," he said, delivering the pre-arranged recognition signal.

"It ought to be; it costs more," Yvette replied with the countersign. Then, identities established, she continued, "I've acquired something of a reputation in here for dining alone; it wouldn't be wise to break character now. There's a bar called the Vortex two blocks away. I'll meet you there in an hour, if it's convenient."

Fortier gave a slight nod, then stood up to play out his part for the rest of the cafe's patrons. *"Khorosho*, be that way," he said, loudly enough for all to hear. "It'll be a cold day in hell before I waste my time on you again."

An hour later they met at the bar under more relaxed circumstances. "How did I do back there?" Fortier asked her.

"A bit melodramatic, perhaps, but it served its purpose," Yvette smiled back.

"What's the assignment this time?"

Briefly, Yvette explained about the problem of Karla Jost and the apparent connection between Gastonia and the pirates. Fortier listened and nodded slowly. "There have been some high-level recruits coming into the upper echelons without working their way through the ranks. I thought something was suspicious but there wasn't any way to hook myself into them. Now that you mention this, though, it all starts to make sense."

Yvette then went on to explain that she and her partner had been assigned to work on the case with Fortier from the pirate end of the operation, and that they were behind the *Paradise*. The commander whistled. "You don't do things by halves, do you?"

"My partner has a . . . shall we say, flair? At any rate, you'll have to convince your boss to tackle it again."

"After losing a whole ship that badly, and not even knowing how it was done? He's given up on it, at least for now. The possible reward isn't worth the sacrifice."

"That's where I come in. As Mila Farese, I was in charge of keeping all the customers happy—and I was the owner's mistress. I know the defenses of the ship backward and forward. The situation as you will explain it to your boss is that my boyfriend and I have had a colossal fight, and I left the ship. You found me here on Bromberg, and I was only too happy to get revenge—as long as I get a substantial enough cut. And of course, you'll have to bring me back to the base with you so I can discuss it with him personally. Think you can manage that?"

Fortier pondered. "The *Paradise* is a rich enough prize that he might just consider it worth another go if he had inside knowledge. Yes, I think he'll bite. I can give him a subcom call tomorrow and argue the case. Where can I reach you?"

Yvette gave him the name of her hotel, and they completed the arrangements for communicating the next day. With business finished, Yvette leaned back in her stool and attempted to satisfy some personal curiosity. "You've got a high-grav body," she said, "and the name Fortier sounds definitely DesPlainian. Are you?"

Fortier shook his head. "My grandfather was, and all his line before him, but he left DesPlaines for a Navy career. He married a woman from Soleban, a normal grav world, and settled there. Both my father and I also followed naval careers—but by the time the genes got down to me, all I've got is the short, stubby body and the thick bones. There are plenty of times I wish I did have the speed and the strength, but . . . no, it wasn't to be. You, I take it, are a true DesPlainian. What's your name?"

Yvette hesitated for just an instant. Her deeply engrained instincts as a secret agent told her not to give her real name to anyone, not even an ally; she was too high-ranking a weapon in SOTE's arsenal to give her identity lightly. If Fortier were captured and subjected to nitrobarb, her cover would be blown—and possibly even the cover for the entire Circus. She thought of giving her code name, Periwinkle, but that was a SOTE code name, and would be meaningless to a Naval Intelligence officer. "For now," she said, "why not just call me Mila Farese? That way you won't have to worry about conflicting identities."

As a secret agent himself, Fortier nodded and gave her a quiet smile. *"Khorosho.* Along those same lines, you'd best forget the name Fortier. The pirates know me as Rocheville. And I'd better be going now—I've been away from the others in my group too long as it is. I'll be in touch with you tomorrow with the results of my call." The two agents shook hands and Fortier left the bar. Yvette waited fifteen minutes to avoid having it look as though they were together, then returned to her hotel, pleased with the outcome of the night's work.

Fortier called her the next day at midafternoon to tell her that he'd arranged for her to be taken back to their base for a meeting with his boss, Admiral Shen Tzu of the "alternate navy," as Shen was fond of calling his pirate band. Shen was at least willing to discuss the possibility of another raid on the *Paradise,* and was looking forward to the acquaintance of the beautiful woman Fortier had described to him.

Yvette met Fortier and the other pirates the next day at the spaceport, and was taken aboard their ship—a small unarmed personal yacht that could hardly be suspected of being a pirate's vessel. The pirates did not bring their loot personally down to the planet; they had it waiting in a ship orbiting this sun far beyond the path of its outermost planet, and prospective buyers were ferried out for inspection. The buyers, many of whom were otherwise legitimate businessmen, could then bring the contraband in as part of their honest import trade, and no one would be the wiser.

The pirates, having concluded their business dealings, were ready to return to base. Out in deep space they and Yvette transferred to the larger ship and set out quickly for the uncharted pirate world.

"It's a jungle planet that doesn't seem to be on any of the charts," Fortier explained to her as they traveled. "They've got the base and the ships hidden away just in case the Empire happens to stumble across it—but there's been no problem so far." He shook his head. "Hundreds of ships—some of them almost destroyer size—and over twenty thousand people to man them. Even a large pirate organization would only need five or ten ships at the most. They's why I told the Navy to hold off their mop-up operations; this base must be part of some larger plan. I've tried to find out more about it, but apart from some rumors about other similar bases elsewhere, I haven't come up with anything definite."

He looked at her with a forlorn smile. "Maybe you'll have more luck than I did, coming at it from a different angle."

It took them three days at top speed to travel from Bromberg to the pirate planet. Yvette was never allowed in the control room, so she did not learn the world's location—but she was sure that was unnecessary. Fortier had probably learned the coordinates long ago and forwarded the information to the Navy. The information she needed was much more subtle and far more important.

Immediately after landing, Fortier escorted her to Admiral Shen's office. Yvette decided it would be perfectly within Mila Farese's character to gawk at the decadence of the Mongol tent office and at the enormous size of the man inhabiting it. The only person she'd ever met who was bigger had been Marchioness Gindri of the gambling moon Vesa—a pale, indulgent slug with only a passing resemblance to humanity. Admiral Shen, however, for all his large bulk, was not soft; there was a cold, hardset mouth above his multiple chins. Yvette had few doubts about this man's ability to handle his obviously high position within the conspiracy.

Shen's eyes were traveling approvingly up and down Yvette's body. "Well, Rocheville," he said to Fortier in a deep, gravelly voice, "what morsel have you brought me this time?"

"Her name is Mila Farese, and she claims to have the key to the *Paradise's* defense."

Shen stopped his ogling and looked instead straight into Yvette's eyes. "Is this true?" he asked.

"You bet it is." Yvette worked up a good show of righteous indignation. "That little weasel has two-timed me for the last time. I'll show him he can't . . ."

"Excuse me," Shen interrupted, "but which little two-timing weasel are we talking about?"

"Brian Sangers, the tonkarat who runs the *Paradise*. I was his top lady until he started fooling with a little jamtart who has less brains than a flea's left foot. I practically ran the whole ship for him, and the only thanks I get is a quick boot in the rear. I'll show him not to mess with a Farese."

"A very commendable spirit, my dear," Shen said calmly, a broad smile illuminating his face. "I presume that is where my organization and I come in."

"Sure. You want to crack it open and get inside, and I've got the knowledge to help you do it. There's millions of rubles floating free in there, if you've got the guts to go for it."

"My, my, Hell certainly does have no fury, does it? And you offer me all this out of the goodness of your heart and your desire for revenge, is that it?"

"Hell, no. I take one-quarter, off the top."

Shen placed his two palms together almost in a position of prayer and buried his face behind the joined hands. "That's a rather high commission, don't you think? I have expenses of my own to meet, after all—there's a payroll and overhead for maintaining this base. The people who go out on the raids always get a percentage of the take—it's part of my incentive program. They wouldn't be happy with me if I gave away such a large share to such a little woman."

"Without me, you ain't ever going to get in," Yvette insisted.

"And without me, you won't have the manpower to complete your revenge," Shen countered. "But I'm a generous man. I'll give you ten percent of the net, after operating expenses are deducted."

Yvette hesitated for effect. "Twenty percent," she said at last.

"Fifteen percent net."

"Fifteen gross."

Admiral Shen considered her latest counter-offer, then slammed an open palm down on his desk with a resounding clap. "Done! It's a pleasure doing business with you, Gospozha Farese. Now, tell me about those defenses."

Yvette shook her head. "I may not be no admiral, but I ain't stupid. If I tell you now, you won't need me at all. I'll go along with your raiders, and I'll give them instructions as they need them."

Shen's smile broadened still further. "Well, well, ever the practical little businesswoman. *Khorosho*, have it your way. When this raid is over, maybe you would consider joining forces with me. I could find a position for a beautiful woman with the brains to match her looks."

Sure, I'll bet you could, Yvette thought as she noticed the lecherous look in Shen's eyes. *I'll bet it's a horizontal position, too.*

But to voice her sarcasm would not be in keeping with the looser, more worldly character of Mila Farese. Instead, Yvette smiled sweetly back at him and said, "I'm afraid you couldn't afford me, honey. As soon as I get my take, I'll be long gone to a life of ease and respectability."

"Suit yourself," Shen said with a shrug of his shoulders. "I'll have one of my other men show you to your quarters; I have a few details to discuss with Rocheville."

Yvette went with her new guide, leaving the two men alone. The next step of the plan was up to Fortier. It would be his job to alter the deal Shen had just made with her, by pointing out that this Brian Sangers must be an exceptional person if he could devise a pirate defense system that worked so well. Fortier would suggest that they capture Sangers and offer him a job in their organization.

Shen must have been impressed by the way the *Paradise* defended itself. It shouldn't take much salesmanship on Fortier's part to switch him around to that way of thinking.

Yvette reached her small cabin and lay down on the bed, staring up at the ceiling. So far, everything had been going according to plan—and for some reason, that disturbed her.

You're too used to having things go wrong, she chided herself. *Lean back and enjoy them when they go right for a change.*

But she found the advice easier to give than to follow.

11

Traps

"You told me to keep my eyes open for anything suspicious," Tanya Boros was saying, "and this certainly was, or I wouldn't have bothered calling you."

A three-dimensional image of Lady A's head filled the screen of Boros's subcom unit. The former Duchess of Swingleton had been a little worried about calling her superior on this matter; Lady A's temper was legendary within the organization, and disturbing her for some trivial purpose was not a recommended practice. Tanya Boros did not think the matter of this interloper was trivial, though, and she hoped Lady A wouldn't, either.

Lady A seemed to be in a good mood today; her expression was almost warm as she looked back at Boros from inside the box. "Explain what happened," she said.

"A man, one of the villagers, came up the hill and was brought into the house by a guard. He looked and acted harmless enough, but there was something about him that was vaguely familiar. I would have killed him outright, but I remembered your instructions so I just let him go and warned him not to talk about this house to anyone. After he was gone, I checked his file with the computer.

"He claimed to be Ernst Brecht from Islandia, and that much did check out—but if he is Ernst Brecht, he can't be nearly as stupid as he acted here. According to the file, Brecht and his wife, acting solely by themselves, took over the entire colony world of Islandia and held it for several days before SOTE captured them. Yet with me, he was practically drooling in his shoes."

"There does seem to be a disparity," said Lady A. "Let me see a picture of him."

Boros obliged. "This is one the guards took of him when he was at their station. The other is from his official prison file, showing him without beard and mustache. He looks even more familiar to me that way, but I just can't place him."

Lady A studied the pictures for a moment, and a smile spread slowly across her face. "Yes indeed," she said, half to herself.

"You know him, then?"

"I've seen him once, at Edna's wedding. He was the rather athletic young man who swung down from the ceiling on a rope and spoiled our little surprise."

"Athletic?" Boros slapped her forehead with her right palm. *"Bozhe moi,* of course. He was an athlete, a bodybuilder . . . what was his name? DuClos, that's it. I was taking training from him just before . . ."

Her eyes narrowed as the picture suddenly swam into focus before her memory. "Then he's the one who . . . and I did it. I betrayed my father and mother. It was all my fault they lost." Her eyes began to fill with tears. Some were actually for the memory of her dead parents—but even more were for having blown her own chance to be heir to the Throne.

Lady A let her cry for a moment, an abnormally tender expression on her face. "It was hardly your fault, child. Your father's plot was not really intended to succeed."

Tanya Boros looked up quickly and drew a sharp intake of breath. "What? How did you . . . you planned it to fail?" She could hardly believe the implications of what Lady A told her. She had grown up with her father's plans for the takeover of the Empire, had seen him work them out with meticulous detail. Never had there been any mention of anyone higher up.

"Not as blatantly as you state it," Lady A said. Under any other circumstances she might have become annoyed at such rude questioning by an inferior, but with Tanya Boros she was strangely subdued. "I had hoped, right up to the last, that he would succeed—and his failure hurt me more than you can guess. But I never really believed he could make it. His attack was much too frontal, and the threat he posed to the Empire was much too obvious. SOTE had been looking for both him and the Patent for over sixty years; it was only a matter of time before they found him. Frankly, I was surprised it took them as long as it did—but then, your father did inherit a certain amount of native cunning from both his parents."

She paused a moment for breath, then continued softly, "No—Banion was at best a feint in the true plan, an obvious decoy set out to keep SOTE busy while we worked the real plan behind the scenes. We now reach into every sector of government, in ways that not even SOTE will realize until it's much too late."

"But . . ."

"Enough of this," Lady A said, suddenly snapping back into her normal behavior. "There are more immediate problems concerning us. It seems you have a SOTE agent on your tail— or possibly two, since you mentioned he had a wife. How do you propose to cope with him?"

"I'll have him killed immediately," Boros replied.

"No, you will *not!*" Lady A's voice was cold and stern. "I've waited too long for him to get there; I was almost beginning to think he wouldn't show up at all. You will keep a close watch on him, certainly, to make sure he doesn't do anything we can't handle. Other than that, we will make him come to us. I'll be out there myself in just a few days, and we'll set a trap with bait he'll never be able to resist."

"What bait is that?"

"Me," said Lady A, and broke off the transmission.

The hunting trip proved to be a total disaster from the standpoint of most of Jules's companions. More than one-third of the total party was killed during the freak storm, and the one wallower that they had managed to catch had been lost, buried somewhere by the blizzard. Jules and Li had been set down about a kilometer outside the camp by the copter, and Jules managed to carry his companion back to the group. Li was at least still alive, and after he came around he was most grateful to Jules for saving him. He had absolutely no recollection of the house or the meeting with Tanya Boros, and Jules—as he'd been ordered—did not discuss it; it was not that he feared what Boros might do, but rather that it was none of these people's business what had gone on there.

Disheartened and discouraged, the hunting party trudged back to the village empty-handed, arriving well after nightfall the next day. Jules collected the minimal pay allotted for such a disastrous expedition and hurried back home to Vonnie.

After their lingering welcome-home kiss, Vonnie started talking quickly to apprise him of what had happened during his absence. "There's a lot more here than meets the eye," she said. "There seems to be a copter somewhere on this planet..."

"I know," her husband said with a slight smile. "I rode in it."

After a line like that, he had to elaborate. He recounted briefly his adventure in the blizzard, spending much more time relating what had happened at that fantastic house. Vonnie had never met Boros, and only knew of her vaguely from Jules's abridged tales of his previous exploits, but she knew full well that Boros's presence here on Gastonia was both a threat and a promise—a threat to possibly expose Jules's cover, and a promise that they were indeed closing in on the mysterious happenings they'd come here to investigate.

When Jules had finished, Vonnie continued her own story of events back in the village—of the copter she had heard going overhead, of the discovery that there were native Gastonians who seemed to be the "forgotten people" of the Empire, and of the offer she had received just yesterday from the mysterious stranger who wanted to challenge the village leadership and establish himself at the top.

Although Jules was tired after the events of the past two days and the long hike back to the village, he knew that time was short. Edna's coronation would be drawing near, and with it came the threat of disruption by Lady A's conspiracy. There were no accurate timepieces on Gastonia and, although the d'Alemberts knew that a day here was about twenty-eight hours long, they had lost track of how time here related to the official Imperial Time which was kept at Earth standard. The two agents stayed up most of the night discussing the possibilities their discoveries had opened.

"If the copter flew over the village, it means Boros or one of her people was visiting someone here; if they were visiting someone at the garrison instead and wanted to keep their presence on this world secret, they'd have flown around the village," Jules mused. "The most likely person for Boros to contact here would be Tshombase, since he controls most of what goes on in the village. That would tie in with what she told me, that she would know if I talked much about her house to anyone back here."

"That seems to make it more important than ever that we integrate ourselves into the village leadership," Vonnie said. "If we can't do it through Tshombase, it'll have to be with this other fellow who asked for our help. From what you've told me, I don't think Boros will be picky about who's in charge of the village; she'll deal with whoever is the mayor, and he'll have to go along because she has the guns and the resources."

"Yes, we'll have to make some plans," Jules said. "When did this guy say he'd talk to you again?"

"He didn't. I just told him I'd have to talk it over with you, and he said he'd be in touch. I imagine it will be within the next couple of days. He seemed pretty eager."

"Eager, eh? I don't like that." Jules paced nervously over the floor. "If he's in too much of a hurry, he may make sloppy mistakes that could cost him when he makes his play for the top. Of course," he added with a smile, "there may be ways we can use that to our advantage as well."

It was two days later when the scar-faced man contacted Yvonne again. She was walking to work in the morning when she heard her name hissed out from an alleyway, and there he was, still partially obscured by shadows. "Well?" he asked impatiently.

"We're in, if you still want us," she said quietly.

"Good. There'll be a short orientation meeting tomorrow night about an hour after sundown at 47 Snowbound Lane. Come unarmed. If you and your husband aren't there, you're dropped from the list."

"We'll be there," Vonnie promised.

Without even waiting for her reply, the man had started slinking away, and within seconds he was gone. Yvonne shrugged her shoulders and continued on her way to work. The plan had now begun to move, however slowly; tomorrow night should be very interesting.

The d'Alemberts arrived at the given address at the appointed time the next night. At Yvonne's knock, the door

opened a crack and a man behind it gave her a quick glance
to make sure she was one of the ones to be admitted. When
her identity had been established, the door swung open wider,
and she and Jules were permitted to enter.

There were fourteen other people in the room. Scarface and
three of his beefy bodyguards stood at the front, while eleven
others—probably new recruits like the d'Alemberts—sat on
the floor facing them. Jules and Yvonne were searched for
weapons and, when it was determined they were unarmed, they
were invited to sit down with the others.

The d'Alemberts were apparently the last expected arrivals,
because as soon as they were seated Scarface began to talk.
He welcomed the recruits to the new organization, and promised them all good jobs when he replaced Tshombase as the
new mayor of the village. He explained to them how he had
studied Tshombase's organization, and knew who and where
all the other's people were. The new organization was still a
little ways from completion; when Scarface judged they were
ready, they would attack throughout Tshombase's network simultaneously in a complete top-to-bottom coup, leaving not
a single one of the old mayor's men alive to stage a counter-
revolution.

He had just begun explaining the roles each of them was
to play in his insurrection when there was a sudden colossal
pounding at the door. Scarface stopped speaking, and the three
bodyguards drew their long knives and turned to face the possible threat. After a second there was another loud pounding,
and the door began to splinter inward. The recruits in the
audience were becoming very nervous, and they all waited
quietly to see what would happen. They were only too aware
that they were unarmed.

At the third pounding, the d'Alemberts sprang into action.
Leaping to their feet, they bounded over the other startled
recruits and raced to the front of the room. The bodyguards,
facing the threat from the door, barely saw them coming. The
two DesPlainians grabbed the men's wrists and twisted the
knives out of their grasp, Jules handling two to his wife's one.
Vonnie disarmed her bodyguard, then turned her attention to
Scarface. The rebel leader had started into the next room for
an escape attempt through a back window. With a flying tackle,
Vonnie caught him and dragged him to the floor.

The door broke apart completely at the fourth impact of the

battering ram, and in charged a host of Tshombase's men, all well-armed with knives. They were expecting resistance, but found little. A few of the unarmed recruits tried to make a break past them and out the door, but were stopped by the threats from Tshombase's men. Sullenly, the would-be rebels returned to their places on the floor.

After a moment, when he was sure it was safe, Tshombase himself strode into the room. The big man put his hands on his hips and looked around, a humorless smile on his ebony features. His eyes fastened on Jules, and he nodded. "You were right, Brecht," he said. "A rat's nest indeed."

The recruits and the bodyguards alike turned to glare their hatred at the two newcomers who had betrayed them. Jules ignored them and looked directly at Tshombase. "I told you we could be of service to your organization."

Scarface was cursing Yvonne loudly as she held him pinned down and helpless. Tshombase turned in that direction and grinned at the man who thought to replace him. "So it's you, Luis. I thought you were smarter than this. Why must I always be disappointed in people?"

He nodded to some of his men. "Take our friend Luis to the office and see if you can't *persuade* him to tell us who else has been playing his little game."

Tshombase's troops herded all their prisoners out the door, leaving the mayor alone with the d'Alemberts. The big man looked at the two DesPlainians and said, "I really had my doubts about you, but you delivered as you promised. Why did you decide to go along with me instead of Luis? He would probably have offered you a higher position."

"I prefer to bet on a sure thing," Jules said, looking unafraid straight into Tshombase's eyes. And, in part, that was the d'Alemberts' real reason. By proving their loyalty to the present mayor, they were sure they could land a job of some sort in his organization, which was already set up, rather than having to wait for Luis to arrange his own administration—assuming that first he succeeded.

But there was more of a reason than that. Tanya Boros must already have contact established with Tshombase, with regular channels of communication. If a new mayor came into the village, there would be delays while new channels were created—and the d'Alemberts had already had their fill of delays. That was why Jules had secretly approached Tshombase and told him of the meeting tonight, to help him smash the revolt before it even began.

Tshombase looked from Jules to Yvonne and back again. "I like the way you two work," he said. "Starting tomorrow, I'm going to make you the guards outside my office. It's a simple job—you just stand by and make sure nobody gets in to disturb me while I'm working. Think you can handle that?"

The SOTE agents were thrilled; that was a far better assignment than they would have dared hope for. It would put them right at the center of village activity, and allow them to see exactly who went in and out of Tshombase's office. "All smooth," Jules said confidently. "No problems."

"Good. I don't like problems. Report to duty first thing tomorrow—and you'll be working at double your present salaries, by the way. Tshombase treats his people right. In the meantime, get some sleep; you've earned it."

Over the course of the next few days, though, the d'Alemberts began to doubt whether they'd been as lucky as they originally thought. Their job of guarding Tshombase's office turned out to be quite monotonous. They never had any trouble with unauthorized visitors trying to intrude; perhaps people had learned long ago that Tshombase did not relish interruptions. Those visitors who did come were either members of Tshombase's gang, with whom they were already familiar, or else villagers who came by to ask the mayor for some favor or another. The walls of the building were thin enough that, by straining a little, the d'Alemberts could hear every word said within the office— but the business was usually so trivial that there was no point. After a while they stopped listening to everything, and only paid attention when there was a chance something important might occur—but nothing important ever seemed to happen.

On a couple of occasions when Tshombase was out and the office was empty, Jules took the opportunity to search the room while his wife covered for him outside. But the searches proved as fruitless as the eavesdropping. There was very little paper of any sort on Gastonia, and Tshombase had no incriminating evidence or useful information lying around. His business dealings were all verbal; he knew full well that no one dared doublecross him, so why bother to keep track of promises?

After more than a week on the job the d'Alemberts were beginning to despair that anything would come of the promotion they had worked so hard to obtain. Then, when they were standing guard one evening shift, they heard a distant humming sound that made them exchange startled glances. As the sound grew closer it became more distinctive: the low buzz of a personal copter coming in for a nearby landing. At last Tshombase was going to have an important visitor.

As the copter landed outside and its motor turned off, Jules and Yvonne drew themselves up to full attention. Moments later two people walked through the door and up the stairs to Tshombase's second-floor office. Both were clad in boots and slacks, with heavy hooded parkas of thick white fur. The first woman Vonnie did not recognize, although she assumed from her husband's description that it must be Tanya Boros. She paid little attention to the erstwhile Duchess of Swingleton, however, because the woman behind Boros was far more important to them. On the other side of the doorway she could almost feel Jules tensing while Lady A walked right up to them as though she owned the building, and perhaps the whole planet. Vonnie had seen Lady A once before, on Earth, but she'd been following someone else and hadn't known Lady A's importance then. She did now.

Tanya Boros stopped before the door and stared at Jules for a moment. "You're the hunter who came to the house, aren't you?"

"Yes, gospozha." Jules was uncomfortable at having her attention focused on him.

"Why didn't you tell me you worked for Tshombase?"

"I didn't, then."

"Congratulations on your promotion," Boros said cynically.

Lady A snorted. "Stop wasting time with the hired help," she said. Brushing past Boros, she opened the door to Tshombase's office and strode confidently in, without either knocking or waiting to be announced. She was obviously a woman used to going where she chose without opposition. Neither Jules nor Yvonne made any move to stop her.

Tanya Boros followed her leader into the office, and closed the door behind them. Since there was no one else in the hall to see them, the d'Alemberts had no qualms about listening in on the conversation through the thin walls.

"Have you got the people I asked for?" Lady A demanded of Tshombase without prelude.

It was amazing to hear Tshombase, the arrogant mayor of the village, speaking in respectful tones to a woman half his

size. "Yes, I've arranged it with the Governor. When do you
want them?"

"I'll be staying at the house until the day after tomorrow.
They can come on the ship with me when I leave. I'll send the
copter over to pick them up sometime that morning."

"Yes, Your Ladyship." Tshombase paused, as though hes-
itant to continue. "Uh, Your Ladyship, about my own trans-
fer . . ."

"You'll stay here for now," Lady A said coldly. "When a
person does a good job for me, I keep him on there to continue
doing a good job. When we are successful, the rewards will
be worth the wait."

"I know, Your Ladyship," Tshombase mumbled. "It's just
that this planet is so miserable and cold . . ."

"And safe," Lady A chided him. "At least here you don't
have SOTE checking down your throat every few minutes. I
don't think they'll ever know how important Gastonia has been
in our plans. They gave us a freedom here that we'd never be
able to get on any ordinary world."

"Yes, Your Ladyship," Tshombase said, having been properly upbraided for his mild insolence. "Who will be on your
list for next time?"

"There won't be a next time." Then—probably in response
to some unvocalized expression—she added, "That's right.
Operation Annihilate is almost ready. You won't have to worry
about staying here that much longer."

"That is good news, Your Ladyship."

But not to Jules and Yvonne. As they stood at their posts
watching Lady A and Tanya Boros leave, they realized how
desperately close they were cutting their margin of safely. Lady
A had sounded most confident that her uprising against the
Empire would succeed—an uprising to be launched by a cam-
paign known ominously as Operation Annihilate.

12

The House on the Hill

The d'Alemberts had a great deal to discuss when they went home from duty that night. "Tshombase mentioned the Governor," Vonnie mused aloud. "He must be on Lady A's payroll, too."

"He'd have to be," Jules agreed. "From the way they were talking, Lady A visits Gastonia fairly regularly. I doubt whether any ships could take off or land here without people in the garrison knowing about it—nor could they have built that big house without attracting someone's attention. The only explanation is that the Governor and some of his staff were paid to look the other way."

He smashed his palm with his fist. "Lady A was right; the Service provided her with the perfect breeding ground for her conspiracy. We rounded up all the prospective recruits and located them here, in one place, for her to take her pick. The planet was so quiet and well-run that we hardly ever thought about it; a person sent here was as good as dead, so we forgot all about him. It's obvious now that they kept it that way on purpose. Where would be a better place to hide a conspiracy than among a group of former conspirators who are now presumably defused and harmless? It makes me so angry that they've fooled us so badly for so long."

Despite the seriousness of the situation, Yvonne couldn't help smiling slightly. It was hardly Jules's fault that this operation had continued this long; someone else in the Service should have reasoned it out long ago. But her husband so identified himself with SOTE that he felt personally responsible for every slip the Service made. But then, she realized, it was that very dedication to his ideals that made her love him so deeply.

"The problem is, though, what are we going to do about it?" By asking her question, Vonnie was hoping to nudge her husband gently onto a more positive line of thought.

"We can't let Lady A escape again, not when she's this close."

"I agree. But she's only going to be here another day and a half; we'll have to move quickly. Once she's off-planet, we won't have any way to get her."

Jules nodded. "We'll have to attack the house tomorrow night, before she leaves."

"Is there time?" Vonnie wondered. "We don't have a copter to take us there, and from your description it's easily a full day's march away. Plus you mentioned guards with blasters and an infrared scanning system. If we were on a civilized planet we could find the equipment to get around all that—but what do we do here on a world where stone axes are the ultimate weapon and running water is but an idle reverie?"

"We improvise, *ma cherie,* we improvise," said Jules—and the smile on his lips told Yvonne he was already formulating a plan.

They had little time for sleep that night, just a couple of hours between the time they thrashed out their attack strategy and the time they needed to leave. It was still long before sunrise when they left the primitive hovel they'd called home for the past few months. Whatever the outcome of their impending assault on Lady A's citadel, they knew they would never be coming back here again.

The initial part of their plan was one that gave them a great deal of satisfaction—stealing the sleigh from old Zolotin, the driver who had cheated them on their arrival. It was a simple enough matter to break into Zolotin's barn and hitch the docile yagi to the sled. With any luck it would be several hours before the theft was discovered. There was little they could do to hide the sleigh's tracks out of the village, but they figured there was little likelihood that anyone except Zolotin would be eager to follow them. Other people had their own work to do, and there were more profitable ways to spend their time than chasing into the hills for a stolen sleigh.

Once they were several kilometers away from the village and dawn was beginning to glow in the eastern sky they relaxed and got the rest they needed before their big adventure that night. They took turns, each driving the yagi for a few hours while the other caught some sleep. The yagi was slightly faster than they remembered it, but still not the speediest of beasts; they could have walked more rapidly, but then they would have arrived at their destination exhausted. This way they would be fresh and ready for action when they arrived.

They stopped twice during the day for the yagi to rest and browse on some of the low scrub vegetation in the area. Jules had been tracing the path from memory, hoping he remembered the various turns and twists in the trail his hunting party had taken—and also hoping he could recreate his wandering pattern during the blizzard. The land started looking more and more familiar, and just as the sun was setting he spotted it. "There!" he cried, pointing at the distant hill where the house reflected the light of the departing sun.

Yvonne squinted until she, too, could make it out. "It's still awfully far away," she said.

"Their scanners have quite a range," Jules said. "We should be safe enough here. We'll wait until nightfall and then move in closer."

Even after it was dark, the house could still be seen as a glimmering light too steady to be a star. Quickly, then, the two agents prepared their makeshift apparatus for fooling the guards' scanners. Yvonne lay face down in the sleigh and Jules covered her over with a fur blanket they had brought with them. After covering the blanket with a layer of snow, he took the reins of the sleigh firmly in his hand and crawled under the blanket with his wife, disturbing the snow as little as possible. Gently, then, he urged the yagi on its plodding way, leaving just enough room out of the top of the blanket for him to see out and guide the beast in the proper direction.

The d'Alemberts were hoping that, because of Gastonia's technological backwardness, Lady A would not have bothered to install one of the more sophisticated infrared detection systems, relying on a simpler one to suit her needs. Infrared detectors worked by sensing the heat difference between an object and its surroundings. If they had chosen to move ahead on foot, they would be radiating energy at the normal body temperature of thirty-seven celsius, and would stand out easily against the much colder snowdrifts around them.

By covering themselves over with snow, however, they hoped to mask their radiative effect. The more sophisticated infrared systems would not be fooled, but a simplified detector would see no further than the snow that covered them. There was no way to similarly disguise the body heat of the yagi—but then, they didn't want to. The yagi was part of their plan.

Minute by minute, meter by meter, Jules drove them closer to the hill and to the guard station at the bottom. If his plan was working correctly, the guards would see on their screens the image of a yagi drawing an apparently empty sleigh, yet coming unerringly toward them. He was hoping that would pique their curiosity enough to come and investigate what was happening.

There was a small stand of trees near the base of the hill, and that was where Jules stopped the sleigh. There were three guards manning the station, and at least one of them would remain at his post while the sleigh was being investigated; if the sleigh were out in the open, he would see two figures suddenly jump out, and he could send the alarm before the d'Alemberts could stop him. But infrared could not see through objects like trees, so whoever stayed back at the station would have no way of knowing what happened here.

Jules and Vonnie waited.

If an empty sleigh had seemed suspicious, its sudden stopping would appear even more so. After ten minutes of silence, the d'Alemberts could hear the sounds of two people crunching through the snow toward them. The guards came slowly, not wanting to take any risks; they probably had their blasters drawn, though the SOTE agents couldn't see them, and they were approaching from both sides of the sleigh to avoid a possible ambush.

Jules carefully gauged the sounds of the footsteps and, at his whispered command, the two DesPlainians leaped into action. They tossed off the blanket that had covered them, sending a fountain of snow rising into the air and startling the two men who'd been approaching them. Even as the guards' attention was momentarily distracted by the shower of white, the d'Alemberts jumped out of the sleigh to either side. The two men could not react half as fast as their DesPlainian adversaries; within seconds they were lying unconscious on the ground— and they had not even had a chance to fire their blasters or in any way warn their comrade back at the guard station.

The SOTE agents exchanged their crudely made village furs for the better parkas worn by the guards, then gagged the men and tied them to a tree. The d'Alemberts took their blasters and felt a little more relieved now that they were again armed with modern weapons. Jules also took one of the guards' pocket phones and, leaving the visual transmitter turned off, called back to the station. "The damned thing's empty," he reported, cupping his hands over his mouth to disguise his voice slightly. "We'll bring it in for a more thorough inspection."

He and Vonnie got back in the sleigh and drove openly toward the boulder that concealed the guard station. The one guard left in the station would see only the two warm figures sitting in the front of the sleigh, and would assume they were his compatriots.

He paid for that assumption with a solid blow to his head a few minutes later. The d'Alemberts were in sole possession of the guard station—and not a shot had been fired to warn the occupants of the house that they were under attack.

"From now on it gets risky," Jules said. "We can't just walk in the front door, and I have no way of knowing whether the windows are wired for alarms or not."

"We'll just have to chance it, then. We've played slash-and-grab before, if it comes to that. It might help if we could grab Lady A as a hostage; they wouldn't shoot at us if we had her for a shield. Where do you think she'd be?"

"Third floor, more than likely," Jules surmised. "On a world without copters, the top story is naturally the safest."

Under cover of darkness, the two agents crept up the steep hill until they stood beside the large house. Silently they walked around it, observing its construction with a professional's eye for detail. When they reached the back—a part Jules had not seen before—they found both the copter pad and the small launching site for Lady A's spaceship. Both copter and ship were waiting there, for which the d'Alemberts were grateful; they would have their choice of transportation out of here.

Finally spotting an ascent route that looked a little more

promising than the others, Jules started his slow climb up the outer wall of the house. The mixed construction materials of brick, stone and timber gave him narrow finger- and toeholds; even so, he needed every scrap of his circus training to cling to the building and make his way up three stories to a perch beside a darkened window.

Yvonne stood by on the ground below, blaster in hand. If Jules's attempt to open the window should set off an alarm, she was prepared to race into the house from the ground floor while Jules was entering from the top, creating havoc from two directions at once and hopefully confusing the occupants enough to let the DesPlainians triumph. But she was hoping such heroics would not be necessary.

Jules inspected the window carefully. A gentle touch proved it was locked, but the lock was merely a mechanical latch, not an electronic mechanism. He saw no wires or electrical connections of any kind around the window—a hopeful sign. With a sigh, he braced himself for the worst and, using the full strength of his DesPlainian muscles, he gave a sudden intense push against the latch.

The latch snapped with a light *sproing* and the window gave the meagerest of creaks as it opened, but other than that there was no sound. The alarm may have been a silent one, keyed to go off only at one specific location, but after waiting at his position for another minute Jules could hear no indication of hurried activity within the house. Maybe they had been lucky after all; maybe Lady A had felt that no one could get past the infrared detectors without special equipment unavailable on Gastonia, and had not bothered with alarms on the house itself. Jules slipped inside the room and looked around.

He found himself in an auxiliary bedroom, currently unoccupied. Crossing to the hall door, he opened it and looked out. The corridor beyond was well-lit but deserted. Jules closed the door again and locked it temporarily, assuring himself some momentary privacy in here.

Stripping the sheets and blankets off the bed, he fastened them together into a long rope that he lowered out the window to his waiting wife below. She tucked her blaster into her parka and scrambled up the makeshift cord; within seconds she was standing beside her husband, who then pulled the rope up after her to avoid leaving telltale signs of their entrance.

Unlocking the bedroom door once more, the d'Alemberts

checked to make sure the hallway was still deserted, then slipped out of their bedroom and along the corridor. They went in separate directions, trying doors along the corridor as they went. Most of the doors were locked, and they chose for the moment not to force their way in; if someone was inside, the SOTE agents might not be able to silence him before he gave the alarm to the rest of the house. They would try the unlocked doors first.

Vonnie found an unlocked door and signaled her success to Jules, who came over to join her. There was no light coming from under the sill, so they quietly opened the door and slipped into the room beyond.

As their eyes grew accustomed to the dark they could see that they'd found an office of some sort, with a desk and computer files standing about the room. With the door closed behind them, shutting off the light from the hallway, the only illumination in the room came from the double windows, where dim starlight filtered in. There'd been no pocketflashes available in the village, of course, and working in this darkness was impossible. "We'll have to risk turning on a light," Jules whispered.

Both agents squinted against the glare as Jules palmed the wall switch and the room was suddenly alive with light. The DesPlainians stood motionless for over a minute, listening for any sign that the light had betrayed them, but when there was none they breathed a little easier. By unspoken agreement, Jules began a quick search of one side of the room while Yvonne concentrated on the other.

Jules's area had a telecom unit and a computer file. Turning on the computer memory, he started playing with it, cuing it almost at random in the hopes of finding some important clue. He had no way of knowing in advance under what headings Lady A and Tanya Boros filed their information, but he could check a few references. He asked the computer for information about Gastonia's Governor, and was rewarded with a long personal file detailing not only the Governor's life and background, but also his involvement with the conspiracy. To Jules's chagrin it dated back more than a decade, almost from the day he was assigned here. Checking some of the listed cross-references, Jules learned which of the Governor's aides were also involved. It turned out to be nearly a third of the garrison's total staff—a dismaying thought indeed.

Yvonne, meanwhile, was searching through the drawers of the desk, and found an item of interest—a small vial of nitro-barb, the most potent truth serum in the Galaxy. Lady A probably kept it on hand in case one of her trusted servants turned out to be a spy from SOTE and she needed to question him. In any case, Vonnie pocketed the vial against possible future need and moved around the desk to a spot behind the door.

Just as she did so, the door flew suddenly open and Lady A stood in the threshold. She had a stun-gun drawn and pointed at Jules before he could reach for his own weapon—but Vonnie was behind the door and out of the woman's sight.

"So," Lady A said coldly, "we have a visitor after all. When Tanya told me about her uninvited guest of a few weeks ago, I thought it might be someone from SOTE, so I set a little trap. I knew you'd be here eventually. I've got a vial of nitrobarb ready for you."

Lady A stepped forward, past the edge of the door. As she did so, Vonnie reached out quickly and knocked the gun from her hand. The instant his wife made her move, Jules made his. Racing forward, he grabbed his adversary, spun her around and gripped her neck in a hammerlock. At the same time Vonnie closed the door once more and locked it. Lady A apparently had been alone, and they wanted to make sure no one else joined the party.

"I've got a few questions I'd like to ask you, too," Jules said. He held his blaster with its nozzle up against Lady A's throat.

Lady A held her nerve. With a voice carved from glacial ice she said, "You know you don't dare use that on me. I know too much that you want to find out."

She was absolutely right, Jules knew, but he had to play out his hand. "I can make life damned unpleasant for you if you don't talk."

"Your puny tortures mean nothing to me. I presume you know that some wills are too strong to be broken by mere physical pain. Mine is one of them. In the end you would merely kill me, and that would avail you nothing."

"It would sure put a crimp in your plans, though, wouldn't it?"

"My personal ones, yes. But as for saving your precious

Empire, my death won't matter in the slightest. The plans are already set, and they will go forward now whether I'm alive or not."

It was painful for Jules to admit that a woman whom he held at gunpoint had *him* over a barrel, but the situation was close to the truth. Calmly, refusing to be angered by her needling tone, he considered his alternatives.

He might try torturing her to get the information he needed, despite her boasts that she wouldn't crack. He couldn't torture her in the house, though, because her screams of pain would bring everyone running—and if he gagged her to stop the screaming, she wouldn't be able to talk. Even if he assumed that he and Vonnie could somehow get her away from the house, they could not guarantee the woman would tell them the truth, even under torture. Lady A, he was sure, was quite capable of constructing smooth lies to mislead them and stall until her plans were already in operation and it was too late to do anything. Even if, by some miracle, they could get Lady A completely out of the house, into her spaceship and off to some other world, the closest planet to Gastonia with a fully equipped Service base was more than a day's flight away at top speed. There would be facilities there for questioning her more throroughly—but invaluable time would have been lost.

Vonnie could read her husband well enough by now to know the processes going on in his mind. Reaching into her pocket, she pulled out the vial of nitrobarb and held it up for Jules to see. "Perhaps this would help," she said, speaking for the first time. "She'd obviously been planning to use it on you."

The existence of the nitrobarb changed things considerably. It was the strongest truth serum ever invented; no one under its influence could lie or withhold information. The drawback, though, was its side effect—the drug proved fatal fifty percent of the time. Lady A was a veritable mine of information; it would be a shame to waste much of it if she should die after only one session. He knew, too, that he and Vonnie were not equipped to give Lady A the most thorough cross-examination; the experts at Headquarters, with all their computer references to back them up could make each answer solve a dozen separate questions. Using nitrobarb on Lady A here would be squandering a potentially valuable resource.

Still, he had little choice. They had to learn more about Operation Annihilate, and it had to be in a hurry. Wasteful or not, there was no other way to learn the truth before it was too late.

Jules looked at the vial of clear fluid and nodded. "We'll give it to her," he said grimly.

He could feel Lady A stiffen as he led her to a chair and forced her to sit down. "No wonder your side will lose the struggle," she said haughtily. "You make too many mistakes. The pawns make their own decisions, and even when they capture the opposing queen they don't know how to use her."

Vonnie had gone back to the desk drawer and found a hyposprayer to administer the nitrobarb. "And what would you do in our position?" she asked sweetly as she returned to the prisoner.

Lady A laughed coldly. "It's not my business to give you advice."

"Then don't criticize, either," Jules said as his wife administered the injection.

Lady A said not another word. She simply smiled at Jules, a cold and evil smile that vanished from her face only when she fell into the stupor that was the first stage of nitrobarb's effect.

It would be another twenty minutes before Lady A passed into the second stage and was ready for questioning. Jules and Yvonne spent the intervening time by continuing the search they'd begun before Lady A had interrupted them. Jules asked the computer files about C, but received no information at all; either the computer had no information about the conspiracy's mysterious leader or else it was filed under a special codeword that he would never guess.

He asked next for information on Karla Jost and received a complete readout on her life story—including the fact that she had left the planet under the auspices of Project Resurrection. Checking this cross-reference provided him with a wealth of information—most particularly the names of the people who'd been removed, the dates of removal, and the planets to which they'd been taken. He asked for, and received, a printout of the list, and tucked the paper into a pocket.

Vonnie, meanwhile, had found nothing new in her search of the desk, and by this time Lady A was starting to come around again. The two agents crowded up close to her so as not to miss a word she said.

"Who is C?" was Jules's first question.

"I don't know his real identity," Lady A said slowly.

"Is he the leader of your conspiracy?"

"Yes."

"Where is he based?"

"I don't know."

Jules was gnashing his teeth in frustration. This was the hard part of questioning a person under nitrobarb; the subject had to tell the truth, but he told no more than the precise answer to the question asked. Knowing the proper question was an art in itself—one that his sister Yvette had been better trained in that he had. "Tell me exactly how you communicate with him, then."

"He has a series of telecom numbers in various sectors that relay through a subcom link directly to him, wherever he is. You call him through those numbers; if he chooses to respond, his answer is printed out on your telecom screen."

A clever way of operating anonymously—and almost impossible to trace, Jules thought. Still, if SOTE could learn the particular subcom frequency C used, they might be able to tap in and monitor some of the calls. "Tell me the telecom numbers," he said.

Lady A rattled off a string of numbers, and Jules copied them down on the back of the Project Resurrection printout. When she'd given him all that she could, the woman stopped abruptly, and it was up to Jules to think of a new question.

"What does C look like?" he asked.

"Tall and thin with thick black hair and gray eyes. High cheekbones, sharp chin, crow's feet about the eyes. He dresses well, but is not very muscular or athletic."

That description narrowed the search down a bit, but it was still far too general. "How old do you think he is?"

"Middle fifties, I'd say."

"Do you have any other superiors?"

"No, he's the only person above me in the organization."

Jules next started a series of questions about Lady A herself. Her name, she said, was really Gretchen Baumann and she came from the planet Kiesel. She was forty-three years old, and had been a member of this conspiracy for the past eighteen years, slowly working her way up the organizational ladder until she reached this exalted position. Her chief asset had been that she'd had no criminal record of any sort, no way for the Service to trace her activities.

The purpose of the conspiracy was quite simple: to destroy the Stanley dynasty and to place C on the Throne as the new Emperor. It was not yet decided whether Lady A would marry him to become Empress, or whether she would take a secondary post as Chancellor. The conspiracy had a navy and armed forces of its own, well-trained and waiting for their cue to move in and take over.

"How do you know what's going on in SOTE?" Jules asked.

"We've had hypnotic instructions implanted in the minds of most top-level secretaries within the Service," Lady A said. "Every few days—or whenever they learn anything of vital importance—they phone a special number and relate everything they've learned since their last phone call. Then they completely forget they've made the call, and go on about their business as normal."

That was a chilling thought. No wonder it had been so hard to trace down the leaks—all the people who betrayed the Service honestly thought they were being loyal and, short of administering tough mindprobes, they would test out truthfully when asked whether they were traitors. Jules wanted to ask for more specifics, such as key names of those under such hypnotic compulsion, but time was pressing and there was still another crucial topic he had to cover.

"Tell me all you can about Operation Annihilate," he said.

"Operation Annihilate is the code name for our attack on the Empire. Our entire navy will rendezvous at a point in space and attack Earth in force. We have more than enough strength to wipe out the fleet normally stationed there. Our own fleet is commanded by Admiral Shen Tzu, who is currently operating as an ordinary pirate. Our original plan was to attack during Princess Edna's wedding. The robot duplicate of Lady Bloodstar was supposed to kill both the Emperor and the Princess, leaving the succession in doubt and causing chaos at the court, while our ships massed and destroyed the Imperial Fleet stationed at Earth. It was you who stopped the assassinations, and somehow the Navy prevented Captain Ling's contingent of ships from achieving its rendezvous. Full implementation of Operation Annihilate was delayed until a better time."

"And when is that better time?" Vonnie interrupted.

"Right after the Princess's ascension to the Throne," Lady A said emotionlessly. "SOTE will be expecting us to attack during the ceremony, so we intend to wait thirty-six hours and hit them after they relax a bit. Confidence in the new Empress's abilities to command will be a little shaky, and she may make tactical mistakes out of inexperience that will give the victory to us. Again, our ships will come from bases scattered throughout the Empire and rendezvous at a given point in space on the day before the ceremony, then depart as a group for Earth."

"Where is the rendezvous point?" Jules asked.

Lady A gave him a string of numbers, which he again jotted down. "How many ships are there in your fleet, and what sizes are they?"

"We have one thousand and fifty-eight. Most are small personal fighters, but we have twelve Galaxy-class cruisers, fifteen Constellation cruisers, fifty Nova superdestroyers . . ."

A sudden uproar in the hall outside interrupted the proceedings. "There must be an intruder in there!" the d'Alemberts heard Tanya Boros cry. "Blast the door in, quickly!"

The door to the room began glowing as blaster beams from outside concentrated their enormous power on it. Within seconds there would be nothing between the SOTE agents and an army of unknown size waiting to gun them down.

Their visit at this house was coming rapidly to an end.

13

Pias's Offer

The three ships drifted in subspace, waiting for their quarry to arrive. The word "drift" was a relative term, for they were really moving at more than a hundred times the speed of light; nonetheless, compared to the speeds that were possible in subspace theirs was a veritable crawl. They didn't want to move too quickly and possibly overshoot their target.

Ordinarily the bridge of a pirate ship was no place for idle visitors, and Yvette would not have been welcomed. But as the woman who had the specialized knowledge of how to combat the *Paradise's* defenses, she was able to insist most forcefully that she indeed belonged here; and since Fortier/"Rocheville" had been put in charge of this particular operation, she had an ally able to accommodate her demands.

They were cruising between the planets Hsoli and Kuragana, waiting for the *Paradise* to come by on its regular run. Its route was known as precisely as though it were on tracks, so there was just the question of waiting for it. This time, much as Yvette hated to think about the loss of money and effort they'd put into it, the *Paradise* would not escape the pirate trap.

There was a blip on the long-distance scanners, indicating the *Paradise* had shown up exactly on schedule. Fortier barked a command and the trio of pirate vessels speeded up to match their target's velocity, simultaneously converging on its position. Coming as they did from three different directions, the *Paradise* would have no option; it could never hope to outrun all of them, so its only choice was to drop back into normal space and play the standard game of pirate and prey.

At first, events followed the same pattern as before. All the ships left subspace at precisely the same moment, and the pirates began their interference pattern to prevent the *Paradise* from beaming a message to the Navy. At the same time, the *Paradise* withdrew its engines into the body of the ship, as it had done before.

"That's a crucial spot right there," Yvette pointed out to Fortier and the other real pirates on the bridge. "As long as the engines and the power source are working, he's in command."

"But we can't use our ships' guns to destroy the engines without blowing holes in the *Paradise*," Fortier said. "We want to take it intact."

"Then send some of your men up inside there with hand weapons," Yvette told him. "You've got to cut his power—and particularly you've got to stop him from turning on the ultragrav. All his crewmembers are DesPlainians, and they'll outmaneuver your fighters every time under high-grav circumstances."

Fortier nodded and gave the appropriate orders. One of the other ships sent out a team of men—not to the open airlock as had happened on the last attack, but to the underbelly of the *Paradise*. There, in their protective sheath, the ship's engines were withdrawn and silent. Using even high-powered hand-blasters was not the most efficient way of destroying them, but the pirates did not want to suffer the fate of their sister ship that had been captured and humiliated. If this slow, painstaking work was the way to win, that was the way they'd do it.

It took nearly an hour of concerted effort, but eventually the pirate forces burned their way through the tough plating of the *Paradise* and were able to dismantle her drive and power systems. Assured, then, that the ultragrav could not be used against them when they entered, attack teams from each of the three ships swarmed through the airlock into the *Paradise* itself. At Yvette's suggestion, though, other pirates remained back on their ships to guard against incursions from the *Paradise's* defenders.

Suddenly the unexpected happened. Like a plant shooting off spores, the *Paradise* suddenly shot off more than a hundred lifepods in all directions. In essence, Pias was surrendering the *Paradise* itself in exchange for the safety of its passengers and crew, knowing how fearsome were the odds against it. The move took the pirates completely by surprise—and Yvette pretended it surprised her as well, though she'd known in advance precisely what would happen.

Fortier now had a choice. None of the lifepods was equipped with a subspace motor, meaning they could only travel at less than light speed; each one did have its own automatic subcom unit, however, transmitting a repeated distress signal and location for the Navy to pick up. Fortier could set his ships to the task of rounding up the pods, since they were moving so slowly—but since they were radiating outward in all directions that would be a very time-consuming job . . . and in the meantime, his ships could not jam all the subcom transmissions the pods were emitting. The Navy could be on its way here before he'd collected even half the pods, and this mission would be as much a failure as the last.

Fortier chose instead to go after the *Paradise* itself. (In actuality the choice was not hard, since it was part of Yvette's plan; but it was good to have a solid reason behind his action when Admiral Shen questioned him about the matter later, as he surely would.) Although the passengers had gone and probably taken most of their money and valuables with them, the ship and its furnishings had an intrinsic value in themselves, and would keep this expedition from being a total loss.

The boarding party was quite surprised, however, to find that an auxiliary generator still maintained a one-gee field within the *Paradise,* and that one lone figure was waiting for them. Pias Bavol was calmly seated in the central casino, playing out a game of solitaire at one of the card tables. He looked up, tipped his hat and waved as the pirates entered. "Good day, gentlemen, I've been expecting you."

"Who are you?" asked the leader of the assault team.

"Brian Sangers, at your service; owner and operator of the once-proud and now temporarily defunct *Paradise* gambling ship. Please be so kind as to inform your captain that I offer him the privilege of making a deal with me."

The pirate waved his blaster at Pias. "You don't look in much position to deal with anybody."

"Oh, put that silly thing away, it's liable to go off. Killing me will gain you nothing. I am a man of small personal fortune, all my cash being tied up in this enterprise. The money and important guests have all departed in the lifepods, and there's no one who'd pay much ransom for me. The Navy will soon be coming in response to the distress calls from the pods, so— since you did such an effective job of ruining the *Paradise's* engines, and since all three of your ships combined couldn't tow this one very far—you'll have to leave my vessel here for salvage. The drapes and furnishings are all quite expensive, but subject to horrible depreciation; if you simply strip the place bare you won't receive even one percent of what it's all worth. The only asset you'll find of any great value is my intellect, and that requires my willing cooperation before it does you any good. So stop pretending you can bully me, and escort me to your captain."

The pirate was stunned. Never before had he encountered anyone with so much raw nerve as the dandy who sat across the room from him, grinning confidently. People in his position were supposed to be terrified, not demanding. Unsure precisely how to react—but not wanting to seem weak in front of his men—he said gruffly, "You'll see the captain, that's for sure. This way." He made a big show of motioning with his gun, even though Pias was obviously not afraid of it.

Pias donned a spacesuit and accompanied the assault team leader back to the main ship while the rest of the pirates were scouring the *Paradise* for anything of value they could find. As Pias was marched onto the pirate bridge, his gaze locked onto Yvette's. Though each was delighted to see the other after such a long separation—the longest since they were married— they had their own particular roles to play that did not allow for tender reunions.

"My dear Mila," Pias said, "you appear to have lived down even below my expectations of you. Small wonder these blasterbats were as successful as they were. They had the queen of treachery as their guiding star."

"Still mouthing off, aren't you?" Yvette retorted. She looked to Fortier. "This guy's mouth will still be working weeks after the rest of him's dead and rotting. He's a stinking liar—don't believe a word he says."

"Coming from you, my dear," said Pias, "that's a high compliment indeed."

Fortier stepped between the two to put an end to the bickering. "I understand you've got something to say to me, Sangers."

"Yes, if you're the man in charge. Your organization is obviously in need of new blood. Your first attempt to take my ship was a dismal failure, and your second attempt, even with inside knowledge, is not going to turn out much better. You lack the imagination and inventiveness to change with the times; you're still doing things the way your grandfather did."

"And I suppose you think you're the man to do this for us, eh?"

"Of course, or I wouldn't be here. I could just as easily have escaped in one of the lifepods, along with everyone else."

"Then why didn't you? You could always have started up another gambling ship."

"The profit margin was too small. Why should I content myself with a meager five or ten percent when, in a pirate organization with talent and imagination, I could rake in far more?"

"I don't have the authority to deal with you on that level," Fortier said.

Pias gave a loud snort. "Then take me to someone who does. I hate doing business with underlings."

In due course, Pias was taken before Admiral Shen and given a chance to explain his plans more fully. He gave a variation of the speech he'd given to Fortier and the other pirates on the bridge, but this one was even more filled with boasts of his intellectual abilities. Shen sat back and listened to this bombast with a barely concealed grin. "So you're offering to become my master tactician, are you?" he asked when Pias had finally finished.

"Not at all," Pias replied. "I'm offering to let *you* become my partner."

"As simple as that, eh?"

"Why not? People sometimes make business relationships much too complicated. I'll accept your handshake."

Shen's grin was broadening. "By Fross, I like you. I don't know when I've been so entertained. If I were a nobleman I might even keep you around as my official jester."

"Then it's you who would be the fool for passing up what I have to offer. With my ideas and your resources we could easily double your income in the next year."

"Do you have any idea what my resources are?"

"Only the vaguest. I imagine a hundred men and maybe a dozen ships."

"Then it's your imagination that's too small. Your numbers don't even begin to approach the actuality."

"I merely estimated what I thought would be standard for a pirate operation like yours. My imagination is quite elastic—it can expand to fit the resources put in."

Shen gave another laugh. "No matter how elastic your imagination is, it would still stretch beyond the breaking point to 'learn of the plans in which I play a major role. In less than a week, I shall be totally beyond the need to play the game of pirate any longer—and so your puny little schemes don't interest me in the slightest."

He pressed a button on his desk and three men, all armed with blasters, entered the room. "I'm sorry to make our acquaintance so brief," Shen said. "You've amused me for a while, but now our ways must part." Then, to his guards, he added, "Take him out into the jungle and dispose of him."

Pias doffed his hat and held it over his chest. "I assure you, Admiral, you're no more sorry than I am. We could have made a pile of rubles together."

Then, before anyone else in the room could move, Pias whipped out the ministunner he kept tucked away behind the rose on his hatband. The tiny gun gave a maximum stun of six hours, but Pias only had it set on number four—a two-hour stun. With three quick bursts he was able to fell the pirates who had come to take him away. He turned back to Shen, but found himself facing down the muzzle of the blaster that had been disguised as the handle of Shen's scimitar. "Good work," said the pirate leader. "Ordinarily after a demonstration like that I might indeed offer you some post in my organization. But time is very short, and I just won't have the chance to run a thorough security check on your background. My original plan still stands, I'm afraid. Would you be so kind as to hand over the stunner so I don't have to burn a hole through you and my office wall?"

Even with his quick reflexes, Pias knew there was no way he could stun Shen before the admiral could blast him. With great reluctance he let the stunner drop from his hand. Shen smiled and called for several more pirates to take Pias away and to clear the unconscious bodies out of the office.

As Pias was escorted out, there was a sinking feeling in his stomach. He'd been sure Shen would offer him a post in the organization. True, the pirate leader had dropped a vital clue that the strike against the Empire would be coming within a week—but unless Pias lived to let SOTE know about it, that clue would do no one any good at all.

14

Escape from Gastonia

The attack on the door interrupted the d'Alemberts' interrogation of Lady A, and they had to think quickly of a way out. There were no other doors in the room, just a pair of windows overlooking the landscape, offering them a three-story drop to the ground. A ten-meter fall, however, was still preferable to a gun battle against unknown odds—especially since they now possessed information vital to the defense of the Empire. They had to get out with it alive.

They glanced at the windows and the same idea occurred to both of them. But Vonnie still hesitated. "What about her?" she asked, nodding in Lady A's direction.

"We'll have to leave her, I'm afraid," Jules decided. As much as he would have liked to take their high-ranking captive with them, it would have been difficult under the best of circumstances; and now, with the two of them under attack and Lady A still deep under the influence of the nitrobarb, it was flatly impossible.

Then the door to the room burst inward, and there was no time for further conversation. As a squad of guards poured into the room, the d'Alemberts made their leap for freedom. There were two simultaneous crashes as the DesPlainians smashed

144

through the twin windows with their arms over their heads to prevent facial injuries. Then they were out in the open air, falling free three floors to the snowy ground below them.

The fall seemed quite slow to their reflexes, trained as they were under high-grav conditions. Jules in particular was an acrobat *par excellence,* and could twist his body around for the best landing position. Yvonne had not been raised in the Circus, but she'd known by her late teens that she would be marrying Jules and entering the Service at his side; as the daughter of a baron, she'd had plenty of leisure time to learn the necessary tricks of staying alive. Her movements as she fell now were not as graceful as her husband's, nor as effortlessly performed—but they were just as practical, and achieved the same ends.

The d'Alemberts hit a level patch of snow without any protruding obstacles. They turned the forward momentum component of their leap to their advantage, rolling over in a somersault that left them, finally, springing to their feet and facing away from the house. They were bruised from the hard landing of their fall, but no bones were broken and no muscles sprained. As the guards appeared in the windows from which they had just leaped, the two SOTE agents began running at top speed.

There was only one destination in both their minds: the small landing field behind the house where both the copter and the spaceship were sitting. There'd been no need to discuss that in advance; it was the only transportation around. Trying to leave on foot or by sleigh would be suicide.

Blaster bolts were sizzling the air around them, melting deep pockets in the snow near their feet. They ran a random, zigzag pattern to avoid being shot, but some of the beams were hitting very close anyway. As soon as the guards realized where the two fugitives were heading, however, most of them stopped firing and started racing down the stairs to head them off.

The small landing field came into view as the d'Alemberts rounded a corner of the building. The copter was at the near edge of the pad, with the spaceship more than thirty meters away at the far side. Nevertheless, Jules gasped, "Ship," to his wife, and Yvonne nodded. Taking the copter would be easy, but they would still be stuck on this planet with no way of getting the information to SOTE Headquarters on Earth. They would have to find some way of breaking into the garrison and convincing the officials there that they really were SOTE agents—and since many of those same officials were in Lady A's pay, that route was not a safe one, either.

As the DesPlainians sprinted across the open field, some of the guards appeared behind them, blasters drawn and ready to fire. Jules, checking over his shoulder for just such pursuit, saw them appear and took a second to stop, turn, draw his own blaster, and fire at the guards. The small knot of pursuers scattered in search of cover while Jules raced on. The Des-Plainians took turns firing back to keep their enemies honest as they ran desperately toward the spaceship that was their only hope of escape.

They reached the side of the ship and Jules stood guard at the base while Vonnie climbed the ladder into the vessel. It was a small ship, built to hold no more than a dozen people; the d'Alemberts were hoping it was empty at present, and fueled for a quick takeoff. It would do them little good to get inside and find the ship cold and completely shut down; starting it up again could take several hours.

Vonnie had reached the top of the ladder and paused there to draw her own blaster once more. Now it was Jules's turn to climb, an exposed target on the side of the ship, hoping that his wife could keep their attackers busy enough evading her fire that they'd be unable to get a clear shot at him. He used the strength of his powerful arms to pull himself up three rungs at a time, but on the last few pulls his hands were sweating so much, despite the cold, that his grasp almost slipped. At long last—less than ten seconds from when he started—he reached the airlock level beside his wife, and the two of them ducked inside and slid the door shut behind them.

They had gained a respite, but it would be a very short-lived one unless they acted quickly. They raced through the ship with guns drawn, on the chance that there might be crewmembers still aboard, but they found themselves alone here. While Vonnie continued the search through the small vessel, Jules went straight to the control room to check the ship's takeoff status.

He was happy to see that the instruments were in the standard format, and that there were controls for weapons as well as for flight. Lady A had a rather sleek little craft here, and he approved wholeheartedly. His eyes quickly scanned the rows of dials, noting their reactions as he flipped some of the toggles. By the time Vonnie returned from her search with the happy news that they were alone in the ship, Jules had completed his systems analysis. "All smooth and roaring to soar," he said happily.

Vonnie slid onto the acceleration couch next to his. Turning on the external field monitors, she said, "We've got company, though. They're not happy about our being here."

Jules glanced over at her screen. The ground around the ship was swarming with guards, trying to figure out some way of getting inside. "Can you use the ship's guns on them?" he asked.

Yvonne checked her gunnery board. "No, they're inside minimum range."

"Then I'll have to get fancy. Hold onto your boots." The ship was not yet ready for takeoff, as it still lacked a course plotting and systems coordination—but, to scare the people around the base, Jules made a quick motion to turn on the engines for a fraction of a second. The roar from the base of the vessel was enough to send Boros's guards fleeing in all directions. The ship shuddered, but stayed where it was as Jules quickly turned the motor off again after he'd made his point. Anything more than an instant of unguided reaction could send the ship toppling over on its side.

Boros's army was scattered around the ship now at a respectful distance, but not abandoning the fight entirely. As Jules continued to run quickly through the preflight systems checkout, Vonnie watched the scene outside with a dubious eye. "I really think we should give them something to keep them busy," she mused. "Do we need that house any longer?"

Jules smiled. "I really don't think so."

With great glee, his wife set about lining the building up in her sights. "Stationary targets aren't much fun," she muttered, "but they're better than nothing."

The ship's guns roared, and the upper floors of the house exploded in a burst of flame. Vonnie aimed again, and more of the structure was demolished. "Think that finishes Lady A and Tanya Boros?" she asked.

Jules didn't look up from his instruments. "It's a nice thought," he said, "but somehow I doubt it. They probably hid in a bomb shelter the instant we got in here. That's what I'd have done in their place."

The display of force from the ship finally caused the guards to scatter altogether and move back toward the house to put out the fires now burning there. With the external pressures removed, Jules was able to finish up his necessary operations in less than ten minutes. "Strap yourself in," he warned— needlessly, for Yvonne had done so long ago. "We are about to take our leave of beautiful Gastonia."

The rockets roared beneath them as their ship lifted skyward with effortless efficiency. Minutes later they had cleared Gastonia's atmosphere and were speeding at top velocity away from the prison planet. Vonnie kept her eyes resolutely on the scanner screens, looking for any sign of pursuit from the garrison, but nothing came after them. Perhaps Tanya Boros and the Governor could not mobilize their forces in time; or perhaps—more likely, in Vonnie's opinion—they didn't want to find themselves in the midst of a running gunbattle with this particular craft. Yvonne could tell from studying her instrument board that Lady A's ship was as well-armed and deadly as the d'Alemberts' own *Comète Cuivré*.

The instant they were far enough away from Gastonia's gravitational influence, Jules slipped their little vessel into subspace. He did not make a long jump, just enough to get them away from the Gastonia system so that their position couldn't be traced. As soon as he was positive they were safe from detection, he dropped back into the normal universe and began warming up the subcom set. He and Yvonne had a long report to send back to Earth—a report that SOTE Headquarters would want as quickly as possible.

The Service, meanwhile, was having plenty of problems just coping with the routine security arrangements for the Coronation that was now just four days away. They had thought that the security arrangements for Edna's wedding the previous year had been difficult—but those were child's play compared to the logistical monstrosity that confused them now.

Only once before in the more than two-hundred-year history of the Empire had a monarch abdicated in favor of a successor. Most of the Stanleys came to sudden, violent ends, and the ascension of their heirs was a much more spontaneous affair. Although it was a tradition to publicly broadcast the Coronation from Earth to every planet in the Galaxy, few people were privileged to be on hand to attend such an event in person.

Edna's coronation as Empress Stanley Eleven, though, had been private knowledge in high government circles for years, and had been announced publicly months ago. People knew in advance that it would be happening—and they knew, too, that they might never see another coronation within their life-times. Stanley Ten had reigned for well over forty years; a majority of people within the Empire had never even lived under another ruler. The excitement caused by the upcoming change in power had electrified the populace throughout the Galaxy.

As tradition decreed, the ceremony would be held at Blood-star Hall in the Angeles-Diego metropolitan complex. Despite SOTE's best precautions, Edna's wedding there had been a near-disaster, with only Jules and Yvonne averting tragedy at the last possible moment. The Head was determined that *this* ceremony was not going to be the fiasco the last one had been, and as a consequence was spending most of his time away from Headquarters coordinating the security precautions with the young Lord Bloodstar. He left his daughter and Girl Friday, Helena, to mind the more routine business back at the office.

It was late at night in Florida, where SOTE Headquarters was hidden, and Helena von Wilmenhorst was having trouble keeping her eyes open. Since her father had gone to Angeles-Diego she'd been averaging only four hours of sleep a night after coordinating his needs with the normal press of Service business. No matter how important the Coronation was, there was still an Empire to be run—an Empire that was rapidly approaching fourteen hundred planets in scope. As one of the people with primary responsibility for the safety of that Empire, Helena had little private life for her own satisfaction.

The words in the daily reports were running into one another in a jumble of jabberwocky. After reading over the same sentence in a manpower requisition for the sixth straight time without comprehending it, she had just about decided to quit for the day. Then the d'Alemberts' report came in—and suddenly, Helena had never been more wide awake in her life.

It was not just the fact that the report was a long-awaited one from two of the top agents in SOTE's retinue; Helena and her father routinely gave d'Alembert reports top consideration anyway. What really made Helena sit upright in her chair was the coding: Class 10 Priority. In all the history of the Service there had been exactly six Class 10's prior to this one. It was an acknowledgement of dire peril to the Empire, an armed attack or revolution either in progress or imminent. Class 10 commanded instant attention at any hour of the day or night.

Within seconds of being notified, Helena had the images of Jules and Yvonne on her screen. She noted with some annoyance that they were not on a scrambler circuit, but knowing the d'Alemberts as well as she did she realized there had to be a good reason for it. Without wasting time on trivial formalities like greetings, she said simply, "Father's at Bloodstar. Let me have it."

Of necessity, Jules's report came in with painful slowness. Lady A's ship was not equipped with a Service scrambler, and he was not about to broadcast such vital information over open ether without some protection. He had to reword everything he wanted to say into one of SOTE's verbal codes, a complex process even under the best of conditions. He had a lot to tell her, too, and he wanted to make sure that every word of it was transmitted correctly. They could not afford any errors at this stage of the game.

Helena took down all the information with a growing feeling of urgency, double-checking the most salient points to make sure she'd understood correctly. The story of impending revolution that Jules was relating was grim indeed, and bound to put a serious strain on the Empire's resources.

She listened for more than an hour as Jules worked his way through the facts. When he was finally finished, she nodded and told him she would pass it right along to the appropriate people. Jules told her that he and Vonnie would rip a seam through subspace and get back to Earth in three days to give a fuller report in person. Then the connection was broken and the screen went blank.

Helena instantly put through a call to her father. She did not use the phrase "Class 10 Priority," not wanting to cause panic throughout Angeles-Diego; but the codeword she used to get through was a personal reference between father and daughter that conveyed roughly the same urgency. Zander von Wilmenhorst was on the line instantly, concern evident on his face.

Since this call was going through double scramblers, Helena did not have to waste time encoding what she said, and she conveyed the information in less than half an hour. The Head did not interrupt his daughter once during her recitation; his superb mind was too busy assimilating data, correlating it with other reports and planning alternate tactics. When she finished, he had only one question: "I know the source, but I still have to ask—is this information one hundred percent accurate?"

"I double-checked that myself," Helena confirmed. "It was obtained under nitrobarb."

The Head nodded. "Good. We may have to commit the disposition of Imperial forces on the basis of this, and we can't take any chances. And put Metzenbach in charge of the office; I want you out here with me by first light tomorrow. We've got work to do."

As soon as he'd ended his conversation with his daughter, the Head was on his way to the palace in Los Angeles where the Imperial family had taken up residence to prepare for the ceremony to come. He would not go into details over the vidphone, but he managed to convey the urgency of his mission. When he arrived at the palace, he was escorted quickly to a small planning chamber that was completely bugproof.

The three other people he'd asked for were already there: Emperor William Stanley, a distinguished man with graying hair, seventy years old with all the experience such an age implies; his daughter, Crown Princess Edna, twenty-five years old but already experienced at wearing the mantle of Imperial responsibility; the Lord Admiral Cesare Benevenuto, the Empire's top military tactician. On these four people, then, the fate of the Galaxy would hinge.

"The conspiracy is ready to make its move," von Wilmenhorst said as preface, then explained the situation as the d'Alemberts had discovered it. The other three listened, their faces getting longer as their predicament grew clearer.

There was a pause after he finished his briefing. It was, by courtesy, the Emperor's right to comment first on the information. William Stanley considered what he'd heard, and finally spoke.

"Even though this information was obtained under nitrobarb," he said, "and was obviously true when it was spoken, it may already be outdated. This mysterious C must know by now that his chief lieutenant has been interrogated, and therefore that there is some chance his plans have been compromised. Couldn't he decide to postpone the entire attack until he can again be sure of surprise?"

"Possible," said Admiral Benevenuto, "but unlikely. A military operation of this scale isn't like a light switch that can be turned on and off at will. Orders must be given, fighting forces mobilized, supplies transported to the proper places. Ships must rendezvous properly, personnel must be brought to the proper fighting pitch—it's an emotional problem as well as a logistical one. From what we've heard, the operation was already canceled once, at the time of the Princess's wedding. To do so again would be most costly in terms of money, manpower and morale. If it were *my* battle, I'd rather sacrifice the element of surprise than lose all my preparations. C does, after all, have a respectably sized fleet on his side, one which is ready for battle while our own forces are scattered all over the Empire. There is no way we can call in our entire fleet in time to counter a concentrated attack on Earth just a few days from now."

"But he may change his plans somewhat in view of the fact that we now know what he's going to do," Edna said.

"He can't be sure we know," the Head spoke up. "Unless he's tapped into our most secure private lines, he can't know how much information we got from Lady A before the interrogation was interrupted. Even if she survives the drug, she won't remember what she said or didn't say. I have a feeling he's going to be watching our movements most carefully in the next few days to find out exactly how much we know and how much we don't. How we react will, to some extent, affect his plans—though I agree with Cesare, I don't think he'd call off the attack completely just because we're expecting it."

The Emperor drummed his fingers nervously on the arm of his chair. "Then we must consider carefully what we do. What alternatives are open to us?"

"I would be remiss in my duty to protect the lives of the Imperial family," said the Head, "if I didn't suggest postponing the Coronation until this affair is over."

"Never!" Edna's voice echoed decisively in the small room. "I don't mean to sound grabby, Father, but I don't think we should let a pack of hooligans decide when Imperial business may be carried out. It's bad enough that they ruined my wedding; if we let them succeed now, then every official function becomes susceptible to their blackmail. I say we continue with the Coronation even if civil war is raging and the Empire is coming down around our ears."

William Stanley beamed proudly and looked at the other two men. "You just heard your Empress's pleasure—and mine too, I might add. Any plans we make *must* take into account the fact that the Coronation will proceed as planned."

"*Khorosho,*" the Head nodded. "I only proposed that because it was my duty to consider it. I wasn't in favor of it either. If we canceled, it would let C know definitely that we're aware of his plans; continuing as scheduled can only increase his doubt and confusion—which is all to our good. Tell me, Admiral, can our regular defensive fleet stationed in the solar system cope with an armada like theirs?"

"One thousand small ships and a few of the larger class?" Benevenuto was thoughtful. "No, not entirely, I'm sorry to say. We could handle their big ships well enough, but some of the smaller ones are bound to slip through our nets and cause damage. I would have to call in reinforcements from some of our nearer bases to handle the threat fully."

"I thought as much," the Head nodded. "And that's exactly what C will be watching for. It would prove to him that we know his plans."

"I'd prefer to do that than leave Earth inadequately protected," Benevenuto harrumphed.

"Forgive me; intelligence work sometimes gets so Machiavellian that I fail to fully explain my thoughts. I'm talking about a feint. C will be watching our nearby bases closely, knowing that only ships from there could be moved here in time to reinforce Earth's defenses. He might not be paying that much attention to some of our more distant bases."

"But what good are they," Edna asked, "if they can't reach Earth in time to defend us?"

"Lady A said that all the enemy ships would be rendezvousing at a given spot. If we were to launch an attack against them there, before they've had a chance to get fully organized, we could wreck their plans before they start and scatter their fleet to the eight corners of the Galaxy."

"That plan has some merit," Benevenuto agreed. "But isn't C likely to at least change the rendezvous spot if he thinks his plans have been compromised?"

"It is a possibility, yes," the Head admitted. "Though that spot was probably chosen for its centralized location; he would have to do a lot of emergency communication to make sure all his divisions were informed of any change. Still, space is big and he could find plenty of other secret places to meet.

"But even if he does change the meeting spot and our ships find nothing there, we can give them secondary orders to proceed immediately to Earth. They should arrive about the same time as C's ships, presenting him with a stronger force than he counted on facing. We wouldn't have much time to coordinate battle tactics between the home fleet and the reinforcements, but we'd have the numbers and the surprise on our side, for a change."

Benevenuto was wavering. "I'm not sure," he said. "I much prefer straight military might to the convoluted maneuvers of the intelligence branch. It may be stodgy, but it would ensure an adequate defense of Earth."

"If we pulled in ships from nearby bases, thus alerting C to the fact we know his plans," the Head argued, "he might decide to go after secondary targets—such as the systems we take our reinforcements from. None of them will be able to withstand C's fleet in their weakened condition. We could end up sacrificing a much larger chunk of our territory than we'd like. I say we lure C into the solar system by pretending not to know his plans, then clobber him. It's a little riskier, but it gives us the chance to break up his fleet in one decisive battle."

"I'd have to run it through our computers to calculate the odds for and against the various alternatives," the admiral said.

William Stanley stood up. "You do that, Cesare, but do it quickly. Personally, I think Zander has handed us a well thought out plan, and I'd like to see it implemented. In any case, I want you in my office with a completed scheme by nine A.M. tomorrow. I want to make sure there's an Empire left to hand over to my daughter on Friday."

15

A Change of Plans

Pias Bavol did not panic when his scheme to work his way into Admiral Shen's organization failed so miserably. He was a man who believed in utilizing all his resources to their best advantage—and one of the best resources he had was his own mind.

Yvette and Fortier were two other resources in his favor, but he could not use them just now. Neither had been with him in Shen's office, and neither knew the trouble he now faced. As far as they were both aware, everything was proceeding according to schedule. He would have to extricate himself from this mess on his own.

There were three pirates escorting him, each with blaster drawn and aimed directly at his back. He could not simply run away, and even his high-gee reflexes were not quick enough to disarm three men before they had a chance to fire at him. There had to be some way, though, of narrowing the numbers a bit. All it took was the right set of circumstances.

He began whistling and walking at a pace much too jaunty for someone under sentence of imminent death. "Come back here," said the leading pirate behind him. "Where do you think you're running to?"

"I'm not running," Pias answered, slowing his pace just a trifle. "Shen said he wanted you to take me up to the surface. I was going to the elevator tube."

"If you don't wait for us, we'll shoot you right here in the hall. I'd think you'd want to take your time. What are you so happy about?"

"Did I say I was happy?" Pias asked. "Just because I refuse to get depressed by the thought of my own death doesn't mean I'm looking forward to it. I've lived a pretty fascinating life, but it had to come to an end sometime, I suppose. Hey, have you guys ever heard of the women of Tartarus?"

All of them had, of course; the courtesans and the fleshpots of that world were legendary throughout space. Pias began weaving the men a fabricated history of his own adventures there, including a detailed account of his night spent with three of the fabled ladies at once. The pirates were practically drooling as Pias graphically described the exotic events of that fabulous evening. By the time the party arrived at the elevator tube the guards were so engrossed in Pias's story that they were less than careful about the way they were guarding him.

As Pias had remembered, the elevator tubes were small ones, holding only two people at a time; since the pirates' ships were in underground silos that could be entered from the base, they had little cause to go to the surface in large numbers. One way or another, the group would have to split up momentarily, and Pias would find himself alone with only one pirate guarding him.

So entertaining had his story been that the men did not consider him a serious threat. They decided that two of them would go up first, training their guns on the entrance so that Pias didn't dare make a break the instant he emerged from the tube. As the first two disappeared up the tube, the third man stayed far enough away that Pias couldn't jump him before he could fire his blaster. Pias waited patiently, seemingly unconcerned about the situation he was in.

When the light came on indicating the tube was ready for them, the pirate motioned Pias to get in and then stepped in behind him. They were now, of necessity, in the confined quarters that Pias wanted. He waited for just the proper moment, and then acted.

There was a jolt as the plate they were on began its rise up the tube. It was a mild movement, but it was enough to joggle the pirate's gun hand. That was all the help Pias needed. He brought his own hand up quickly to deflect the other man's weapon. The blaster went off, but its bolt was spent harmlessly against the wall of the tube, and he never got a chance for a second shot. Pias's elbow shot up, catching the man with a vicious blow to the windpipe that rendered him instantly unconscious. The blaster dropped from his hand and Pias, with his high-gee reflexes, picked it out of the air and gripped it securely. He turned facing the door, prepared to blast the other two pirates the instant he reached the surface.

It was quite fortunate for him that his reflexes were so fast, for the two people he faced were not the pirates who had gone up the tube before him, but his own wife and Commander Fortier. Had he fired point blank, he might well have killed the only two allies he had on the entire planet—but, when he saw who they were, he was able to hold his fire in time.

Yvette saw her husband armed and ready for a fight, and smiled. "We came to rescue you," she said, indicating the two guards who lay unconscious on the ground before her, "but I guess you beat us to it."

"We have a saying on Newforest which translates roughly, 'The hangman loves a person who's expecting a reprieve.' I wasn't going to my execution quite that docilely."

Yvette clucked mockingly. "And how many times have you told *me* to be patient and have faith in you?"

"Faith is all very well," Pias said, holding up the weapon in his right hand, "but give me a blaster any time."

Fortier saw his chance here to break into the conversation. "It's a lucky thing for you I planted a bug in Shen's office, or we wouldn't have known you were in trouble and been able to head it off."

Pias dropped his gaze for a moment. "I really miscalculated this time, I guess."

"That doesn't matter now, anyway," Fortier said. "There's been a change in plans. I just received a subcom call from Headquarters back at Luna Base. They know when the attack is going to take place, and they've issued us a new set of orders."

Fortier explained that somehow the high command had learned that the enemy fleet would be making its rendezvous at a particular spot in just a couple of days. Fortier and at least one of the SOTE agents were to go on ahead and wait there, while the Navy kept its own ships just a short distance away, out of detection range. The instant the pirate fleet showed up, the scout ship would call the Navy, who would then sweep in and destroy the enemy before it had a chance to attack Earth.

"You're the logical choice to come with me," Fortier told Pias as he concluded his explanation. "You're dead if you're seen on this world any more."

"What about her?" Pias asked, pointing at Yvette. "Doesn't she come, too?"

"Someone has to stay with Shen in case he tries something unexpected," Yvette said, shaking her head. "The commander was the logical choice for that, except for one thing—he's the only one among us who can pilot a ship. Therefore he has to go. It's a shame to blow the cover identity he's worked so hard to build, but there's no other choice. The same goes for you. I at least still have a chance here—Shen may still think I'm useful to him. That's why I'm staying."

Both husband and wife knew how slender a thread of hope that was. Shen was unpredictable, and could order Yvette killed tomorrow for some reason real or imagined. Pias hated the thought of leaving his beloved spouse to such an uncertain fate, but he knew she was right—if someone had to stay behind, she was the only choice. And both had long ago resigned themselves to death if they should make any mistakes in their job. It was not a pleasant alternative, but it was a necessary one.

Fortier showed them the way to another elevator tube, one that was seldom used, and the trio descended once more into the depths of the pirate base. Already, now that they knew what to look for, they could see that activity within the base had stepped up, that teams of workers were laboring furiously to get all the ships into fighting shape. There was going to be a big move coming quite soon, just as Headquarters had said, and the rebel forces were readying for the push.

The increased activity made it a little more difficult to steal a ship, as there was scarcely a vessel that did not have someone checking it out. While Yvette and Pias remained in hiding, Fortier strolled boldly out among the workers, secure in his identity as Rocheville, Shen's top assistant. He returned to the SOTE agents half an hour later to say that he'd located a scout ship with only two mechanics working on it, and that it would be the best they could find on short notice. Time was crucial now; it could not be much longer before Shen learned that Pias had not been killed, and then an all-out hunt for the fugitive would begin.

The three undercover agents crept furtively through back corridors of the base to the ship Fortier had chosen. It was a matter of only a few seconds' fighting, and the ship was theirs. "These people have already done most of the work," Fortier commented as they tied the mechanics up and left them in a seldom-visited storage area. "It should only take me about ten minutes or so, and we'll be all set to leave."

Ten minutes did not give the Bavols much time to say all they wanted to say to one another. They had been separated for the first time since their wedding when Yvette left the *Paradise*, and had only been reunited a few days ago when the pirates captured that ship—and even that had been a less than satisfactory reunion, because they were playing roles that forced them to act as though they hated one another. Now they were to be separated once more—and there was a strong possibility that they might never see each other alive again.

Words were totally inadequate to express the feelings flowing between them as they stood in the ship waiting for Fortier to announce he was ready for takeoff. They looked in each other's eyes and caressed each other's face. Then, drawn as though by a powerful magnet, they embraced tightly and surrendered themselves to a passionate, lingering kiss that continued unabated until they heard Fortier clearing his throat discreetly behind them.

"All smooth," he said simply.

With great reluctance, Yvette pulled herself away from her husband's embrace. "Take care of yourself, *mon cher*," she said quietly. "I'll see you back on Earth." Then abruptly she turned and walked out of the ship, before her eyes betrayed her and she showed the tears she felt were coming.

She moved quickly away from the area without looking back. A few minutes later she felt, rather than heard, the vibrations from the ship's departure. Alarms began ringing through the base almost instantly at the unauthorized takeoff. The confusion as people ran through the halls helped cover her own retreat back to the quarters that had been provided for her. It was almost certain that the pirates would mount some sort of chase after the fleeing ship—but, caught unaware as they were, they should be no match for Fortier's skills as a pilot.

The naval commander would be off their screens before they could get very far—and once off, he was unlikely to be found again.

Yvette returned to her room and waited. She was expecting Shen to call her soon and let her know that she'd been right about "Brian Sangers," that he was dangerous and not to be trusted. What she *wasn't* expecting was the tirascaline gas that came seeping slowly through the ventilator over her doorway. She tried to rise from her bed at the first whiff of the sickeningly sweet sleep drug, but fell back limply in a matter of seconds, totally unconscious.

She awoke with a ringing in her head and the room swimming around her. At first she was disoriented, but came slowly to the realization that she was lying on her back atop a table. It took her another few minutes before her head cleared enough to note that her arms and legs were chained to the four corners of the tabletop.

As she started stirring, testing the strength of her bonds, a man entered the room. He was small, and uniformed as a pirate, but she'd never seen him before. "Who are you?" she asked groggily. "What happened to me?"

"I'm keeping you here until the rest come back. We've had our fill of spies from SOTE."

A cold chill went down Yvette's spine, but she refused to let it show. "What do you mean? Let me out of here. I demand to speak to Shen!"

"That'll be a little hard, gospozha. He's parsecs away by now, along with the rest of the fleet."

Out of the corner of her eye, Yvette saw a shape moving in the doorway toward her captor. She kept talking, trying to distract him. "You're overstepping your orders. When Shen comes back, he'll have your ears as bookends for daring to talk to me this way."

"It was his orders that put you here. He . . ."

The pirate got no further in his speech, as he was cut down from behind by a sharp blow to the base of his neck. Yvette lifted her head to see who her mysterious savior might be, and saw to her amazement that it was Fortier. He'd disguised himself by shaving off his mustache, letting his hair grow long and darkening his skin pigment, but it was unquestionably the same man who had taken off in the ship with her husband. "I'm glad to see you again," Yvette said. "Did everything go smoothly? Why did you come back?"

Fortier cocked his head and eyed her curiously, as though he didn't know her at all. "State the nature of our business," he said sharply.

It was Yvette's turn to be suspicious. Could this somehow be an imposter? She decided on a test. "I'm afraid the drug disoriented me. What does the timepiece say?" The word "time-piece" was Fortier's codename; the real Fortier should react to that, but an imposter wouldn't.

She could see Fortier relax visibly, and he stooped over her unconscious jailer to find the key that would unlock her chains. "Are you from NI?" he asked as he searched through the pirate's pockets.

That question did nothing to allay Yvette's suspicions. "No, SOTE," she said. "Which you should remember perfectly well."

Fortier had found the key and was freeing her of her bonds. "I'm sure that damnable doppelgänger does, but I've never had the honor of meeting you, gospozha."

A chill of premonition ran down Yvette's spine. "What do you mean, doppelgänger?" she asked, making the question sound much more casual than it really was.

Fortier took a deep breath and began his story. "Several months ago I was alone on the surface when I was ambushed by that . . . double. I hid in a small cave behind a waterfall and shot at him with my stun-gun, but nothing happened—he just kept coming at me. Then he fired a blaster and hit me on the right side of my chest. It should have killed me, but it didn't; I think some of the beam's energy must have gone into heating the water from the waterfall before it reached me. My chest is badly scarred up, and I passed out from the pain, but I lived.

"When I came to I was buried beneath a pile of rubble. I can only imagine that my double, whoever he is, used his blaster to cause a rockslide and bury what he thought was my dead body. Again, the rockslide should have killed me, but it didn't; I suppose I should thank my DesPlainian heritage for giving me such a tough body.

"I was alive, but I was in pretty wretched shape. I lay there in pain for a couple of days before I could gather enough strength to push the rocks off me and crawl out. There was plenty of water flowing past to wash my blaster wound and the cuts and bruises I got from the rockslide—but it was another day and a half before I could stagger to my feet and wander into the jungle to find something to eat.

"I spent a week in the jungle, living off whatever I could scavenge while I waited for my strength to return. I had plenty of time to think. The only reason a duplicate of me would want to kill me is to take my place—which means someone went to a great deal of trouble to learn a lot about me. That someone thought I was dead now, and I saw no reason to let him know otherwise; I might learn more this way. As soon as I felt well enough again, I slipped back into the base.

"One of the best things about this place is that it's so crowded that no one really knows anyone else. I was able to darken my complexion with the juice from some berries from the jungle, and I let my hair grow long and shaggy. I shaved my mustache at the first chance I got, and just started mingling with the ordinary men. Unfortunately I couldn't get too close to my double to see what he was up to; I was afraid he might spot me. I saw him with you a couple of times, but that didn't mean anything—I had no way of knowing which side you were on. I spent months roaming around the base, but I haven't really learned anything I didn't know before.

"Then, just a short while ago, the order came down that all ships would be sent into battle. I didn't want to get trapped on one of them, so I hid until they were all gone. I figured the base would be practically deserted, and I could put in a subcom call to Luna Base to warn them. I was on my way to the Communications Room when I heard the voices in here and stopped to investigate. That's about it so far."

Yvette had been rubbing her wrists and ankles while he talked, massaging life back into them. Fortier's story had a ring of horrible truth to it—a truth she didn't want to believe because of what it implied. "It's a nice story," she said noncommittally.

Fortier smiled. "I see. You want some proof that *I'm* not the double, right?"

"Exactly."

"Khorosho, what would it take?"

"I've worked against those doubles before. They're carefully constructed robots. If you're the real thing, you'll bleed; if you're not, you won't."

Fortier thought for a moment, then looked around for something to use as an instrument. Picking up the key to the chains again, he scratched one edge along the back of his left hand. He squeezed the flesh and a satisfactory thin line of red appeared. "How's that?" he asked.

"I'm convinced," Yvette said. "But I wish I weren't."

Because that meant that her husband had just gone off alone in a spaceship with the fourth of Lady A's deadly robots—on a mission that had suddenly twisted itself beyond her ability to understand.

16

——————— *A New Empress* ———————

The d'Alemberts' ship, traveling at top speed all the way from Gastonia, made it back to Earth in time for the Coronation. Jules and Vonnie landed at the Vandenberg Spaceport shortly after dawn on Friday morning, and the Head had a special jet waiting there to take them into Angeles-Diego. The two agents were tired after their ordeal and long trip, but exhilarated at the same time by the thought of actually attending this ceremony normally reserved for the highest of the nobility.

They arrived at Bloodstar Hall three hours before activities were to start, and found special admittance passes in their names waiting for them. They were escorted to the backstage area and SOTE's security control checkpoint, where conditions were chaos incarnate. People were running around busily, giving orders right and left, seemingly at random—yet the d'Alemberts knew that there was indeed a rationale behind every action, no matter how hectic the scene looked.

The Head and his daughter were in the center of a mob, being bombarded with questions of where to go and what particular assignment to carry out. Nevertheless, when he noted the arrival of the DesPlainian team, the Head squeezed his way through the throng and over to their side. "I'm glad to see you've made it," he said. "We've acted on your information, though I don't have time to explain it all now. Do you think you would be able to help our security contingent here? I'll understand perfectly if you say you're too tired."

The thought of actually taking part in Edna's Coronation, no matter how far behind the scenes, overcame any feelings of fatigue. "We'd be delighted to help," Jules said quickly, and Yvonne added her own, "Only too happy."

The Head smiled. "Good. I hope it'll be an easy assignment. We're not expecting any trouble within the hall itself, and we're making constant scans for weapons. So far we haven't found any. If C sticks to his plans, the attack won't come until tomorrow, so today's events should go well.

"As Grand Duke of Sector Four I'll have to be in the audience and Helena, as my daughter and heir, will be with me. Have to keep up appearances, after all, though I'd be much more useful back here. Ima Takanabe will be running the checkpoint; I'll take you over and introduce you. She can give you your assignments for the day."

He led them over to a woman directing much of the backstage traffic, in her forties and about the same height as the d'Alemberts themselves. She was the picture of efficiency. "Colonel Takanabe, these are agents Wombat and Hedgehog. Use them wherever you need two exceptionally talented people." Then, with only a slight nod, he was off again to round up his daughter and take their seats in the audience.

Colonel Takanabe was impressed. Like everyone else in the Service, she knew the codename Wombat as one of the top people in the organization—and while she had never heard of Hedgehog, she knew that any partner of Wombat's had to be among the best. She needed but an instant's thought to decide where to station the two newcomers to best effect.

Jules and Yvonne ended up behind the scenes, one on either side of the enormous platform that served as both altar and dais for the Coronation ceremony. Their job looked easy, but it was deceptive. They were to be constantly scanning the audience for the slightest sign of trouble—and if anything untoward occurred, it was their task to remedy it without disrupting the ceremony if at all possible. The job required absolute concentration throughout the many hours of the ceremony, and could not be taken lightly. It was also a job that, if performed correctly, would receive no notice at all except in Takanabe's efficiency report.

The rites had actually been going on for many hours before the d'Alemberts had arrived at the hall. Emperor Stanley Ten had gone on Galaxy-wide live broadcast the night before to announce his official abdication, to become effective upon the crowning of his daughter. He then made the *pro forma* call for the nobles of the Empire to gather together to proclaim Edna as Empress Stanley Eleven, supreme ruler of the Empire of Earth.

There followed, on that same broadcast, a rare televised meeting of the Chamber of Thirty-Six wherein the grand dukes of all thirty-six sectors of space unanimously issued a proclamation requesting Crown Princess Edna to assume the Throne. The scene then shifted to the College of Dukes, where the planetary rulers met in council. Not all the 1,368 dukes in the Empire were present, of course; only twice in history had every duke been in attendance simultaneously at the College, and both occasions occurred early in the Empire's history, when there were far fewer dukes. Nevertheless, the College managed a splendid turnout, and their pomp rivalled that of the grand dukes as they issued an identical proclamation.

The scene then shifted back to the Imperial Palace, where Edna Stanley acknowledged the proclamations and agreed to become the new Empress. She then made a speech to the people of the Empire, while her father stood proudly behind her—one of the few times in the last five decades that he had ever stood in the background. Edna gave a glowing tribute to the peace and prosperity during her father's reign; she called him "the greatest of the Great Stanleys" and pointed out that during his reign the Empire expanded by nearly twenty-three percent.

Moving from the past to the future, Edna spoke in general terms of the goals she wanted to accomplish for the Empire. Her speech was simple and distinct, delivered without a trace of nervousness or self-consciousness. All her life Edna had trained to become empress; she now looked and acted the part to perfection. Those who heard her speak that evening—and the vast majority of people within the Empire did, no matter what time it was on their respective worlds—could have no doubts at all about her capacity to administer the largest empire man had ever created.

At no time did Edna allow her audience the slightest inkling that the Empire was under the threat of imminent attack from a navy that could very well rival her own. Only the positive was mentioned that night, and only smiles could be seen on official faces.

When the broadcast ended, the public observance of the rites went into abeyance—but the traditions went on nonetheless. It was traditional for the Empress-designate and her husband to spend the night awake, fasting and meditating. In part this was a practical measure, since few incoming rulers were able to get much sleep the night before the Coronation anyway, and were glad of the chance to rehearse their part in the next day's festivities. In Edna's case, part of the time was spent in consultation with her top military advisors, going over plans to thwart the impending attack by C's forces; the rest of her energy was indeed devoted to meditation, under the guidance of her husband Liu, a fully trained mystic from the planet Anares. The two of them spent many hours that night kneeling face to face on the floor in a dimly lit room, surrounded by servants and courtiers. The royal couple held hands, but did not speak a word; in the months since their marriage, they had reached a development in their relationship where words were unnecessary.

Shortly before dawn the meditations were broken along with the fast. The couple was led to a banquet table where a sumptuous feast had been laid out for them. Custom required, however, that they only taste from each of the plates; they had to take in some nourishment to face the long day ahead, but at the same time they knew that too heavy a meal might tend to make them feel logy or sick. Their selections and portions were carefully chosen by the Imperial physician ahead of time for best effect.

Edna and her husband were then separated for the ritual bathing and dressing. Each was anointed with scented oils and perfumes, then dressed ceremoniously by teams of attendants. The official coronation robes worn by the Empress-designate and her consort were centuries old, dating back to the very beginnings of the Empire. Edna wore a sideless surcoat of cloth-of-gold, heavy with jewels, over a white satin dress with a three-meter train; around her shoulders was a scarlet mantle edged with ermine. Her hair, undecorated, hung straight down her back to her waist.

Liu was in a scarlet houppelande open down the front to

show a robe of gleaming white. He wore no jewels, and the fur trim on his houppelande was plain white mink. At his waist was a gold chain belt and a sword of gold set with jewels—the consort's sword, deliberately blunt. Like his wife's, his head was bare.

Once dressed, the royal couple were brought down to the entrance of the Imperial Palace in Los Angeles, where the carriage was waiting to take them to Bloodstar Hall. This was an actual horse-drawn coach, gilded wood with enormous gems set in it, pulled by a team of six snow-white horses. It took close to four hours to travel from palace to hall in this primitive conveyance, and the route along the way was jammed with loving, screaming subjects all craning to get even a glimpse of their new monarch. Edna waved to the crowds until she thought her arm was going to fall out of its socket, and she and Liu tossed out handfuls of tiny coins that had been minted especially for this occasion.

Lord Bloodstar was waiting for them on the front steps of the hall when the carriage pulled up. He carried with him the ceremonial sword of state, and he ordered her to halt while they went through a traditional challenge and response, at the end of which he acknowledged her as the rightful ruler of the Empire. Then, carrying the sword before him, he led her up the stairs and inside the front door where he announced the arrival of the Empress-designate to the assembled lords and ladies of the Empire.

At this point, Edna accepted the sword from Lord Bloodstar and began her long, slow march down the aisle while the nobles in attendance rose to their feet and watched her in silence. All across the Galaxy, trillions of people were glued to their trivision sets, watching the incredible spectacle at home, at their jobs, or wherever they happened to be. Behind Edna as she walked came her retinue of ladies-in-waiting, carrying her train; then her husband and his retinue; and finally Lord Bloodstar bringing up the rear.

Normally the Archbishop of Earth would have been waiting alone on the platform ahead of her—but that was because the preceding emperor seldom had the chance to attend the coronation of his successor. Today, William Stanley stood there beside the Archbishop. He was clad in a white silk shroud, a garment symbolizing his ceremonial "death," which allowed

Edna to succeed him. In his hands, he carried his own personal Great Seals of State which had been purposely defaced; this act signified that he could no longer execute documents and laws as the Emperor, and his power was at an end. Edna had her own official seals. At any given moment, there could only be one person holding the supreme authority, or the Galaxy would dissolve into chaos.

William Stanley stood proudly on the platform, watching through mist-laden eyes as his daughter made the same long walk he had taken forty-six years ago. Scores of memories, happy and sad, flashed through his mind as he waited for her to reach the platform, but he did not regret in the slightest his decision to hand over the power to her. He'd seen his daughter in action often enough to know she would make a wise and fair ruler—and how many monarchs had ever been blessed with such knowledge of their successors during their own lifetimes?

Edna reached the base of the platform and started slowly up the stairs, aided by her ladies, being most careful not to make the slightest slip in these unfamiliar clothes. This moment must not be spoiled by anything so trivial. When she came to the top, Edna walked to the center of the platform, placed her sword upon the altar next to the crown of state that was already there, and knelt with her head bowed. Her ladies removed the mantle from her shoulders and retreated backwards down the stairs. The archbishop then came over and stood on her right side, her father on her left, and together both men began the invocation to start the ceremony.

The d'Alemberts had seen almost nothing of the rites; their duty kept their eyes focused on the audience rather than on the ceremony itself. It was at this point that both were relieved by others and told to report back to Colonel Takanabe at the security checkpoint. Puzzled—and a little alarmed by this unexpected change—they obeyed.

Takanabe was terse as she took them aside and explained the situation. "There is a fleet of spaceships materializing in the solar system, out of the ecliptic plane and beyond the orbit of Mars—but they are coming toward Earth in a hurry. Do you know anything about this?"

The d'Alemberts exchanged startled glances. "They weren't supposed to attack until tomorrow!" Vonnie exclaimed.

"Well, someone forgot to tell them," Takanabe said grimly. She turned to a special microphone and repeated what she'd told the d'Alemberts. This connection went to a receiver planted in the Head's ear, so small as to be unnoticeable unless one knew precisely what to look for. The Head had also been equipped with a subvocal microphone so he could speak to the checkpoint if necessary without disturbing those in the audience around him.

The Head listened quietly to Colonel Takanabe's terse recitation. "Are Wombat and Hedgehog there?" he asked when she'd finished.

"Yes, sir," Jules spoke up instantly.

"What do you make of this?"

"I don't know. I suppose it's possible they changed their plans—but that information we had was gotten under nitrobarb."

"Are you sure?" Those three words came across the air waves and hit the agents like so many bullets.

Vonnie slapped a hand to her forehead. *Mon Dieu!* We could have been injecting her with distilled water!"

As the magnitude of what had happened began to sink in, the d'Alemberts felt sick at heart. They had been so proud of themselves for finally capturing Lady A, for finding out how the leaks from SOTE were accomplished, and especially for learning the details of the plan to attack Earth. They had escaped from Gastonia alive and delivered their vital information on time. And all the while they had been operating under a ruse perpetrated by one of the craftiest villains who'd ever lived.

Looking back on it, they could see step by step everything that had gone into setting them up. Shortly after Jules discovered the house—something he was bound to do eventually—they had been elevated to a high position within Tshombase's regime . . . a position that just happened to put them in the right place to overhear Lady A saying that she would be staying at the house for a few days. Their attack, with almost no resources, against a well-defended house had been absurdly simple, and they encountered no resistance once they broke in. The one door unlocked on the top floor had been the entrance to Lady A's office, where a vial of "nitrobarb" was conveniently lying in a drawer, waiting to be found!

As soon as the scene was set, Lady A stumbled in alone and allowed herself to be captured most easily, knowing the only real alternative the agents would have was to use the planted "nitrobarb" on her. Under the influence of the supposed truth drug she could tell them anything and they would believe her implicitly. Then, when she had told them precisely what she wanted them to know, guards broke in and chased the agents away to a conveniently waiting spaceship.

Jules felt like a classic fool. "I've seen rookies fresh out of the Academy with more brains than we have," he moaned.

"I refuse to let you wallow in self-deprecation," the Head said sharply. "It's no dishonor to lose to the best—and now we know exactly how good our Lady A is. She took great pains that you would believe her. At every step of the game she made sure it was just hard enough to give you a good challenge, so you wouldn't think you were given things too easily. She played every hand perfectly; I only hope we survive to win a rematch."

"But what can we do about it now?" Vonnie asked.

"At the moment, the principal fight is out of our hands," the Head said with remarkable calm. "It's the Navy's job to fight these battles, not ours. We'll have to leave it up to them and hope they're better at their job than we've been at ours.

"The Service has its own tasks at the moment—security during the Coronation. No matter what's happening in space above us, our Empress needs protection right here in this room. Lady A tried a two-pronged attack during Edna's wedding; she might use that tactic again. Take up your posts and make sure nothing goes wrong—let the Navy handle the rest."

At that moment a mighty cheer went up throughout the building, a cheer that shook Bloodstar Hall to its very foundations. The enormous crowd, unaware of the drama that was soon to take place in the vacuum between planets, was reacting to the archbishop's placing the purple robe of state around Edna's shoulders and her father's placing the heavy silver and gold crown upon her head. At that moment, the other peers in the audience put on their own crowns and coronets. It was official now. Princess Edna had become Her Most Imperial Majesty, Empress Stanley Eleven, sovereign ruler of the Empire of Earth.

The d'Alemberts took up their posts once more as the archbishop's benediction was pronounced over the newly crowned empress. The next four hours would be filled with various ranks of nobility, councilors and officials appearing before their new monarch and swearing, individually and collectively, their fealty to her and all her line and heirs. But though the Des-Plainians kept their sharp eyes alert for any signs of danger within the hall itself, their minds were millions of kilometers away, far out in space where the battle was to be joined—a battle that, because of their mistake, could well mean the end of the Stanley Dynasty and, indeed, of the Empire itself.

17

The Fourth Robot

Yvette explained to the real Commander Fortier exactly what the Bavols' mission had been here while she and the naval officer were on their way to Shen's office. "What I can't understand," she said, "is what Shen expects to gain by all this. Why did the robot take my partner with him? If they knew all along that we were SOTE agents, why go through with this elaborate charade?"

"There are only two reasons for letting any spy live once you know his identity: to find out who else he contacts, and to feed him misleading information. They certainly accomplished the first objective here; perhaps they're after the second as well."

Yvette nodded grimly. Authentication was always a problem in the intelligence business. If the fake Commander Fortier told something to Headquarters, it would carry so much weight; if Pias Bavol of SOTE confirmed the same information, it would be worth that much more. Lady A and her cohorts might indeed have a reason to keep her husband alive a while longer; at least until he had unwittingly done what they wanted. Then, Yvette was sure, the robot would kill him without mercy even before her husband could react.

The two agents had their guns drawn as they moved through the halls of the pirate base, but they avoided confrontations with the few pirates they encountered by hiding until the others passed. The place was not totally deserted, but the silence was eerie when contrasted to the bustle that had been the rule until just recently.

They reached Admiral Shen's office in short time. They made quick work of the two guards and set about searching the room for any clues to the conspiracy's plans. Yvette checked for physical evidence in desks and cabinets while Fortier, more familiar with the computer filing system the pirates used, checked the electronic records. At last he came upon a particular code heading that pleased him, and he spent several minutes skimming it before announcing his discovery.

"It's not good for our side," he said when Yvette came over to see what he'd found, "but I have to admit it's clever. They're going to leak to our people the 'fact' that they'll attack the day after the Coronation with a certain sized force. The Navy, trying not to tip its hand, will not order reinforcements from nearby bases to cope, but rather have ships come from the more distant bases. These ships are supposed to go first to a spot where all the enemy ships are thought to be conducting a rendezvous; if they're not there, the reinforcements are to go on to bolster Earth's defenses."

Yvette nodded. "That's where my partner and the robot went, to the rendezvous point to act as a beacon for the Navy ships."

"The only trouble is, that plan is a fraud. The attack is scheduled for the day of the Coronation, rather than the day after. The pirate fleet is more than double the strength Headquarters thinks it is. If the reinforcements ever do arrive, the battle will be over and the pirates can cut them down at their leisure."

"*If* they arrive?"

Fortier pointed to a section of the display screen. "That rendezvous point is a trap. Your partner and my lookalike are there to lure the fleet in by telling them the pirates are on their way and an ambush can be set. Actually, that area is crammed with spacemines, mass activated. The scout ship's too small to set them off, but if the Navy's ships drop in there from subspace most—if not all—of them will be blown out of the sky. There won't be enough left to reinforce Earth's defenses."

"We've got to send out a warning. We've got to let someone know the truth."

"Whom do you suggest? It's almost time for the Coronation; Headquarters will know very shortly anyway. And as for your partner or the reinforcement ships, they're in subspace right now and couldn't receive a message."

"Then we'll send a message to the near-Earth bases," Yvette said resolutely. "If they start now, they may be able to reach Earth in time to help out."

Fortier nodded and raced out of the room. Yvette was at his heels as he ran down the deserted corridors to the Communications Room, and fortunately their paths did not cross any of the few pirates left on the base. They waited what seemed to them an ungodly long time for the subetheric communicator to warm up, and then Fortier began sending out calls to the bases that ringed Earth's solar system. After a few desperate moments, he looked up at Yvette.

"I can't get through," he said. "This subcom looks to be in good condition, but I can't get through to any of the bases close enough to Earth to be of any help. Could there have been sabotage on that large a scale?"

"Where Lady A is concerned," Yvette said dismally, "nothing seems to be impossible."

Fortier rubbed his forehead worriedly for a moment, then looked up quickly. "If we can't call, we'll take the message to them in person," he said. "A few ships were left behind here because their guns aren't working, but otherwise they're in running condition. We can each take one and..."

"I can't fly a ship," Yvette said.

"Then we'll both go in one. We'll get to the nearest base and if the subcoms are still out they can dispatch personal message ships to the other bases. We'll get the alarm out somehow."

Yvette bit at her lower lip. "You go on without me and come back to pick me up later."

"What can you accomplish here alone?"

"I can wait until my partner's ship gets out of subspace and send him a message warning him about the robot."

"But the robot will hear the same message, and it can act faster than any human can."

Yvette's jaw was firmly set. "I'll think of something."

Fortier wanted to point out what a risk she was taking. If the pirate fleet were defeated, they might come running back to this base to make a last stand—and any spy they found here would bear the full brunt of their ire. If the pirates won the battle, a SOTE agent here alone would be cut off from any possible allies; the pirates might return triumphantly and kill her.

He wanted to tell her all those things and more—but looking into her eyes, he could see that she already knew them. Still, her feeling for her partner was so strong that she was willing to take the risk anyway to save his life.

So, instead of lecturing her, the commander merely nodded and said, "Doesn't SOTE have some sort of official toast?"

Yvette gave him a weak grin and quoted the Service salute: "'Here's to tomorrow, fellow and friend. May we both live to see it.'"

Fortier smiled back at her. "I can't think of a better wish right now—or a better way to say goodbye." And, without further ado, he turned and went out of the room, leaving Yvette alone with the subcom set.

The scout ship in which Pias and his supposed ally were traveling took four days in subspace before reaching its destination. Then they dropped back into the real universe and waited for things to happen.

It did not take long. Within an hour of their arrival, a coded message came in from the reinforcement fleet, asking for a status report. The Fortier-robot told them he expected the pirates to rendezvous at this point within six hours, and that they should time their own arrival here shortly before that. Then they could be waiting to pick the pirates off like so many insects. Pias gave his concurrence in that opinion, and the scout ship signed off.

"What do we do now?" Pias asked.

"We wait," his companion replied. "The fleet may get in touch with us again, or they may just decide to move right in. We have to be here to help them in either case."

Fifteen minutes later, another call came in, this one from Yvette. Pias handled the subcom, while the other stood behind him, looking over his shoulder. "What's the matter?" Pias asked. "Why are you calling?"

"Status report," Yvette said. "The pirates took off several hours after you did—you should be expecting them very shortly now."

"Thanks, but what about you? We thought you were going to stay with them," the Fortier-robot said from over Pias's shoulder.

"They must have distrusted me or something. They tried to set a trap for me right after you left, but I managed to escape, and they didn't want to hold up their invasion looking for me. I've been trying to reach you ever since, but I just got through."

"We only came out of subspace ourselves a little while ago," Pias said.

"*Eh bien*, be careful, darling," Yvette said, looking straight into her husband's eyes. "And be glad you've got Commander Fortier with you. He's as good a friend as Elspeth FitzHugh."

Pias was about to remark that Elspeth FitzHugh could hardly have been called a friend when he realized that that was the exact point his wife was driving at. Elspeth FitzHugh was the robot he'd destroyed several months ago during their work on the planet Purity. Yvette was saying that the other person in the scout ship with Pias was one of the deadly robots Lady A had planted against the Empire—but Yvette was saying it in an oblique way that only Pias would understand, because she knew the robot would overhear.

"He probably is," Pias smiled back, "or the Head wouldn't have assigned us to work with him."

"You can be positive of that."

Yvette's reply to his implied question of how certain her information was convinced Pias. There was no doubt in Yvette's mind at all about this Fortier's status. Pias wondered how she had learned this, but he knew by now how much faith he could put in his wife's word. When she said "positive," she meant it.

"You couldn't have said it better," Pias told her. "We'd better break the connection now; Fortier and I have a lot of planning to do."

"*Khorosho*. Take care of yourself—and remember, I love you."

"I love you, too," Pias smiled back. "That's what keeps me going." And as her face disappeared off the screen, he closed his eyes to hold the afterimage for as long as he could.

Fortier, a robot! They had known that the fourth of the creatures had been built like a male DesPlainian—but Fortier wasn't *quite* a DesPlainian, and he'd come so highly recommended that they overlooked that fact. For this robot to have taken the real Fortier's place, it would have to know the inner workings of Naval Intelligence, including all the codes—and the implications of *that* were frightening.

Pias forced his mind to put aside such thoughts and concentrate on only one thing: how to destroy this robot. Both of them had come aboard with blasters they had taken from Pias's pirate captors, but they had stored them out of the way on a lower deck. Neither had thought he would need them inside the ship; Pias had not expected betrayal from his ally, and the robot had probably planned to kill the SOTE agent with a surprise snap of the neck. The situation had changed, and Pias knew he'd have to find some way of going below and arming himself. The robot could not be overcome simply by brute force.

"I don't know about you," he said aloud, "but waiting makes me hungry. I think I'll go aft and fix myself a snack. Can I get you anything while I'm back there?"

"No, I couldn't eat right now. Too nervous."

"Suit yourself." Pias left his seat in the control cabin and climbed down the ladder into the small galley/storeroom below it. He started clattering noisily around to convince his companion he was indeed working in here, meanwhile trying to remember where they had stored the blasters. He recalled, to his chagrin, that they were one more level down, in the small ship's engine room. He couldn't think of any reasonable excuse for going down there.

"What was that?" Pias asked suddenly.

"What was what?"

"I thought I heard a noise down in the drive room. I'd better go have a look." And without waiting for an answer Pias practically dove down the ladder as fast as he could. At this point he didn't care whether the robot's suspicions were aroused or not; he wanted to get to a blaster as quickly as possible, while he still had a slight headstart on his enemy.

At this point the robot peered down from the control room and saw that Pias was moving far faster than he should have been for performing this kind of check. Whether the robot knew now that Pias was aware of its identity, it did know that this behavior was suspicious. Pias was not so essential to the robot's plans that suspicious behavior could be at all tolerated. The killer machine thus came to the conclusion, in a fraction of a second, that Pias was now to be dispensed with immediately.

Having decided, it acted. Despite Pias's headstart, the robot was so agile that it was down the ladder into the galley before Pias had even made it completely into the drive room. The SOTE agent could hear his enemy's approach and knew every second counted. He leaped directly from the ladder to the cabinet in which the blasters had been stored.

Grabbing both weapons at once, he turned around, fumbling the guns into firing position. Even as he did so the robot reached out one hand and grabbed the pair of barrels, crushing the weapons in its powerful grip. The move was a dramatic one, possibly intended to impress Pias and demoralize him. But the Newforester didn't have time to be impressed; he was too busy struggling for his life.

The instant the robot grabbed the guns and destroyed them, Pias ducked under the other's outstretched arm and came up behind it. The man from SOTE knew he was stuck in this chamber; if he tried climbing the ladder again, the robot could grab his leg and the fight would soon be over. Similarly, he could not hope to beat the creature in simple hand-to-hand combat—it was too quick and too strong, even for a person from a high-grav world. He had to have some kind of a weapon and, even more important, a strategem.

There was a long steel wrench sitting on a shelf against the far wall. Pias swiped at it, grabbed it, and danced out of the robot's reach as it came at him again. Pias was not sure how well-constructed the robot was, but he was willing to bet a wrench would do some damage if he could manage to land a solid blow. If . . .

There was very little room to maneuver in the cramped drive room, a fact that worked to the robot's advantage. Two of the side walls were banks of dials and switches, manual overrides for the control systems normally run from the pilot's console. The floor was thickly plated and corrugated, shielding the room's occupants from the deadly energies of the atomic drive beneath them. The other two walls were for shelves and cabinets, holding miscellaneous tools and items the occupants of the ship wished to store. And in the center of the room, dominating everything, were the large black drive housings—floor to ceiling in height and so thick that a man embracing one could not fit his arms even halfway around. These immense machines operated with little more than a gargling sound, but with his senses heightened for this battle they sounded to Pias like twin waterfalls pounding at his brain.

The robot came at him with impersonal determination, and Pias had to keep backing away, circling around the room in and out of tight corners, trying to maneuver for better position. But there was no better position, not in these narrow spaces. Even under peaceful conditions, ship's engineers had difficulty maneuvering themselves through the cramped confines of the drive room to check on or repair any component of the ship. Pias looked for a good place to stand and found none. He dared not even swing his wrench until he could be assured of a solid blow; with the robot's amazing reflexes it could easily wrest the weapon away from him given any chance at all.

This should be Jules's fight, one small detached part of him thought. *He's the physical one. I'm the one who likes to think his way out of things.*

The robot kept coming, quick as lightning, relentless as the sea.

In backing up, Pias bumped his left elbow hard against the protruding knob of a small hatch labeled "Contaminant Flush." Luckily the wrench was in his other hand, or he would have dropped it as he yowled with pain. The robot only smiled and kept advancing—but in the middle of the pain, the flash of an idea occurred to Pias.

It would be too late to try it right now; the positions were wrong. He backed up again, continuing around another circuit of the room, trying to maneuver his opponent into exactly the configuration he wanted. He only prayed he would have enough strength in his right arm to make it work.

As they reached the Contaminant Flush hatch again, Pias planted his feet firmly and refused to back away any farther. The robot smiled, seeing this as a positive sign that the fight would soon be over, and rushed forward even faster. Its eyes watched the wrench in Pias's right hand, confident that was the only danger it faced.

As the machine came toward him, Pias reached out with his left hand and pulled open the hatch cover for the Contaminant Flush chute. The robot, seeing this sudden move, tried to slow down to avoid running into the open cover that was now between itself and its target—and in that instant, Pias swung his wrench downward at the robot's head with all the strength his body possessed.

The robot reached up quickly, grabbing the handle of the wrench before it could reach its head and gripping it tightly to yank it out of Pias's grasp. Pias continued his downward momentum so hard that his feet actually left the ground. So strong was the follow-through that it pulled the robot off its feet and banged it against the side of the open hatch. Before it could recover, Pias pushed it toward the opening and shoved it into the chute, swinging the hatch shut behind it and locking it with a decided *clang* that rang through the room.

The chute was meant as an emergency disposal tube for anything within the spaceship that became contaminated by radiation from the drive. Before the robot could react and fight its way out, Pias pressed the button at the side of the hatch. With a silent *whoosh* of air, the robot was ejected from the tube and out of the ship into the dark depths of space beyond the hull.

Pias leaned against the wall and found himself collapsing into a sitting position on the floor. His arms and legs were trembling with the aftershock, and it took a moment for him to steady them. *That,* he decided, *was entirely too close.*

The job was not finished though, he knew. The robot did not need to breathe, and had not been "killed" simply by being ejected into space. It was helpless for the moment, hanging in the void with no means of getting back to the ship, but it was still functioning and potentially dangerous. He would have to take care of that.

As soon as his legs were steady enough to stand on, he climbed back to his feet and returned up the ladder to the control room. He checked the gunnery screen, and soon had the robot lined up in his sights. The scout ship was equipped with short-range spaceblasters, and Pias made ample use of them. The robot was a very small target for the aiming computer to zero in on, but four shots were sufficient to blow the robot apart.

That done, Pias turned on the subcom once more and beamed a message back to the pirate base. "Yes?" Yvette answered cautiously.

"I got it," Pias said, and went on to describe in detail his fight with the robot.

Yvette was beside herself with joy. "I knew you could do it. I'm proud of you, my brave, clever husband. That means that all four of Lady A's robots we know about are destroyed."

"Leaving perhaps many more that we *don't* know about," Pias cautioned, trying to keep a sense of proportion. "It also leaves you alone at the pirate base and me alone out here. Neither of us can pilot a spaceship, so we're totally at the Universe's mercy. Tell me, what was the robot's plan in getting me out here?"

Yvette explained what she and Fortier had learned, that the area where Pias's ship was currently floating was booby-trapped, waiting to destroy the Navy ships that blundered into it.

"We've already told the fleet to come on in," Pias said. "They may be on their way here this instant."

Yvette's face was grim. "They'll have to be stopped if we're going to save the fleet and send them on to reinforce Earth."

"Don't worry," Pias said. "You've done your job by warning me about the robot, and Fortier is doing his by warning the near-Earth bases. Now it's time for me to do mine by warning the fleet. Never fear, my love, I'll think of something."

But as his wife's image faded from the screen, he had to admit to himself that he'd projected more confidence than he truly felt. He made a quick try to raise the fleet by subcom, but there was no response. As he'd feared, the ships had already gone into subspace on their way to this rendezvous point. They would be unable to receive subcom calls again until they materialized here—at which time it would be far too late.

Pias sat for several minutes staring at the complex assemblage of dials, meters, buttons, knobs, switches and blinking red, green, blue and amber lights that comprised the instrument panel. He'd seen other people maneuver those controls, but they were a total mystery to him. That one over there looked as though it might activate the engines; this set here probably put the ship into subspace; and those switches at the top seemed to be the directional jets. There were others whose functions he couldn't even guess at. And of course, the ship was not equipped with an instruction manual.

"I'll think of something," he said to himself under his breath. "But it had better be good and it had better be fast!"

18

—— *The Coronation Day Incursion* ——

While the eyes of the Galaxy were focused on the events at Bloodstar Hall, the Empire's fate was actually being contested in space many kilometers away. Lord Admiral Benevenuto, though he'd been expecting the attack tomorrow rather than today, nonetheless had all his forces on the alert, ready for signs of trouble—and, while he would have liked to attend the Coronation himself, he stayed at his post on Luna Base to handle anything that might come up.

Thus, when the pirate fleet dropped out of subspace into the solar system, he was not exactly surprised by its appearance. What did startle him, though, was its size. The attackers were two thousand strong, nearly double the numbers that the information from SOTE—supposedly obtained under nitro-barb—had led anyone to suspect. *"Bozhe moi!"* exclaimed the admiral under his breath. "It's a regular armada!"

He had known that his forces would be outnumbered, but not this badly. The reinforcements that were scheduled to arrive from the faraway bases wouldn't be here until tomorrow—and even they would be barely sufficient to counter this much larger force he was facing.

His first order of business was to mobilize the forces of

Earth. Luna Base was suddenly so alive with bells and sirens that the whole moon seemed to ring with the alarms. Many of these warning signals had never rung before except during drills—but, as the admiral's voice was now informing everyone on the base, this was no drill. War had come to the Empire, on a scale not seen since the infamous Dukes' Revolt shortly after the Empire's foundation.

Men and women scrambled madly to their battle stations. Security had kept a tight lid on the knowledge of this attack, and none of them had been expecting anything out of the ordinary. Many of them, off duty, had been watching the Coronation themselves. Now some were confused and many were frightened by the startling turn of events; but—in tribute to their training and dedication—they carried on despite their confusion and their fear.

Within five minutes of the enemy fleet's appearance, the advance ships of the Empire's forces lifted off the moon on an intercept course. Other ships under Earth's command, in orbital positions around the solar system, began converging on a given spot where the defenders intended to engage their adversaries in the coming battle—a spot well above the ecliptic plane and as far from Earth itself as could be managed.

The attackers had the advantage of numbers, which also gave them a choice of the attack formation they would use. As their fleet sailed relentlessly toward the Earth, the ships clustered together in a large ball, with the smaller ships around the perimeter and the bigger guns in toward the center.

Odd, thought Benevenuto. *That's a defensive formation, a formation you use when you're outnumbered and under attack in open space. It doesn't make sense here. They've got so many little ships clustered about that they don't even have room to fire off the big ones.*

Arguments were flying fast and furious through the War Room at Luna Base as the board of admirals sat around the conference table and watched the three-dimensional representations floating within the screens. Standard procedure when the enemy clustered that way was to form the defending ships into a loose-knit globe around the center, firing in from all angles and pouring as much energy as possible into the cluster's heart. Several admirals argued that the Navy should be doing just that, but Benevenuto demurred. "Let's stay spread out for now," he said. "We'll see if they make their move."

At Bloodstar Hall, there was a scheduled break in the ceremony during which the Empress was to have a small snack and refresh herself. She was informed of the attack at this time, but merely nodded gravely and said, "The Navy will do its job. Meanwhile, the ceremony will continue as planned.

Edna also took this opportunity to change her outfit, so that when she returned to the dais she was wearing a more modern long silver gown, heavily jeweled. Over this she wore her robe of state, and her crown atop her head. Liu appeared beside her, now wearing a white robe and purple mantle. She presented him with a real sword now, symbol of his role as her defender, and the two sat side by side through the proceedings.

Even if her personal presence could have made a difference in the battle, Edna would not have called a halt in the coronation ceremony that was laboriously grinding its way through the afternoon. Her facial expressions were kept under rigid control all the way as the speeches and the formula recitations droned on. She would accept a noble's oath of fealty with the graciousness of a born ruler, give that person a half-smile of personal warmth, and then sit back to await the coming of the next. Most monarchs called the Coronation the longest day of their lives, and Edna could easily understand why. The extra tension in her case only made it worse.

She was determined, though, to go through with every last word and gesture of it. *We are all born with our various duties in life,* she thought during a lull in the ritual. *The men and women of my Navy are doing theirs this minute; should they expect that I would do any less than mine?*

The hours dragged by, too, in the War Room as the two fleets slowly narrowed the gap between them. The pirate armada continued to fly in its tight cluster formation, contrary to all rules of custom and logic. Three-quarters of the high command voted to englobe. To silence them, Benevenuto had simulations run in the war games computer. The result of each simulation was the same: the computer also said to englobe.

"If we wait too much longer," one admiral insisted, "they'll break through our lines and we won't be *able* to englobe."

Benevenuto stood firm in his decision. The pirates' cluster was not an efficient attack formation. It was a feint, it had to be. He knew, as surely as he drew breath, that englobing would be a tactical mistake of the worst order. Resolutely he kept his ships aligned on a plane perpendicular to the cluster's course, a wall that was always between the invaders and the Earth.

In the computer simulation, they watched the lights representing the pirate armada approach the wall formed by Earth's Navy. Soon the two forces would be within firing range and the battle would begin in earnest. The Empire ships on the wall near the point of contact would be able to fire at the cluster, but those farther away would be out of range and ineffective. The cluster, like a demolition ball, would punch right through the plane of defense and keep on going.

"Commence firing as soon as the cluster is within range," Benevenuto ordered. "And tell the defense to retreat, keeping a constant firing distance between our wall and their cluster. Any ships in the center damaged or destroyed are to be replaced by vessels from the periphery—but we stay, at all times, between Earth and the invading force."

"Retreat is suicide!" Admiral Carswell cried. "We want to keep their ships as far from Earth as possible. We must englobe and attack now."

"May I remind you that we're outnumbered, Admiral?" Benevenuto said calmly. "In our present formation, all of our ships are between Earth and the enemy; if we were to englobe, the majority of our ships would be on other sides, leaving only token resistance in the enemy's path. That cluster is not an attack formation. They're only using it to draw us into a globe so they can make their real move. Gentlemen and ladies, we will not be drawn. We will force them to make their move first, even if it means strategic withdrawal."

The two fleets were now within firing range, and the simulation on the screen showed that a fight was definitely taking place. It was still at a low level because only a few ships were involved on either side. For the pirates, only their ships in the outer layer of the cluster on the side facing the wall had any chance of hitting anything; and for the Navy, only those ships at the contact point of the wall could fire back at the attackers. Slowly the wall was pressed backwards toward the Earth as the pirate cluster, with its superior numbers, pushed forward trying to break through the line of defense.

On Earth, the sun was setting on the western coast of North America as the formal acceptance ceremony at Bloodstar Hall was drawing to a close. After the last oath of fealty was given and acknowledged, it was customary for the new ruler to give a speech. Edna had had a long one all prepared, but the situation now seemed to require her presence elsewhere. She abandoned her prepared text and instead made a few off-the-cuff remarks. She thanked all who had attended and all who wished her and the Empire well. She praised her father for the wisdom and the peace that characterized his reign, and made a solemn promise to do all within her power to continue in his course. She concluded by asking for everyone's courage and support during the Empire's current crisis—a request that startled her Galaxy-wide audience, since most people hadn't known there *was* a crisis. They were soon to learn otherwise.

The official ceremonies concluded, Edna swept out of Bloodstar Hall, trailing majesty behind her like the train of her gown. Traditionally she should have taken the same horse-drawn coach back to the Imperial Palace where the Coronation Dinner and Ball were to be held. Edna, however, had paid enough compromise to tradition today, and had no patience for more while there was a war on. She and her father instead boarded the official copter and sped back to the palace, where Edna announced that the celebrations were postponed for a week during the emergency.

Once back in the palace, Edna and her father went directly to the Council Chamber, where a direct link-up with Luna Base was already waiting for them. While Benevenuto and his staff kept abreast of developments, a senior aide filled the new Empress in on everything that had happened so far. The arguments for and against englobement were summarized, and Edna listened gravely. Her father sat down beside her, out of camera range, and squeezed her hand to give her confidence. The decisions were all hers to make, now, but he let her know he was there to lend his opinion if needed.

When the situation had been summarized, Edna called Benevenuto over to the line to talk personally. "Are you sure this cluster of theirs is just a feint?" she asked her Lord of the Admiralty.

"They can't attack Earth in that formation," Benevenuto replied. "All their big firepower is in the center; they haven't enough artillery on the surface of their sphere to do much damage. They're just trying to entice us into committing ourselves before making their move."

"The bulk of the advice seems to be in favor of englobement."

Benevenuto drew himself up proudly. "I can only go by the

accumulated instincts of forty years in the Navy. I'd stake my reputation on that opinion."

"You are staking your reputation," Edna said coolly, "and a whole lot more, besides. The Empire itself may be riding on this battle."

"All the more reason, Your Majesty, to act the way I know is right."

"I'll pray for both of us, Admiral. Carry on."

The Empress broke the connection and turned to look at her father. The look of imperious command she had affected for her officers' sake was gone now, replaced by one of indecision. "Did I do the right thing?" she asked.

"Time will tell you better than I can," William Stanley said, putting an arm around her shoulders to comfort her. "But I didn't appoint Cesare Benevenuto Lord of the Admiralty just because I liked his mustache. When you know someone's an expert, you trust him in his field of expertise." He smiled. "If it's any consolation, I would have done the same thing you just did."

At Luna Base, Lord Admiral Benevenuto was unaware of this vote of Imperial confidence. As minutes dragged into an hour, and then two, his problems only increased. The pirate cluster was coming closer and closer to Earth's orbit, and his wall of defense was retreating at an equal pace. The enemy had made no move to disperse its cluster. More and more of the admirals were crying for englobement. Computer simulations were saying that englobement was the only strategy, and that its implementation was urgent.

Sweat was literally dripping off Benevenuto's brow as he watched the points of light move slowly across the display screen. Behind him, he knew, some of the admirals were discussing the possibility of going to the Empress and asking that he be replaced by someone more reasonable. He shut out those whispers, shut out the noises, shut out the entire world except for those steady little lights in front of him. *Make your move,* he implored the pirates. *Break out of your thrice-damned cluster.*

As though willing it had made it so, the cluster suddenly exploded on the screen, sending pinpoint fragments of light in all directions. Each dot represented a ship, and their numbers were beyond counting. Benevenuto almost collapsed with relief. His gamble had paid off; the pirates had broken first.

The advantage of Benevenuto's tactics now became apparent: If the Empire forces had englobed the cluster they would, because of their smaller numbers, have had to space themselves widely around the surface of their imaginary sphere. The sudden "explosion" of the cluster would have been disastrous. Dozens, if not hundreds, of the attacking vessels would have slipped through the lacy globe. Some, assuredly, would have been destroyed, but the majority would have dispersed throughout space, and would have outflanked the defenders. The Navy would be both outnumbered and outpositioned.

Benevenuto's wall could do nothing to change the relative numbers, but it had prevented the enemy from getting around the defense. Those members of the cluster who exploded out towards Earth found themselves being fired upon the instant they approached shooting distance of the wall; those who expanded in the opposite direction were not as immediate a threat, and could be discounted for the time being.

Benevenuto spent little time gloating about the success of his strategy. All he had done was prevent a crisis from becoming a catastrophe. His forces were still woefully outnumbered, and there was little that could be done about it any more except trust to fate. Now that the battle had been joined in full, strategy took on a secondary importance. Although his forces would try to hold the wall as best they could, the fighting now belonged to individual ships and the fighting prowess of the two navies.

The morale boost in forcing the pirates to commit themselves first was a big one for the Empire's fighters, and gave them an initial surge into battle. Their guns blazed across the emptiness of space as they ripped out against the rebel invaders. There was a small flurry of flashes on the computer screen at Luna Base as the first real volley of the war wiped several pirate vessels off the board. The pirates recovered their equilibrium in a minute, though, and a more accurate tenor of battle established itself.

There were simply too many pirate ships to be contained easily. As more and more of them spread out from the center of the original cluster, they moved parallel to the wall in an effort to skirt around and behind it. At Benevenuto's order, the ships comprising the wall spread apart a little more—but never so far apart that an enemy ship could slip between the spaces and get past them.

When the wall had expanded to its maximum permissible size and still the pirates were circling around, the edges of the wall bent backward as the Navy once more gave way—but again, the "retreat" served a specific function. At no time was an invading ship allowed to slip behind a defender; the Navy's vessels were always between the pirates and the planet they were defending. Eventually, Benevenuto knew, his wall would be twisted into a sphere surrounding the Earth—at which point, the pirates would have successfully englobed *them*. The Navy was saying to the attackers, though, "If you want to harm Earth, you'll have to go through us first."

It was a noble sentiment—but unfortunately, the pirates had enough ships to do the job, given the time. Earth's only hope was that the reinforcements would arrive and not give them enough time.

Hours passed, and the insurgent forces hammered relentlessly at the Navy's positions. Back and back the defenders were pushed, giving way reluctantly, until, as Benevenuto had known would happen, they circled the Earth like a sphere of fireflies. The moon itself was outside the sphere of defense; several of the pirates' bigger ships came overhead and began pounding at Luna Base. But though all Earth's ships were busy in defense of the mother planet, Luna Base was not completely helpless. Its big surface-mounted guns blasted forth, crippling one of the pirate ships and making the others back off to a more respectful distance. The blasts from the ships did some surface damage to the base, but the command levels, buried deep beneath the lunar soil, remained protected.

The Earth was bathed in a web of fire as the pirate forces picked at it, probing constantly for some weakness, some hole they could slip through to the surface below. The Navy fighters held up their shields and locked together in tight formation, refusing to let the enemy pass. Whenever an Empire ship was hit and disabled, the others around it quickly closed up to block the opening. They did their share of damage, but there were many more of the attackers than there were defenders. Slowly, the sphere around the Earth was tightening—just like a noose.

By now, the news had spread throughout the Empire that Earth was under attack by an insurrectionist movement "of unknown origin." The general call was put out for Navy vessels not on urgent duty elsewhere to rally to the capital planet's defense—but no hope could really be put there. The battle would be over before most of them could reach the solar system. By that time, either the Stanley Dynasty would have been upheld . . . or chaos would rule in the Galaxy.

The inhabitants of Earth hardly had to be told that something out of the ordinary was happening; their eyes provided ample evidence of the war of fire. People living in the nighttime hemisphere saw their sky alive with new stars and meteors as the two opposing fleets battled for supremacy. The ships themselves were invisible to the naked eye, but the trails made by their energy beams were spiderwebs of light crisscrossing the constellations—and when a direct hit was made, the bright explosion was a nova against the dark sky.

The defending ships were sorely pressed. Already some of them were dipping slightly into the upper levels of Earth's atmosphere. They could not shrink back any further—but if too many more of their number were destroyed, there would be holes in their shell of protection that the enemy ships could penetrate. The havoc those ships could wreak on the surface of a highly populated planet like Earth was almost inconceivable.

Then, when the high command at Luna Base was beginning to despair, other ships appeared on the screen near the orbit of Venus and closing in fast on the Earth. Benevenuto's first thought, that these were the reinforcements he'd been expecting, was crushed as he realized that those ships could not possibly arrive for another ten hours. His next thought was that these might be more pirate ships, brought in to reinforce the already dominant fleet. But that idea, too, proved to be wrong as the incoming messages began to arrive.

These were ships from near-Earth bases, the ones that had been bypassed in the initial strategy discussions between the Navy, the Emperor and SOTE. Their incoming communications had been sabotaged in some unknown manner, but they were warned of the upcoming invasion by the arrival of Commander Fortier in person, bringing with him documentary proof of what was to occur. Rising to the occasion in the best tradition of the Imperial Navy, the ships set out at once to assist the beleaguered forces of Earth.

Because of the sabotage to their communications equipment, the various bases had been unable to coordinate their efforts. Scout ships were sent to each individual base, alerting them of the danger and requesting help. As a result, the reinforcements arrived in groups of five, ten or as many as fifty ships at a time—but even so, each newcomer was a welcome sight indeed to the admirals of the high command. Each new ship meant that much more life for Earth, that much less domination by the traitors.

The pirates were obviously surprised by the late arrivals, and seemed unsure for a little while how to cope. The attack on Earth did not abate, but the rebel leaders deployed some of the ships that had been backing up the attack to take care of the threat from the new direction instead. This cheered the weary crews of the defense ships; they'd been on duty for close to a full day without letup, while the attackers had had sufficient numbers to relieve one another every so often. Now that more pressure was on them as well, the pirates would not be quite so relaxed.

Reinforcements from the near-Earth bases straggled in during the course of the next eight hours. These new forces were fresher than either the pirates or the Earth-based naval units, and brought a renewed vigor to the fighting. Even counting the newcomers, the Navy's forces were still slightly fewer in number than those of the attackers; but the ferocity with which the reinforcements fought more than made up the difference. The rebel leaders realized at last that they had a fight on their hands.

At this point the battle—which had begun to look like a rout by the pirates—could have gone either way. The rebels had superior numbers and a slight edge in position, but they were now fighting on two fronts at once and could not concentrate on breaking through the last of Earth's defenses. The Imperial forces, on the other hand, were hampered by an apparent breakdown in their computer system. Reports that should have been tallied instantly were taking too long to reach the high command; simulations were either incomplete, inaccurate, or too late to do any good. Confusion somewhere along the line of programming, it was assumed, was fouling up what had been touted as an infallible network for strategic calculations. More and more often coordination broke down, and individual commanders had to make spot decisions on their own. In some cases, this cost the Imperial forces key tactical positions, but they made the best of it nonetheless.

As the battle dragged on into its second day, both sides were wearing down appreciably. The pirates had hoped to win the war with a quick, decisive stroke so that they could proclaim their new regime before the outlying sectors of the Empire could respond to the crisis. That dream had died, now, and with it had gone much of the rebels' spirit. The Navy had a cause to fight for, while the insurgents had only their own greed propelling them forward. If they did not capture their goal soon, they would not have time to consolidate their gains before the rest of the Empire rose in protest.

With this in mind, Admiral Shen decided on one last bold stroke: an all-out assault on Earth. Ignoring the Navy ships at their rear, the pirate vessels dived at their target in a suicidal charge. Their blasters were firing continuously, pouring incalculable amounts of energy down at the harried remnants of Earth's defense. Perhaps it might have worked if they hadn't been so successful before at pushing the defense net in tightly against the atmosphere; but the ships protecting the mother planet were now packed so closely together that their firing ranges overlapped. The destruction of even three ships in a given area made little difference; their neighbors were able to hold up the net and prevent a single attacker from slipping through. The rebels ended up losing fully ten percent of their ships in that one attempt to break through—and still the Earth was intact.

Then, dropping out of subspace barely fifty million kilometers away, came the reinforcements Benevenuto had been expecting—a compact grouping of more than a thousand ships, all fresh and eager for battle. In the War Room, still tense after the narrow escape from the suicide charge, a rousing cheer went up as the new arrivals were spotted on the screens—and this cheer was echoed all down the line of command as the word was spread.

The rebels' reaction, needless to say, was quite different. Their attack, which once had looked so unbeatable, had failed. There was no way they could expect to hold their own against the now-superior Imperial forces, nor could they expect to be shown any mercy if they surrendered. Their only course lay in flight, and Admiral Shen was wise enough to take it. He gave the general order to retreat, and his ships fled from the Earth at top speed.

The Navy, smelling blood, hastened in pursuit. Crews who'd thought themselves nearly dead of exhaustion suddenly found renewed strength to join the chase. The tight defense net that had ringed the Earth suddenly evaporated. There was no longer any use for it; the attackers were on the run.

All told, nearly two-thirds of the enemy fleet was either destroyed or captured by the end of battle. Many of those who escaped did so in disorganization; there is no evidence that they ever rejoined the conspiracy against the Throne, their crews contenting themselves, instead, with becoming ordinary pirates once more. Most of them were eventually rounded up by the Navy during the course of its normal anti-pirate activities. Only twenty-five percent of Admiral Shen's once-mighty armada remained intact and returned to some hidden base to lick its wounds and prepare—perhaps—for new battles.

While the Navy pursued its duty of rounding up the remaining rebel ships, it was for Earth—and indeed, for the entire Empire—a moment of great relief. Once again the unity of Mankind among the stars had been maintained. The battle that was to be known forever afterward as the Coronation Day Incursion was over.

19

Breathing Room

When the commanding officer of the final contingent of reinforcements had a chance to make his report to Command
Central—after the pandemonium brought on by the victory had
died down in the halls of Luna Base—he had a strange tale
to tell. His fleet, as per their orders, had been waiting in the
vicinity of the supposed pirate rendezvous point. They had
checked with the intelligence operatives at the scene, and had
been told that everything was going as it had been planned.
Accordingly, the fleet set out to intercept the pirates at the
rendezvous point.

They never made it there, and it was fortunate they didn't.
They learned that the entire region of space had been mined,
and their force would have been decimated had they materialized there. Instead, they altered course and flew directly to
Earth, where their presence decided the outcome of the battle.

What had stopped them was, in the words of one captain,
"the craziest damned pilot I ever saw in my life." While still
in subspace, the lead ships detected the presence of another
vessel. It was flying in circles, spirals and indescribable, ir-
rational patterns, like a housefly on LSD or durambitol. No
natural object could move like that, and no sane pilot would.

It was as though whoever controlled that ship were pushing buttons at random to make it go.

And that was exactly what it was. Unsure what to make of this apparition, the fleet stopped to investigate, and found a small scout ship manned by an agent of SOTE who warned them of the danger ahead. He told them they must proceed to Earth at all possible speed. They took him aboard with them, and he explained the story in more detail along the way, omitting only those classified items for which the captain did not have a "need to know."

Mop up operations were begun a few days later, as soon as the Navy had time to recover from the near fatal battle. A contingent of small scout ships was dispatched to the phony rendezvous site to sweep the field and destroy all active mines that could pose a hazard to future astrogation. Commander Fortier—assured of an imminent promotion to captain for his outstanding work in this case—returned to the secret world of the pirate base to pick up Yvette Bavol. The SOTE agent had not been idle while the battle was going on. All told, nearly thirty pirates had been left behind by Shen to guard the base; Yvette had rounded them up single-handedly and had waited, confident an Imperial ship would soon come to take the prisoners off her hands. She and her prisoners were transported back to Earth in triumph.

On the planet Gastonia, SOTE agents rounded up the Governor and his crooked aides, holding them on charges of treason. There was no trace, however, of either Lady A or Tanya Boros; both women had made good their escape once they were sure their plan had worked.

Throughout the Empire, the mood of the people was one of elation. Not only did they have a new Empress, but she'd already weathered one of the most frightening challenges a monarch could be called on to face. Not once had she lost her composure. Not once had she behaved as anything less than the Empress her people had a right to expect. The people of the Galaxy knew now that Emperor Stanley Ten had made one more wise decision in passing on his title to such an able and dedicated young woman.

The elation did not extend, however, to the office at SOTE Headquarters where the d'Alemberts and the Bavols reconvened with their leader and his daughter. The faces there were long indeed. Though the events of recent days may have seemed a triumph to the rest of humanity, the people in this room knew better. From the very beginning they had let Lady A lead them around by their noses, doing exactly what she expected of them—and in the end, only the good fortune of Commander Fortier's surviving his double's ambush enabled them to weather the experience.

The Head could read the dejection so plain on his agents' faces, and refused to let them dwell on their failures. "In a way," he spoke up, "Lady A was paying us a high compliment. It was only because she knew you were such good agents that she could make her plans that intricately. Lesser people might have fumbled along the way, and couldn't be counted on."

"Somehow," Pias said, "that doesn't make me feel any better."

"The fact remains," Jules agreed, "that because of us, the Navy was underprepared for one of the most decisive battles in history."

"What's to keep us from falling for her tricks again?" Vonnie added.

"The same stubborn pride that makes you feel so bad now," the Head smiled. "*Khorosho,* you were fooled—badly. Anyone can be fooled once. The best of us don't make the same mistake twice—and Lady A knows that as well as I do. If she were to set you up this way again, you'd spot it in a second and her plan would backfire in her face. I don't think she'll try that trick again."

"No, she'll think up new ones," Pias agreed. "She's funny that way."

"How much of what she told us *can* we believe?" Vonnie asked. "Anything?"

The Head leaned back in his chair and clasped his hands behind his neck. "The best liars know how to combine just enough truth with their lies to make them believable. She told us quite honestly that they were going to attack, but her date was slightly off. She told us they had a large fleet, but she understated its size enough to mislead us. I'm willing to bet that she was telling the truth when she said she'd never met C, but her physical description of him is not to be trusted— and those telecom numbers she gave you for reaching C are pure gibberish."

"And that identity she gave us as 'Gretchen Baumann' is equally phony, right?" Yvette said.

"The identity is real enough," the Head said. "Gretchen Baumann was born on the planet Kiesel forty-three years ago; but she quite died at the age of seven from a fall down the stairs. She quite obviously did not grow up to be our Lady A—again, an ingenious blending of fact and fiction.

"As far as we've determined to date, the story about implanting our people with posthypnotic suggestions to inform her conspiracy what we're doing is pure fabrication. We'll check it out, of course, but I think it unlikely she would have spilled her actual source of information. Even if she thought her victory in that battle was inevitable, she still would have kept something in reserve."

The Head stood up, walked around to the front of his desk and sat down on its edge. "In the meantime, we have to concentrate on the positive. No matter how close a call we had, we still ended up with a brilliant victory. The enemy fleet was decimated, and the survivors have to be demoralized. If nothing else, we've gained ourselves some breathing room. It'll be quite some time before C can build his forces up again to a high enough level to pose much of a threat; he and Lady A will have to content themselves with harassing tactics in the meantime. And there's always the chance that after this defeat they'll give up their conspiracy plans altogether."

"There's always the chance DesPlaines will turn to chocolate," Yvette said dryly, "but I wouldn't put much faith in it."

At this point Helena stuck her head in the door from the outer office. "That call's coming in from Luna Base, Father."

The Head nodded. "*Khorosho,* I'll take it in here."

Jules stood up nervously. "If it's something personal, we could leave."

"I wouldn't hear of it. It is personal, but not for me. Please stay, all of you."

He turned to his screen, which was beginning to flicker, and in another moment the image of the caller appeared. It was none other than their new Empress, who was interrupting her inspection tour of Luna Base to talk specifically to these superb secret agents.

Jules and Yvette knew Edna rather well, Pias and Yvonne less so—but none of them had spoken to her since her ascension to the Throne. All were a little flustered at this unexpected contact, but Pias—ever the gallant—recovered first. He stood and bowed deeply with a sweeping gesture. "Your Majesty, I'm honored," he said.

Edna watched with amusement as the others echoed his behavior. "I'm still the same person I was before," she told them. "I expect my friends to treat me in private as a friend, not as some fragile china doll on a shaky pedestal. I called because I wanted to thank you for all you've done so far, and to wish you continued success."

"Thank us?" Jules said. "Our failure nearly wrecked the Empire."

"Zander showed me your report on Gastonia, and I think it's remarkable," Edna said. "I'm not talking about your being duped into carrying false information, or the fact that Lady A and Tanya Boros escaped. The information about the planet itself was fascinating. I'd had no idea that kind of thing was going on. And particularly to learn of the many innocent people condemned to a life of barbarity simply because they were born of traitorous parents—that's not the kind of thing I want occurring in *my* Empire. I think the concept of Gastonia as a prison world has outlived its usefulness; Stephanie was never my favorite ancestor, anyway. I intend to call a meeting of the Imperial Council to discuss alternate ways of dealing with traitors—and all this reform has come about because of your work. Hardly a failure, I'd say.

"And as for Yvette and Pias, the information you obtained with Captain Fortier, and the actions the three of you took, helped keep my reign from being the shortest on record. Pias in particular." She turned to look directly at the Newforester. "I'm told that the piloting you did was . . . quite remarkable."

"Never had a lesson," Pias replied.

"You might try a few," Edna scolded lightly. "If you hadn't had such heroic success, I might now have to consider grounding you permanently on some rather serious charges."

Pias's face fell. "Reckless flying, I suppose."

Edna smiled, taking all the sting out of her words. "No," she said. "Actually I was thinking of saving an Empire without a license."

FROM E.E. "DOC" SMITH
The man who invented space opera and made laser-blasters part of intergalactic life
SKYLARK SERIES

MS READ-a-thon—
a simple way to start
youngsters reading

Boys and girls between 6 and 14 can join the MS READ-a-thon and help find a cure for Multiple Sclerosis by reading books. And they get two rewards — the enjoyment of reading, and the great feeling that comes from helping others.

Parents and educators: For complete information call your local MS chapter. Or mail the coupon below.

Kids can help, too!